This book
completes

THE LOST ARTIST

THE LOST ARTIST

GAIL LUKASIK

FIVE STAR
A part of Gale, Cengage Learning

To Sue —
Best
Gail Lukasik

GALE
CENGAGE Learning

Detroit • New York • San Francisco • New Haven, Conn • Waterville, Maine • London

**GALE
CENGAGE Learning**

Copyright © 2012 by Gail Lukasik.
Five Star Publishing, a part of Gale, Cengage Learning.

ALL RIGHTS RESERVED
This novel is a work of fiction. Names, characters, places and incidents are either the product of the author's imagination, or, if real, used fictitiously.

No part of this work covered by the copyright herein may be reproduced, transmitted, stored, or used in any form or by any means graphic, electronic, or mechanical, including but not limited to photocopying, recording, scanning, digitizing, taping, Web distribution, information networks, or information storage and retrieval systems, except as permitted under Section 107 or 108 of the 1976 United States Copyright Act, without the prior written permission of the publisher.

The publisher bears no responsibility for the quality of information provided through author or third-party Web sites and does not have any control over, nor assume any responsibility for, information contained in these sites. Providing these sites should not be construed as an endorsement or approval by the publisher of these organizations or of the positions they may take on various issues.
Set in 11 pt. Plantin.

LIBRARY OF CONGRESS CATALOGING-IN-PUBLICATION DATA

Lukasik, Gail.
   The lost artist / Gail Lukasik. — 1st ed.
     p. cm.
   ISBN 978-1-4328-2576-8 (hardcover) — ISBN 1-4328-2576-3 (hardcover) 1. Women performance artists—Fiction. 2. Lost works of art—Fiction. 3. Farmhouses—Illinois—Fiction. I. Title.
PS3612.U385L67 2012
813'.6—dc23   2011049912

First Edition. First Printing: May 2012.
Published in 2012 in conjunction with Tekno Books and Ed Gorman.

Printed in Mexico
1 2 3 4 5 6 7 16 15 14 13 12

To my friend, Nancy Cirillo, whose continuing support made this book possible; and, as always, my husband, Jerry, whose steadiness keeps me on course.

ACKNOWLEDGMENTS

The author wishes to acknowledge the invaluable assistance of the following people: Restoration Artist, Barbara Magnum; Sandy Boaz; Sue Glasco; Gary Hacker; University Archivist, Leah Broaddus; Professor Marion S. Miller; Ranger, Laura Heiden; Curator/Assistant Professor, Sara Hume; Environmental Educator, Jean Weeg; Mary Gaunter; and my children, Christopher and Lauren, whose interesting lives inspired several of the book's settings.

Prologue:
Anna, Illinois:
Present Day

The empty grave changed everything.

She stood on the porch, watching the car's taillights disappear down the gravel road, until only darkness and thunder remained, and the old house looming over her with intent.

She could smell the rain coming, feel the electricity sizzle the night air.

Rain; it had begun with rain—insistent, unrelenting, washing away the soil, loosening the old oak roots, exposing the empty grave.

The local press would be all over the story, all over her, all over her house. She could see the front-page headline: "Early settler's body missing from grave." Below it, a grainy photo of her house. And the tag line: "The 1836 Braun house still stands in Anna, Illinois. Professor Karen Caffrey is the house's present owner."

But there was no way anyone could tie her to the theft. She'd been too careful.

Suddenly a scissor of heat lightning illuminated the landscape, and a dark figure appeared at the edge of the woods near the house. He was back.

"Sick, sick, sick," she said, digging in her skirt pocket, yanking out her cell phone. She held it up in his direction so he could see it. Then she flipped it open. "I'm calling the sheriff," she shouted. Even as she said it, she knew it was an idle threat.

The restraining order said "one hundred feet." The woods

were more than two hundred feet from the house. Besides, the police were the last thing she wanted now.

The phone rang off to message and she heard her sister's voice, then the beep. She must have mistakenly hit Rose's number. With her eyes still riveted on him, she finished the charade, then put the phone back in her pocket. Slowly he disappeared into the woods, until all she could see were the trees swaying in some silent dance only they knew.

Quickly she opened the front door, her hands shaking. Once inside she locked the door, went into the front parlor, shut the windows, locking them and drawing the curtains. For a moment, she stood listening for his footsteps on the porch, wondering if the fake phone call had scared him off. Or would this be the night he would follow through on his threats? She ran her hand over the cell phone in her pocket. Maybe she should call the police.

When she didn't hear anything, she peered through a slit in the curtains. Nothing. She let out a deep sigh. Her ruse had worked. She was safe.

Intimidation, that's what he wanted. He wouldn't risk touching her again.

The kitchen door. Damn, she said to herself, running down the hall. She turned the back-door lock and shut the windows. Another flash of heat lightning blazed the kitchen with light and rain started pinging the windows.

As she walked back down the hall, and up the wide plank stairs, she realized she was shaking again. I can't let him get to me like this.

Once upstairs, she paused outside her study and glanced across the narrow hall. Her desire to gaze at the murals was so strong she almost gave in to it. There was no time for that now, she told herself, turning and walking into her study.

The rain was falling in sheets now, glazing her windows with sound. She switched on the overhead light, sat down at her computer, and powered it up, nervously tapping her foot. Tonight her cocoon-like study with the walls of books didn't have its usual calming effect; instead it intensified her sense of things closing in on her. She was finding it hard to breathe.

When the screen appeared, she typed in her password, clicked on her hard drive, scrolled down to the file entitled Syllabi, and opened it. There were her meticulous notes in chronological order from the purchase of the farmhouse to the discovery of the diary to the restoration of the three mural walls.

July 3, she typed. *Emily Braun's grave is empty. Lawrence claims the oak tree tumbled over and exposed the empty grave. What happened to Emily?*

She closed the file, renamed it, and sent it to her Newberry Library account in Chicago.

As she waited for the e-mail to be sent, she took an envelope from her top desk drawer and addressed it to her sister, the only person she trusted. Irresponsible and feckless as Rose was, she was also fiercely loyal. She dashed off a quick note: "Rose, Keep this in a safe place. I'll explain later." And shoved the note inside the envelope.

Once the file was safely sent, she moved the file to trash and then emptied the trash. Another rumble and flash of lightning startled her, sending her heart racing. She stood up, pulling down on her short skirt.

Maybe I should change first, she thought, glancing at the rickety wood ladder resting against the closet door.

No, let's get this over with.

She dragged the ladder across the wood floor to the towering bookshelves against the back wall. As she struggled to open the ladder, a splinter caught in her thumb.

"Great," she said aloud, biting at the splinter.

She gazed up at the top shelf, which nearly crested the ten-foot ceiling, her fear of heights making her woozy. What had possessed me to hide it there of all places? Then she remembered that day she'd stolen the diary pages, the euphoria like a drug coursing through her body, sustaining her as she'd climbed the ladder, the pages snugly hidden inside the book *Obsessed*, her little joke. She'd finally done the unexpected, and it was a heady feeling.

All fear gone, she shook the ladder to steady it, kicked off her spiky shoes, took in a deep breath and began to climb slowly. Not looking down, she kept her eyes focused on the books in front of her as she went from one step to another, her hands clutching the ladder, the uneven rungs digging into her bare feet. With each step, the ladder shuddered and she waited until the shuddering stopped before taking the next step.

Finally, she was at the top step, her short compact body leaning against the top rung. She put one hand on the bookcase and with the other she reached for the book. The ladder shook, swaying with her effort. She stopped, took in another deep breath and reached up again, this time stretching her body farther, the rung digging into her thighs. But she couldn't reach the book.

Then, tentatively, she raised her left leg and put her foot on the open rung, her one hand inching up on the bookcase, the other stretching toward the book. Her fingers caught the edge of the book, and carefully she eased it out. Now the ladder was swaying and shuddering precariously. Almost there, she reassured herself.

She shoved the book under her arm, and brought her foot down to the top step, sighing with relief.

Just as she took another step down, the room went dark. The shock of the darkness paralyzed her. Then lightning tore the room open with light and she saw him.

He was standing in the doorway, a hulky shadow.

"How did you get in here?" was all she managed to say before he lunged for the ladder and jerked it backwards away from the bookcase.

For a moment she was airborne, then her body hit the hard floor with a thud, the book falling with her, scattering the loose pages like snow.

She tried to sit up, but nothing happened. She tried to call out, but no words came. Her body was dead to her. As he stood over her, she gasped for breath that didn't come. Then she looked past him toward the dark watery window. She didn't want his face to be the last thing she saw.

Chapter One:
Anna, Illinois,
Present Day

The house was as dark as stone, not a light shining anywhere. I rang the doorbell again; its echo chimed with a hollow sound. Annoyed, I cupped my hands to the front-door glass and saw nothing but a dim hallway and a staircase on the right.

Suddenly, a cascade of fireworks went off, sending a shot of adrenaline up my spine. I walked to the edge of the creaky porch, watching the reds and blues and whites rain down over the countryside, illuminating the rolling hills, the gravel road, and the decrepit farmhouse.

Where was Karen? Her ancient foreign car was parked beside the house; the upstairs windows were open. I stepped back to the front door and banged on it out of frustration. Nothing.

This was looking like a bad idea. Last night's eerie phone call from Karen came back to me. No words, just thunder and wind gusting. Then a click. When I'd called back to tell her I was coming for the July Fourth weekend, her phone went to voice mail. She never returned my phone call.

What was going on? I wondered. No matter how angry my sister might be with me right now, and I knew she was, she'd never take off on me. We always had each other's backs.

I jumped as another burst of fireworks exploded like gunshots, pelting the darkness—pop, pop, pop. Instinctively I touched the bruise on my right cheek, hidden under heavy makeup, its tenderness bringing back last week's mugging, the sudden yank from behind as the assailant tore the backpack from my shoulder, then shoved me to the pavement like I was nothing.

In the dark alley beside the Elevated Theater, I never saw him. But he knew everything about me—where I lived, that I was a Chicago performance artist, age thirty-three, with auburn hair and hazel eyes, name Rose Caffrey, 135 pounds, all the intimacies of identity.

My hands shook as I retrieved my cell phone from my purse, speed dialed Karen's number, and listened to its ring inside the house. Car and cell phone here, but no Karen. Maybe she's gone to the fireworks display with a friend and forgotten her cell phone. Not likely but possible.

Okay, what now? It was too late to drive back to Chicago. I could either wait in my car or use the spare key Karen had sent me right after she'd bought the old house. I shoved the cell phone in my shorts pocket and started digging in my purse for the key.

It took a while, but I finally found the spare key in one of the zippered compartments. What had her note said? "Front door or back door?" I looked down at the key; she'd painted a red B on the key for her clueless sister. Did she always have to remind me of my failings? Did I always have to prove her right?

As I trudged through the muddy weeds toward the back door, I stopped to peer into Karen's car. Empty.

When I reached the back door, another explosion of fireworks rained down in bright confusion, reflecting my image in the glass. My shorn head, a casualty of last night's performance, Skin Deep, gave me pause. It's only hair, it'll grow back, I told myself, as I slipped the key into the lock and pushed on the door.

A cloud of warm air engulfed me in a rank odor. I stood on the threshold and took in a deep breath, immediately regretting it. I'd only smelled something like that once before on a hike in the Wisconsin woods where I'd stumbled upon the rotting carcass of a deer.

Old houses smelled funny, I reassured myself, putting my hand over my nose as I stepped inside the country kitchen and switched on the overhead light, which cast a sickly yellow glow. On the table were a cup stained with coffee and a newspaper. I glanced at the date. July third.

Either Karen had left in a hurry or . . . I pushed the alternative from my mind as I quickly walked down the hall, switching on lights going from room to room, my hand firmly over my nose.

"Karen?" I called.

When I reached the staircase, I hesitated, waiting to catch my breath. Then I took my hand away from my nose and sniffed. The stench was stronger here as if it were embodied.

Whatever was causing that odor was upstairs. Now a million dark thoughts began whirling through my head as I stood at the bottom of the stairs looking up. My unanswered phone call, Karen's car, the locked house and open upstairs windows, and that horrible smell.

I should call nine-one-one, I told myself. There's no reason to go up there alone.

Then I shook my head as if I could free myself of those thoughts. There had to be another explanation. Karen was fine. She had to be.

I hurried up the wide plank stairs, the sound of my flip-flops like the beating of a heart. When I reached the upstairs landing, I was breathing hard and feeling light-headed.

She's at the fireworks, I told myself as I entered the first room on the right, a bedroom. The window was open, curtains moving in and out as if breathing. I switched on the light, stared at the bed as if I expected Karen to be lying there. Nothing; just a wrought-iron bed neatly made with a blue-and-white quilt, white eyelet shams and bed skirt.

Now my heart was pounding in my head as I walked across the hall to the bathroom, turning on the light, again finding nothing.

Two rooms remained. I didn't want to go any farther, afraid of what I might find. I turned around and headed toward the stairs. Then I stopped. This is what you always do, run away. What if Karen is in one of those rooms?

I turned back and walked slowly toward the last room on the right, telling myself that an animal had gotten into the house while Karen was away.

"You're such a baby," she'd tease me later when we'd laugh about the dead raccoon I'd imagined was her.

When I reached the room, I stopped. For a moment, I couldn't register what I was seeing. Then the realization made me stumble backwards into the hall.

"No!" I cried.

Karen's crumpled body lay across the wood floor. Her eyes were open. Her neck twisted at a strange angle. She was clearly dead. The smell of feces, urine and decomposing flesh was everywhere.

I stared at the broken body that had been my sister. Karen was no longer there. But still I cried out her name as if that could bring her back, half expecting her to blink, sit up, and scold me. When she didn't, I shut my eyes on the horrific scene. When I opened them, Karen was still there, still dead. A ladder beside her, books strewn everywhere.

There was nothing I could do for her now.

Another blast of fireworks lit up the room, casting it in an unbearable light. I felt my stomach roil. I ran from the room, down the stairs and hallway, out the kitchen's back door and into the night. Then I vomited. When there was nothing left to vomit, I collapsed into the muddy grass and sat there, traumatized, holding my knees to my chest and rocking back and forth.

The sounds of a band playing "America the Beautiful" wafted across the countryside, reaching through my shock.

"There's been an accident," I said when the nine-one-one operator picked up. "My sister's dead."

"Ma'am, where are you?"

"Her house."

"Ma'am, you'll have to give me an address."

I rubbed my forehead, trying to think. "You turn right on Campground Road, go past the Campground Cemetery, and bear right on Old Cutoff Road. The house is on the right. There's a silver mailbox with a . . ." I started to sob.

"Ma'am, I need an address."

I struggled to my feet and walked around the house, across the weedy grass to the gravel road. "One, two, one."

"What is your name?"

"Rose Caffrey."

"Rose, you stay there. We'll have the police and an ambulance there shortly."

"I said she was dead," I whispered.

"I have that, ma'am. You sit tight till the police get there. And don't touch anything."

I sat in the back of the police car, staring blankly out the open window, the feel of the leather seat on my bare legs and the crackling of the police radio the only sensations keeping me present. Every once in a while a tremor ran through me like an aftershock. I wasn't sure why I couldn't wait in my car. "Just until we sort everything out," Officer Dade had said.

"Watch it," someone shouted. I looked out the car's window toward the house.

Two EMTs were maneuvering the gurney with Karen's body down the front steps toward the waiting ambulance. "My sister's body," I said aloud to no one.

The image of her crumpled on the floor, her short skirt hiked up around her thighs, the swell of her breast where the chemise top had slipped down, wouldn't leave me. Like a monotonous tune, it kept repeating and repeating in my head.

"Do you have a place to stay?" Officer Dade was leaning inside the back window, his muscular arms rampant with dark hair somehow comforting.

"What?" I stared up at him as if he'd materialized out of the warm night air.

"Didn't mean to startle you," he apologized. He was a squat man with a barrel chest, a small head and an open face. "But I wanted to let you know that there's a motel on Route One Forty-Six across from the Trail of Tears stop 'n shop. You can follow me there. It's not fancy, but it's clean."

"I gotta get back to Chicago."

"Ms. Caffrey, you're in shock. Not a good idea to drive that far. And as next of kin, you'll need to make arrangements for your sister."

"Did she fall? Is that what happened?"

"Looks that way. But we won't know for sure until the coroner completes the autopsy."

"Can I go now?"

Officer Dade opened the car door. "Sure. We're about through here. You want to follow me, then?"

As I got out of the car, I felt my legs wobble under me and put my hand against the car to steady myself. "No, it's okay. I know where I'm going."

He called after me, "Remember you'll need to come by the police station tomorrow and fill out a report."

Driving away from the farmhouse, I opened all the windows. The night had finally cooled and a few stars glittered the sky. I needed the reality of night; the hum of the cicadas, the rustling of the trees, and the loamy scent of deep summer, which seemed to whisper across the farmland and the forests as if the night were restless and full of secrets.

"Nick, Karen's dead." I huddled under the blanket and the brown quilted bedspread with the air conditioner cranked and the television on, shivering and sweating.

"What are you talking about? What happened? Are you okay?"

"I found her. She must have fallen from a ladder and broken her neck. It was so awful—and the smell. I'll never forget that smell." Though I hadn't eaten for hours, my stomach rolled again with nausea. The first thing I did when I got to the motel room was stand in the shower, scrubbing and scrubbing until my skin was red and raw.

"Tell me where you are? I can be there by morning."

Dear sweet Nick always ready to rescue me. Of all my former lovers, he was the only one I'd remained friends with, which I credited more to him than me.

"No, I can handle this. Besides, don't you have rehearsals starting next weekend for your new play with the homeless women?"

"Forget the play. Just tell me where you are." I knew the play was important to him, and I wasn't going to let him pull his white-knight routine and jeopardize it.

"Listen, there is something you can do for me. Stavros is threatening to put my things on the curb if I don't come up with the two months' rent I owe."

"Why didn't you tell me before? I could have loaned you the money. What's a trust fund for if not to help your friends?" Nick's grandfather, Nicholas Baxter the First, had made his fortune in steel and sold the company for an obscene amount of money. Nick's trust fund supported his passion, Elevated, an avant-garde theater in the south loop, where the roar of the elevated train punctuated every performance.

"Just tell him what happened. I've lied to him so many times, I don't think he'll believe me."

"Don't worry about it."

"Thanks." I started to cry.

"C'mon, RT, you know I hate it when you do that." Nick was the only person who called me RT, short for Rose Theresa.

I hung up, swiping at my tears and battering my bruised cheek, not caring if I did. Anything not to remember, not to feel those familiar feelings I'd kept buried for so long.

The swift loss of my parents on that icy night in Chicago, their car skidding across the highway, had turned me inside out.

Never again, I'd decided, standing over their graves in the cold January wind, would I care for anyone this deeply. Better to skim the surface of people; then, when they left, and they always did, it would be like shedding old skin.

This certainty had kept me safe, and if I was honest with myself, had stood between Karen and me. And now she was gone, too.

Chapter Two

The old farmhouse loomed over me, its shadow like a stain across the tall weedy grass. I didn't want to go inside. I didn't want to relive the horror of finding Karen's broken body. But, like it or not, this was now my house. And I couldn't wait to get rid of it.

"Don't let the outside fool you." Dan Yeager, Karen's realty agent, now mine, said, tugging at his tie as if it were strangling him.

Under the full light of day the house looked even worse than I'd remembered—clapboards peeling to raw wood, sagging front porch, shingles missing, and a tilting chimney.

"I don't get why she bought this . . . this . . ." I gestured toward the house as if I could make it disappear. "This ruin."

That question had plagued me through the difficult week of coping with Karen's death, from the coroner's ruling of accidental death to the reading of her will to the cremation of the remains that once were Karen. By week's end, I'd fallen into a fugue state, answering when spoken to, offering nothing, and at night barely sleeping. And when I did sleep, I dreamed of Karen.

"I tried talking her out of it, told her the rehab would cost more than the house," Dan explained, glancing down at the realty papers he held in his hand like an apology. "But you know Karen. Once her mind's made up."

I thought I did. I was still smarting from my meeting with

Karen's lawyer. Besides the house, I'd been left the old car and nothing else. All the money from her life-insurance policy had been willed to a scholarship fund for Native American studies, as well as all other monies. The house felt like a punishment.

"Just how old is it?" I asked. All that was missing from this wreck was a condemned sign plastered across the front door.

"One hundred and seventy-five years old, give or take a few years. But after one hundred and fifty, who's counting?" he joked, pushing his steel-rimmed glasses up his short nose. In his early fifties, Dan had light-brown hair and eyes amazingly alike in color. His large, square-shaped head seemed at odds with his short, stocky body.

I smiled weakly at his lame joke. He didn't want to be here any more than I did.

For some inexplicable reason, an angry jolt shot up my spine as I recalled Karen's description of the house as untouched and real. Then she'd added, "Of course, I don't expect you to like it," which meant, "I don't need you to like it."

I dug the toe of my thong sandal in the muddy ground and watched the mud ooze around it, muting its hot pink color. She knew I'd hate this house, and she'd left it to me anyway.

"She was going to do the exterior this fall, when it got cooler," Dan said as if I'd asked him about it. He seemed so defensive of Karen, I wondered if they'd been more than acquaintances. She'd never mentioned him to me. I glanced down at his left hand: no ring.

I tried to picture my short, pugnacious sister with this short, diffident man. She would have eaten him alive, then used the bones to clean her teeth. What my sister liked was a challenge. And Dan Yeager of the black sport coat, gray trousers, and blue tie offered little of that.

"Maybe we should get out of the heat and discuss the details inside," I suggested. Looking at him was making me hot. Beads of sweat bubbled near his hairline and his pores oozed a lime scent, probably his aftershave. I kept thinking, why doesn't he take off his sport coat. It had to be in the high nineties, and the humidity was so thick you could taste it.

"We can sign the papers out here. No need to go inside. I know you've been through a lot, what with finding Karen's body and all." His eyes swept over my ultrashort hair.

"I cut my hair like this for a performance," I said, not wanting him to think I'd had chemo.

He looked at me quizzically. "Oh, yeah, right. Karen did say something about you being some kind of performer. Anyway, if you want, I can even get someone to box up her stuff for you." He rocked from foot to foot nervously, like a boxer.

I could feel my resolve seeping away. "Just my signature and that's it? I'm done?"

"Got the comps right here." He rustled the papers in his hand. "We just need to set an asking price."

Wavering, I stared at the house. Sign the papers, head back to Chicago today, and get on with my life. Karen's last words played in mind.

"Honestly Rose, this is no way for a grown-up to live." She'd been lecturing me on my financial failings and my poor career choice.

I'd hung up on her. When I called back, she never returned my phone call.

"Let's get this over with," I said, hurrying toward the house before I changed my mind. A flurry of grasshoppers flew at my face like second thoughts.

Standing in the cool dark hallway, a wave of nausea rippled through me as that terrible night came rushing back, and with it that sweet, sickening smell of decay and death. A cold, clammy sweat broke out all over my body and I swayed with dizziness.

"You okay?" Dan asked. Though he meant well, his doe-eyed stare so full of pity was making everything worse.

I swallowed my nausea. "I'm fine." And if I said it enough times, maybe I would be.

"Everything's been cleaned up, if that's got you worried."

"Cleaned up?"

"Well, you know, upstairs." His eyes glanced up toward the ceiling. "But, like I said, we don't have to do a walk-through. I can go over the comps with you, explain everything, and we can be on our way."

"Don't you think I owe my sister more than that?" I snapped, instantly regretting it. "Sorry. It's just . . . well, you know. I have to do this."

He patted my arm as if I were an elderly relative, making me feel worse. "No problem. I'm used to people losing it. Goes with the real-estate territory. A guy once took a swing at me because I suggested he lower the price of his house."

When I didn't respond, he cleared his throat and continued, "Okay, then. Hardwoods throughout the house, both downstairs and up. Most buyers want hardwood floors. So that's a definite selling point."

In the waning afternoon light, the floors and wood trim glowed as if lit from within. The effect was quite lovely.

"And that staircase, isn't it a beaut?"

My eyes followed the ornately carved flowers that tangled up the staircase like tendrils. I was seeing it for the first time. Rushing up the stairs that night, I hadn't noticed anything.

My stomach lurched with the memory. I swallowed again.

"You probably know Karen restored all the wood in the house herself. She told me she didn't trust anyone else to do it."

"Karen did all this?" That was a surprise. The most physical thing I ever saw Karen do was crack open a book.

He nodded his head. "Wait till you see the parlor." He

gestured toward the front parlor on the left.

From the green marble fireplace to the chandelier's carved medallion to the creamy white settee and two wing chairs flanking the fireplace, the parlor had the look and feel of an earlier century. I was astonished by the sharp contrast between the house's interior and exterior. No one would ever expect the interior to be so perfectly pristine.

Intrigued, I walked to the fireplace to get a closer look at the angelic cherubs that embossed the mantel's sides.

"That green mantelpiece there, Karen found it hidden under a pile of trash in the cellar. Lugged it upstairs herself," Dan bragged.

I ran my hand over the cherubs as if they held some secret I could uncover by touching them. "Hard to imagine her doing any of this."

"Yup. Let me show you the rest of the downstairs."

As Dan escorted me through the first-floor rooms, all meticulously restored, my stomach settled and I began to think the house might be sellable, and maybe at a decent price.

Then we were back at the carved, flowered staircase, my stomach once again in knots.

For an uncomfortable moment we stood listening to the sounds of the old house, the summer breeze rattling the windows, the sigh of an appliance, the creaks and moans of age.

"You really don't need to go up there." Dan's tone was sharp. "It's not like you haven't seen it." He yanked so hard on his tie, the knot loosened.

Why the sudden change? I wondered. He almost sounded angry. Was he afraid I was going to snap at him again?

"I told you I'm fine."

"Well, you don't look fine. And Gary—you know the guy who cleaned up everything? He said, you might notice a little"—he wrinkled his short nose—"odor, which should go away over time."

That gave me pause. "I'm going to have to go up there eventually to clear out my sister's things," I countered, my contrary nature erupting suddenly. When someone told me not to do something, I instantly wanted to do it, hang the consequences.

He shrugged his shoulders as if to say, I warned you.

"Is there a reason I shouldn't go upstairs?" Something in his demeanor seemed off. Now I wanted to go upstairs.

"No, no." He waved his hand. "Just what I said about the odor. Don't want you more upset."

For all his protests to the contrary, he didn't want me upstairs, and it wasn't because of the odor. I was sure of it. "Like I said, I'm fine." I wasn't fine, but I was going upstairs.

"Okay, then," he said, with more cheer than I felt. "I guess you know what you're doing."

As we walked up the plank stairs, Dan kept up a constant chatter. "There's over an acre. Used to be over two hundred acres. But, you know, through the years the Braun family sold most of it off."

All the while he was talking, I kept wondering why his attitude had changed from affable to anxious and why I didn't just sign the papers and be done with this house.

When we reached the landing, I stopped. I was breathing heavily, sweat running down my back, making my fuchsia T-shirt cling to me.

"Whew," I said, pulling my sticky shirt away to circulate air. "Is it always this hot here?"

"Yeah, it takes some getting used to."

I took in a deep breath, searching for a trace of that putrid odor. All I smelled was a piney scent. If Gary the cleanup guy had smelled something, he had a keener sense of smell than I did.

Though the house felt too close, as if it were pressing on my chest, I started going from room to room, half listening to Dan's narrative about Karen's restoration work, trying not to see the details of my sister's life—from her perfume bottles to her toothbrush to her white terry robe hung on the back of the bathroom door—and failing miserably.

As we left the bathroom, my heart felt like it would pound itself free of my body. Suddenly Dan stopped and turned toward me. "Look, before we go any farther, I have to say I've never been in a situation like this, so I'm not sure what you want me to do."

So that's why he'd tried to talk me out of coming upstairs: he was as nervous as I was. Did he think I'd get hysterical, burst into tears, faint?

All my senses were on overdrive. "The worst has already happened," I said, not sounding at all like myself. Now it was my turn to pat his arm, offering him comfort. I walked past him, down the hall and into the room where Karen died.

Dan was right; Gary had cleaned up everything.

The ladder now leaned against her antique desk. No books lay scattered about on the floor. A halo of dust motes spun in the light. It was as if Karen had never died in this room.

I looked up toward the built-in bookcases that reached to the ceiling. "It's almost poetic, you know, the way she died."

Dan had come into the room. "What do you mean? I don't follow you."

"Reaching for a book." I realized by the stare he gave me, I'd said something inappropriate.

"Sorry. My emotions are all over the place."

"Understandable."

"And the last room?" I pointed across the hall.

Not waiting for Dan, I walked the short distance. Then I

stopped just inside the room. I couldn't believe what I was seeing.

It was as if I'd walked into another world and another time. Three walls were painted with vivid scenes of beauty, delicate brushstrokes, and pastels so light and hued as if they'd been breathed onto the walls.

"Wow," I whispered, turning around slowly, seeing how each scene blended into the other as if a story was being told on the walls, each wall another chapter of that story. And only one chapter remained untold on the wall nearest the door, which was still covered in dark-blue paint, its ragged edge like an invitation to be peeled back.

One wall was the story of this farmhouse, for surely this was a painting of the farmhouse right down to the shutters. The only difference was a large tree, which dominated the foreground, totally out of proportion to the house.

In the tree sat a blackbird with open mouth and open wings. What looked like a road rippled from the house to a rolling hill where cows grazed, then on to another hill dotted with blackbirds that looked like tiny bows.

Another wall was a scene of a town set on a hill, complete with steepled church, Georgian-style homes, and what looked like a town hall or a school. Behind the town was a volcano-like mountain, spewing smoke that trailed toward the doorway wall. Below the town was a large lake where several large boats drifted, their sails billowing.

The third was the starkest of the three: gray-green monochromatic colors, a large tree again in the foreground, a lone house off to the right in the distance, four cows in a field, one very small tree beside the house.

The paintings were done in a style I recognized from my art-history courses as American primitive, characterized by naive themes and simplistic, stylized drawings.

What were these magnificent murals doing in this decrepit nineteenth-century farmhouse?

Dan's footsteps on the hardwood floors broke my concentration.

"Are these murals original to the house?"

He shrugged. "Got me. I didn't even know they were here until Gary told me when he returned the house key. I was going to drive out and take a look but never got around to it."

"So Karen must have found them after she bought the house?"

"Yup, looks that way. This room was painted blue, just like that wall by the door. Why? Do you think they're valuable or something?"

I went over to the mural of the farmhouse, marveling again at the artistry. "That depends on a lot of things."

"Like what?"

"Who the artist was, the age of the murals, stuff like that."

"Just looks like some old drawings to me," Dan said, dismissively.

"Karen couldn't have done this restoration herself. She must have hired someone."

"Well, I don't know anything about that. Why don't I show you the comps, and then let's talk about an asking price."

As we made our way downstairs and into the front parlor, my mind was still on the murals. If they were painted one hundred and seventy-five years ago, was it likely that someone with this obvious talent would be living in rural southern Illinois? Not likely. Then how did they get here? It didn't make sense. And even more perplexing: why hadn't Karen told me about them?

We sat on the white settee while Dan shuffled through his papers, found the ones he was looking for and handed them to me.

"That's your competition."

Most were newer houses in nearby developments. The houses looked raw and aggressive with their faux brick and multiple peaked rooflines. The lawns manicured like green crew cuts.

"So, how long do you think it'll take to sell it?" I asked, feeling somewhat more confident now that I'd seen the interior.

"If you look at the listing prices of the newer homes, which are close to what this house is worth, you'll see what you're up against. And most buyers in your price range want new. Not to mention we have a very limited buyer pool."

He handed me the listing sheet for this house.

"Are you telling me Karen paid that much for this house?"

"Like I said, I tried to talk her out of it. I even told her the house had maybe twelve more years to live. But her response was, 'From the moment I saw it, I knew it had to be mine.'"

Who was this Karen he was describing? Not my practical, frugal sister.

I thought again about my overextended credit cards, my late rent payments, and the only thing I owned outright, my ten-year-old SUV with 100,000 miles on it that was in need of new brakes and a tune-up.

"How much would I have to come down in price for a quick sale?"

He looked up toward the ceiling as if the price were floating above him. "Eighty grand."

"Then list it for eighty grand less."

"Okay, but you have to understand that's no guarantee of a sale. And if you get an interested buyer, they're going to bid under that, especially since the rehab's not complete. That limits your buyers. You'd have to find someone who's into fixer-uppers."

Something is better than nothing, I reassured myself. "Look, I need the money. This house"—I gestured with my arm—"is all Karen left me."

He had the decency to look embarrassed.

I studied the house's listing sheet, this time carefully reading over the entire sheet as if some magical explanation for Karen's purchase would appear. Seller: James Braun, Sr.

"Didn't you say the Braun family built this house?"

He nodded his head yes.

"So it's been in the family all these years. Why sell now?"

He looked away for a moment. "Well, Braun, Senior, put the house on the market a few years ago when he moved to Florida. Why he didn't give it to his son Jimmy, I don't know. But Jimmy was living here when Karen bought the house. You probably know about the problem Karen had with Jimmy."

"No, what problem?"

"Karen had to have the sheriff evict him from the property."

"What happened to him? The son? Afterwards?"

"Oh, he's around somewhere, living with friends and whatnot. Probably still dealing drugs."

"You gotta be kidding. What kinds of drugs?" I'd heard stories about rural meth labs, the destruction and violence they fostered.

He waved his hand in dismissal. "That I don't know." Dan stood up. "You heading back to town?"

"I'm going to start packing up Karen's personal items first." My mind was still on the angry, drug-dealing son Karen had evicted.

"Well, you have my number if you need anything. I'll put the For Sale sign up now and bring the lockbox by tomorrow. Oh, one more thing. Karen's car. If you're interested, I might be able to find you a buyer. What with your money situation."

"That would be great."

"Okay. And, again, I'm really sorry about Karen."

After Dan left, I went outside to my car and retrieved my suitcase. I couldn't afford another night in a motel—even at the

$49.99-a-night motel on Route 146. If I hustled, I could clear out Karen's things in a day or two, then be back in Chicago.

I was about to close the hatch when I spotted the urn with Karen's ashes. It didn't seem right to leave it in the car. So I grabbed the urn along with my suitcase and headed back to the house. Just as I got inside the door, my cell phone jangled.

It was Nick. "First off, it's all taken care of."

"What happened?" I could tell from his voice that something was up and it wasn't good.

"All your stuff's at my place."

I let out a sigh. "That bastard threw me out?"

"Sorry, RT, there was nothing I could do."

"What about the dresses?" My fantastically proportioned dresses, each handmade, were my art, integral to my public performances.

"Would I let you down? First things I grabbed. I stored them at the theater. When you coming back?"

"Soon as I pack up Karen's personal stuff. At the latest Monday."

"You okay?"

"Other than my sister being dead and me being homeless, just great."

"You always have me."

"Yeah, I always have you. Thanks, Nick."

I hung up, wondering where to start.

It was after eight o'clock when I lifted the last of my sister's skirt suits off the closet pole and tossed them into a box, releasing that flowery, old-fashioned scent that was Karen: lily of the valley with a strange undertone of citrus. Just like the flattened and stacked boxes I'd found in the cellar were Karen, each one's contents noted in black marker: kitchen dishes, linen, clothing.

Quickly I taped the box shut and dragged it out into the hallway. Though the suits were expensive looking, and I didn't have a suit to my name, I couldn't see myself in any of Karen's cautious, sad clothes, even if they fit me, which they didn't. Tomorrow I'd drive the clothes to the nearest Salvation Army or Goodwill.

Standing in the hall, staring at the five boxes, I listened to the grumble of my stomach. The only room left to pack was Karen's study, the room she'd died in. The sun was almost down, and with it went my waning courage. I could finish packing tomorrow. I went downstairs and into the kitchen, looking for something to drink and eat.

In the back of the fridge behind a quart of OJ, milk, and iced tea, I found one light beer, surprisingly a domestic beer. I twisted the bottle cap off and took a swig. Then I rummaged around for food, finally settling on a block of very-pricey-looking French cheese that hadn't expired and some fancy crackers cut in a variety of alluring shapes.

The day's heat still lingered in the kitchen, and the ladder-backed chairs looked torturous. So I took my meal to the parlor and dragged one of the wingback chairs near the bay window to enjoy the breeze. Before sitting down, I gazed out the window at the land, which rolled away from the house in green verdant waves of tall grass, lovely and lonely as a green sea. Then I plopped down in the chair and put my feet up on the polished wood window seat.

As I ate my meager dinner, I glanced around the room. I could see Karen's clever, careful mind at work. I knew if I searched her bookshelves, I'd find the historical books that had inspired the room, if you could call it inspiration.

If it had been my room to decorate, I'd have gone against every notion of history and blazed the room with incongruity, so that it rebelled against the very notion of itself. Karen had been right in saying I wouldn't like the house. It felt old and weighted and sad.

My stomach churned when I spotted the black-and-white photo of Karen and me on one of the tiger-maple side tables. In all the confusion of her death, I'd missed it. I went to the side table and picked up the photo. Karen's arm was slung around my shoulders. She had to be about fifteen, which would make me five. We were standing in front of the two-story flat on Kenmore. Karen was squinting into the sun, and I had my head down. Both of us were laughing. I didn't remember the photo and now she wasn't here to tell me about it.

I put the photo facedown, not wanting its painful reminder, and went back to my chair, taking a long swallow of my beer as I tried to reconcile the Karen I'd known with the Karen I'd recently discovered.

Packing up her clothes, I'd found three black lacy bras with front clasps and matching panties stashed in the back of a drawer like a dirty secret. If she'd had a lover, I never knew about it.

I looked around the room again, so precisely preserved. This house seemed like another secret Karen had been keeping. She'd told me she'd bought an older home. She'd never said anything about it being one hundred and seventy-five years old, or that she'd had to evict the owner's drug-dealing son. Then there were those mysterious murals. Why hadn't she told me about them? As an artist, she knew I'd find them fascinating.

Well, maybe soon the house would be someone else's mystery to solve.

I finished my beer and leaned back in the chair, finally letting exhaustion take over.

Karen and I were sitting in an empty church, the sharp smell of incense clouding the air. Karen wore an old flannel shirt, her blonde hair a rat's nest, her neck set at an odd angle. As she reached out to me, her fingers curved like claws. Then she opened her mouth and exhaled a cloud of smoke.

I jolted awake, not knowing where I was. A faint trace of cigarette smoke, like a distant memory, seemed to linger in the warm summer night air as if someone was outside smoking. As I looked at the lacy panels gently moving with the breeze, it all came tumbling back into me. Karen was dead. I'd fallen asleep in her chair.

I got up and peered out into the darkness, listening, hearing only the rustle of trees, an owl's plaintive song somewhere in the distance.

Suddenly the mantel clock chimed twice, making me jump. Too wired to go to bed, I went into the kitchen, got myself a glass of milk and sat in the dark at the kitchen table. Again a whiff of cigarette smoke prickled my nose. Was the drug-dealing son back?

I went and checked the lock on the kitchen door. It was still locked. Why did it feel like someone had just been in the house?

Before heading upstairs for bed, I grabbed my cell phone and shoved it in my pocket. As soon as I turned on Karen's bedroom light, I knew I couldn't sleep there. It's only for a few nights, I told myself, as I bundled up the blue-and-white quilt and went downstairs to sleep in the wingback chair like a sentry.

Chapter Three

A bell was chiming over and over, and I wanted it to stop. Still half asleep, I groped for an alarm clock on the side table, then realized the chiming was coming from the front doorbell.

"Hold on," I shouted, getting up stiffly from the chair and rubbing the kink in my neck. I couldn't find my flip-flops, but at least I was dressed. I'd slept in my T-shirt and shorts. When I reached the front door, the ringing had stopped. Through the door's glass I saw a tall, lanky man dressed in faded jeans and a white T-shirt, an angry scowl on his face.

I inched the door open hoping this wasn't the drug-dealing son but a potential buyer. Though from the rigidity of his shoulders and the hard set of his jaw, I had my doubts about him being a potential buyer.

"Can I help you?" I asked.

For an uncomfortable moment, he gawked at my stubby head, his eyes traveling from my bruised cheek and back to my head, then said gruffly, "Where's Karen?"

"What do you want with Karen?" He didn't look like a drug dealer, but then again what did a drug dealer look like? I positioned my foot against the door in case he decided to push his way in. Like that would stop him.

"Just tell me where she is, okay? If she changed her mind, she should have said something and saved me the trip." With every word his anger ratcheted up. "And what's with the For Sale sign?"

"Karen's dead," I spat at him, resisting the urge to slam the door in his face.

It was as if I'd thrown cold water on him; his whole demeanor changed from anger to shock. "What? I just talked to her."

"She died over a week ago. Now, who the hell are you?" I didn't like being yelled at, especially by some strange man who clearly had me at a disadvantage.

His broad shoulders slumped as if all the air had been forced out of him. "Alex Hague. I've been restoring the murals." He glanced down at his sandal-clad feet as if he'd dropped something, then looked away.

So this was the guy who'd brought those murals back to life. It was as if I'd willed him here, and that made me nervous. I almost asked him if he smoked but held my quirky thoughts in check.

"I can't believe she's dead," he continued. "I should have known something was wrong when she didn't answer my last e-mail. That wasn't like her." He seemed to come back to himself. "Are you a friend of hers?"

"I'm her sister, Rose."

He seemed perplexed. "She never mentioned she had a sister."

I was too tired to go into the complexity of our relationship. "Yeah, I've been getting a lot of that lately."

He stared at me, and I could tell that he was comparing me to Karen, wondering why we didn't look alike. "Look, I'm sorry for being such a jerk. I'm still jet-lagged. I just got back from London, then flew to Boston for a day, and came straight here."

"You want something to drink?" I said in way of forgiveness. And I wanted to know about the mysterious murals.

"Sure."

"Let me brush my teeth. Then you can tell me about the murals."

★ ★ ★ ★ ★

The oak kitchen table was covered in photographs, reports, clumps of paint-covered wallpaper and a plastic sleeve that contained a narrow piece of faded cloth, which Alex Hague had placed on the table as if it were the original Magna Carta. The warm breeze from the window ruffled the papers, but did little to alleviate the kitchen's oppressiveness—a musky blend of coffee, humidity and a sweet cloying scent I'd yet to put my finger on—rotting fruit, dead mouse. But at least the smoky smell was gone.

I'd explained to Alex that I was now the owner of the farmhouse and was selling it. That had sent him scurrying to his rental car to retrieve a bulging green duffle bag. As he emptied the contents on the table, I'd thought of Pandora's Box—chaotic, intriguing and sure to cause trouble. Or was that Alex Hague who was sure to cause trouble, with his swimmer's body and earnestness?

I rested my chin in my hand, listening to Alex talk about the murals as if they were children he was inordinately proud of, explaining to me every detail of their lives from conception to adulthood. His enthusiasm was like a tonic. I felt myself being drawn in to his world of paint chips and binding techniques. It didn't hurt that his deep-set green eyes had flecks of gold and his hawk-like nose gave him a rakish look. With two husbands under my belt, so to speak, and a miscreant lifestyle, I was better served concentrating on paint chips and not on Alex Hague, whose passion for his work was his most attractive feature.

"The original owners would have had a whitewash put on the walls."

"You mean the Braun family?"

"Yeah, that's who we think were the original owners. At least that's as far back as Karen was able to trace the deeds of ownership."

He held my eyes a beat too long.

"Anyway, it was believed that whitewashing a wall would act as a disinfectant to keep down bacteria. As to the murals, they were painted with a tempera paint or casein. Then the walls were wallpapered. Judging from the condition of the murals, I'd say that was done fairly soon after they were painted. See this."

He picked up a clump of the paint-covered wallpaper and held it out to me. "You can see the layers, each layer is a moment in time captured. It's sort of like when you cut open a tree and count the rings. Only in this case, the first ring is wallpaper, then paint, then another layer of wallpaper, then layers of paint. Each layer was put down by people living in the nineteenth, then twentieth, then twenty-first century."

I took the sample from him and fingered the compressed layers, then turned the clump over. On the back was a faint patterning of what looked like leaves.

"Wow," I said, like a starry-eyed teenager, not sure if the wow was for the leaf patterning or Alex Hague. I shifted in my chair.

"Yeah, pretty incredible, huh? That paint is a mixture of lead white, yellow ocher, and a clay substance that might have come from the wet clay soil of a nearby creek."

"And you know this how?"

"I dropped off the micro samples of the paint at the Museum of Fine Arts lab in Boston, before I took off for London. They confirmed the paint's substance. These are watercolor murals, which is much better than oil, in terms of them being better preserved. I also had the wallpaper's adhesive analyzed. The initial wallpaper was applied with a water-soluble starch glue, and that wallpaper pattern was one commonly used in the early to mid-nineteenth century. And, as I suspected, the wallpaper was available around the same time the murals were painted."

"Which is?"

"About eighteen thirty-six."

"So the murals are authentic?" I handed the clump back to him.

He examined it, turning it in his hand, then put it back down on the table. I waited for him to say something. When he didn't, I gushed again. "That's amazing."

He cocked his head. "How so?"

"You don't find it extraordinary that there was an artist this talented painting a wall mural in a southern Illinois farmhouse around eighteen thirty-six?"

"Yes and no." He glanced over my head toward the open kitchen window.

"What do you mean?"

He leaned back in his chair, stretching out his long legs. "I can explain it better if we're actually looking at the murals. Do you have a minute?"

His question was clearly rhetorical. Hadn't I been sitting in the stifling kitchen for over forty-five minutes, letting him gab on about tempera paint and clay soil? Why did I feel that that was where this conversation was leading from the moment I told him I'd inherited the house? I knew what was coming next; he wanted to finish the murals. Okay, let's play this out. I was curious to see how he would handle me. And how I would handle him.

Upstairs the heat was so thick it seemed to be a presence. As we walked into the mural room, I almost expected the large trees to be drooping in the heat.

Alex went to the farmhouse mural as if pulled by an invisible magnet. Standing in front of it, he ran his long, surprisingly slender, fingers over the surface as if it were the skin of a lover.

"Come closer," he said. His fingers outlined the farmhouse. "More than likely this house was drawn from a stencil, which wouldn't have been that difficult to get back then. It was a lot cheaper to decorate with paint than wallpaper. Also, wallpaper made a home for insects."

"But what about that enormous tree and that blackbird in it? Those don't look like stencils to me. And the composition, you have to admit that took some ability."

"You've got a good eye." He turned from the mural and stared at me as if he were seeing for the first time.

I felt my face flush under his gaze. "That's what I get paid the big bucks for."

"You're not a painter, are you?"

I laughed. "Performance artist."

"That have anything to do with your hair or lack of hair?" He swirled a finger over my head.

"All for my art. You were saying about the artist?" I coaxed, not wanting to talk about my shorn head. I was going to have to start wearing a bandanna.

"You ever hear of the nineteenth-century muralist Rufus Porter?"

"He couldn't have painted these," I answered. "He was a New England painter." I'd seen a few of his murals in an art-history book, but didn't know much else about Porter.

He turned back to the farmhouse mural. "Right, but don't you agree that it's as if he did? And that's what's so mysterious about these murals. As an itinerant painter who traveled throughout New England during the eighteen-twenties and thirties and into the forties, painting farmhouse and tavern walls, most of the time for the price of lodging and meals, he never set foot in Illinois. His murals are noted for their large trees, foreground plants, houses with steps, clouds, and"—he moved to the adjacent mural—"incongruent elements like this volcano and the Spanish galleon."

I joined him and took a closer look at the mural. Sure enough, one vessel was a Spanish galleon with sails billowing in the wind.

"Did he have students?" I turned toward Alex.

"Yeah, but the ones we know about stayed in New England as well. But he published a book in eighteen twenty-four called *Curious Arts,* which might explain our mystery artist. The book gave basic instructions on how to paint murals, and it was one of the most read of the early art-instruction books."

"So your guess is that the mystery artist was someone who lived here and had a copy of the Porter book?"

"More likely, some unknown itinerant painter who traveled through the Midwest and had a copy of Porter's book."

I walked to the monochromatic mural on the opposite wall. "Okay, maybe. But how do you explain this mural? Only a few stencils used here, mostly drawn freehand. Gray-green monochrome colors, remarkable composition. There's a different feel with this one, too."

He crossed the room and stood beside me. "You forgot historically significant."

"Aren't they all historically significant because of their age?"

"Yeah, but there's something peculiar to this particular mural." He took a magnifying glass from his back pocket and handed it to me. "Look at that downstairs window."

Under the magnification of the glass, I saw a person standing in the full-length window, a most unexpected person.

"Is that a Native American child?" The child had black braids, a feather in his hair, but was dressed in a blue suit of the time period.

"Now, look at the top window on the right."

A Native American woman was in that window, with a similar feather in her hair, and a dark-blue dress, also of the time period.

"It's not that unusual to see Native Americans in nineteenth-century murals. What's so significant?"

"If you take the time period the murals were painted, sometime in the mid-eighteen-thirties, and the fact that the

Cherokee came through this part of southern Illinois in eighteen thirty-eight during the forced march from their homelands to Oklahoma, we might be looking at miniatures of two Cherokee who were here then."

I studied the two portraits again. "You're talking about the Trail of Tears."

He turned toward me with an expression of incredible longing. "I can't explain the artistry in these murals, just like I can't explain why there's a volcano in this landscape or two drawings of Native Americans in this one. I'm positive that last wall will solve the mystery. You have to let me finish the restoration. It's what you sister wanted."

I stepped back out of the range of his intensity. "How do you know what my sister wanted?"

"Because she told me. You said that your sister died over a week ago. Well, check the date on this e-mail she sent me." He pulled a paper from his jeans pocket and handed it to me.

I unfolded the paper and read the date: July third, the date she died. The e-mail was sent at six-forty A.M. Later that night she would be dead. My hand was shaking as I read the e-mail.

Alex,

Yes, go ahead with the analysis of the fabric. Hang the cost. I know this is the real deal. I feel it in my gut. Looking forward to your return on July 11. If there's a change in your plans, let me know.

K

"What fabric is she talking about?" I was stalling for time, trying to think through if what Karen had wanted was what I wanted, because my knee-jerk reaction was to go against Karen's wishes, even if they were what I might want.

He must have slipped the clear sleeve from his pocket while I was reading Karen's e-mail, because now he was holding it carefully by his fingertips, taking the brownish fabric from the sleeve. He walked over to the farmhouse mural, took the fabric by its ends and placed it over the white road that ran from the house to the hill dotted with birds. It fit perfectly.

"What is that?" I asked, looking over his shoulder, inhaling his clean, soapy scent.

"It's a ribbon, a grosgrain ribbon to be exact. You can't tell, but it once was pink, made of silk. If you look real close you can see the two punctures."

I leaned in. Yes, there were two small dots piercing the ribbon.

"I didn't see them because there was wallpaper glue on the ribbon obscuring them. The textile lab in Boston found them. They're consistent with a pin, maybe from a brooch. The artist used this ribbon as a road."

"But why? When he could have used paint?"

"Maybe the ribbon had some special meaning to him."

Now it was my turn to run my fingers over the mural. I traced the road from the house to the field of blackbirds and felt a shiver of electricity.

"I can't pay you," I said.

"Your sister paid me up-front for the restoration. It's the only way I'd accept the commission."

"How long will it take to finish the last mural?"

"A week, maybe a little more."

"I'm not planning on sticking around that long. Once I finish packing the rest of my sister's things, which I hope to do today, I'm heading back to Chicago."

"You don't need to be here."

"Okay, but I can't take the house off the market while you work." I was putting hurdle after hurdle in front of him, not sure why, acting out of some primal instinct.

"I wouldn't expect you to. I can start right now."

"Sure, okay, sure. Just let me know if you need anything." I was through the doorway when something occurred to me. "Do you think these murals are worth anything?"

His eyes looked away as if he were seeing the answer. "Depends on what you mean by worth? Historically they're worth a lot, but from a collector's point of view, probably not much. Unless you could prove they were painted by Porter or someone of that caliber."

"Say I could, then what?"

"Then we'd have them removed and sold at auction. The last Porter murals sold for around twenty-five grand each."

I stood there not moving, my brain reeling with possibilities. Four walls at twenty-five grand each was a tidy profit. "Do you think Karen knew who the artist was?"

He hesitated, which made me think he was holding back something. "No, but I got the impression she had a hunch."

"Do you have a hunch?"

Again, the hesitation. "Not yet. Maybe once I uncover that last mural and see what's there, I'll know more."

Then it hit me. Duh—the most important question. Why hadn't I thought of it from the start? "You never said how Karen knew the murals were here in the first place? If they were buried under layers of paint and wallpaper for over one hundred and seventy-odd years, how could she have known about them?" I may not be the sharpest knife in the drawer, but eventually I cut my way through.

He came so close I could smell coffee on his breath as he reached toward me. Instinctively I stepped back. But instead of touching me, he reached over my head to a spot above the doorway.

I turned and looked up to see where he was pointing. "See how there's only traces of the mural here? She'd started removing the layers over the doorway first. When she pulled away the first chunk, she saw bits of the mural underneath. At least that's what she told me."

Then, before I could stop myself, I said, "You don't smoke, do you?" Did I really think he'd been outside the house last night spying on me?

He titled his head and smiled. "No, why?"

"No reason."

Chapter Four

By eleven o'clock the solvent smell of Alex's chemicals wafted through the house, mingling with the rising humidity in a toxic brew that was giving me a throbbing headache. Even with all the windows open to the max, I felt like my lungs were being seared with every breath. How could he stand being in that room? I thought. As far as I could tell he'd taken only one break to use the bathroom.

I'd puttered around in the parlor and the kitchen, packing up loose personal items, taking countless breaks to drink water, and walk outside to fill my burning lungs with fresh air.

Only Karen's study awaited me like some siren call, but instead of rocks I'd founder on books, day planners, bills and letters—the essence of Karen's life. And even worse, the memory of her broken body sprawled across the study floor.

There's no one else, I told myself, as I took in another chemical breath and strode down the hall toward Karen's study. As I neared the study, the chemical smell grew virulent, drawing me toward the mural room, where I stopped to watch Alex work.

If he knew I was standing inside the door, he didn't acknowledge me. His whole body leaned into the ladder, his gloved fingers holding what looked like a slender silver scalpel, which he inched meticulously behind a flap of painted wallpaper. He wore a pair of goggles, probably magnified, and a high-powered lamp was focused on his work area. Scattered around the room was an assortment of tools.

I was about to ask him if he wanted something cold to drink, but something about the delicacy of what he was doing and his absolute focus changed my mind. Instead, I walked across the hall and into Karen's study as if it were any other room, going straight to her desk and avoiding all eye contact with the area of the floor where she'd died.

Sitting at her desk, I opened the middle drawer and found her checkbook and day planner. Beside the checkbook was a paper-clipped pile of the month's bills. From what I could see, every bill was paid and duly noted in her checkbook; the last check was to the electric company dated June 29. The check to Alex Hague was there—a hefty sum that made me gasp.

"Wow," I said aloud, forgetting Alex was across the hall earning this money. Then an angry jolt shot through me as I remembered Karen's words. "I can't keep enabling you."

I closed the checkbook and threw it into a box. "No chance of that, sis."

Her day planner was already written in for the fall, a fall she would never see. She was scheduled to teach Native American Studies and a seminar on European Colonialism in the sixteenth century, on Tuesdays and Thursday—her life was a testament to everything I wasn't—organized, responsible, reasonable.

I flipped forward a few pages, noting that every first weekend of the month like clockwork, she'd written the words Newberry Library. When I reached November my stomach tightened at the sight of my name. I'd been penciled in for Thanksgiving with a question mark after my name. I picked up a pen and scratched out my name, ripping the paper. Then I threw the day planner at the checkbook with such force the box moved. I pushed the chair back and stood up. My jean shorts and chartreuse chemise top clung to my sweaty body like wet paint and my head was pounding.

I'm outta here.

I stomped across the hall to the mural room and stood in the doorway with my hands on my hips.

"Listen, I have to run into town. Call me on my cell if you need anything." I didn't wait for an answer, but hurried down the stairs, grabbed my purse from the hall table and left.

Driving away, I watched in the rearview mirror as the house slowly disappeared as if devoured by the trees, the land, and the sky. Then it was gone. I swiped at my eyes, the tears another betrayal.

Get a grip, I scolded myself as the gravel road turned to asphalt darkened with the shadows of trees arching overhead, dabbling the car with a wavering light that pulsed with uncertainty. Not unlike the uncertainty I'd been feeling since I'd stepped inside that house. Nothing made sense. What had the dilapidated house, the black lacy underwear, the mysterious murals, to do with my sister, a woman who to outward appearances wore one of three somber colors almost every day of her life? But underneath she'd been hiding a different self, a self that I hadn't known existed, a self I'd like to have known. Maybe if she'd shown me a glimmer of this other self, then we could have been sisters not just in name only but in feeling. Was I partially to blame for her secrecy, with my guardedness and the massive chip on my shoulder I wore like a badge of courage? Who could blame her for not wanting to trust me?

As the road curved right and flattened, I gripped the steering wheel tighter as if the car were driving me, searching for the white steepled church, my marker to bear to the right. There it was, rising clean against the fading blue of the spent sky.

I loosened my grip and slowed the car, wanting to read the two stone markers edging the church grounds. On my way to the house, I'd only glimpsed the stone markers near the modest cemetery, but I recalled seeing a date etched into the stones, eighteen something. A little local research would get my mind off my jagged relationship with Karen.

Union County Church Est. 1850, the first stone marker read. That was well after the Braun house was built.

Easing my foot off the gas pedal, I let the car roll forward to the second sign: *Campground Cemetery Since 1836 Trail of Tears.*

I leaned back, still staring at the stone marker. The cemetery had been established around the same time as the farmhouse was built. Was there a connection?

Abruptly I pulled the car off the road onto the grass, grabbed my old SRL camera from the backseat where I kept it, and jumped out, my mind spinning: Campground Cemetery, 1836, Trail of Tears, the Braun farmhouse mural, painted around the same time period.

Could the Braun descendants be buried in this cemetery? Surely Alex had checked it out. If there'd been a connection, he would have mentioned it to me. Well, if nothing else, I could walk off my nervous energy taking what I called "gut shots."

The heat was like an assault, the sky troubled with clouds that seemed to make it only hotter as I walked toward the church and the cemetery grounds, snapping a few quick random shots, not bothering to check the viewfinder, just letting the camera be an extension of my subconscious.

As if in an undertow I was submerged into the landscape, the soggy emerald-green grass, the white-framed church, which resembled a child's drawing, the headstones, their rippling stone—all of it melting into the midday heat. Later when I developed the film, I would be there: the smell of wet grass, the keen cut of blue sky, and the quiet of bodies long dead.

When I reached the cemetery, where about forty headstones were placed in neat rows behind the church, I slung my camera over my shoulder, taking in a deep breath as if I'd finally surfaced, and walked from headstone to headstone searching for the Braun name. As I walked, it was as if I walked back and forth through time and people's lives, 1856, 1903, 1869, 1873—Werman, Fowler, and Davis. But no Braun.

The last row of headstones ended next to an upturned tree, an enormous oak that had fallen away from the graves, exposing a snarl of twisted roots that looked like a nest of snakes. A large shovel rested against the tree.

When I neared the end of the row, I stopped.

Charles Braun, beloved son of Edward and Emily Braun, Born 1832, Died 1838.

The headstone was badly worn and simply etched, the words barely visible and haphazardly carved into the stone as if grief had shaken the carver's hand.

I knelt down to get a closer look, drops of sweat running down my nose. An angel had been etched into the stone, at least it looked like an angel—the face gone, only an outline of wings and body.

Next to his headstone was: *Edward Braun, dearest father, Born 1800, Died 1860.*

Then, *Captain James Braun, soldier, husband and father, Born 1843, Died 1895.*

The fourth headstone said, *Leticia Braun, wife of Edward Braun. Born 1820, Died 1885.*

And the last was, *Emily Lord Braun, wife of Edward Braun. Born 1812, Died 1842.* The ground around her headstone was disturbed as if the grave were newly dug. From the position of the fallen tree and the grave, the disturbance must have happened when the tree fell.

I sat back on my heels staring at the five headstones, thinking about what the dates told me. Charles Braun, the only son of Edward and Emily, had died at age six. After Emily's death, Edward had remarried and fathered another child, James, in quick order. James Senior and his drug-dealing son were direct descendants of Edward and Leticia.

Slinging my camera around, I aimed it at the headstones, snapping photo after photo, as if I could somehow bring these people back to life, as if they would rise out of the ground and tell me their secrets.

"Whatta you doing there, babe?"

So intent on what I was doing, I hadn't heard anyone approach. When I twisted around, I saw a man lurking over me holding a chain saw, a cigarette dangling from his mouth. His black baseball cap was on backwards and behind his thick glasses, his eyes seemed vaguely blue. Tufts of hair sprouted from the hollow of his collarbone.

"Just taking some photos." I raised the camera at him indicating I was harmless. Then stood up and wiped my dirty hands on my shorts. "Hope that's okay."

"Well, well," he said, as if he couldn't form a sentence, staring at my flimsy chemise top. "That tree's my job, sweet cheeks." His hands were mud-caked and both knees of his jeans were thready and worn through. Under the reek of alcohol, I could smell his body odor.

"What happened to it?" I asked, resisting the urge to cross my arms over my chest to block his leering gaze.

"Duh, fell over," he answered, chuckling to himself. He spat the cigarette in the direction of my sandaled feet. It landed on my big toe and bounced off.

That tore it. "You work here?" I asked sharply, switching into my city attitude.

"You gonna report me to the reverend?" He taunted, grinning and showing two missing lower teeth.

"You want me to?" I shot back at him, a rush of anger dampening my common sense. I should have walked away instead of engaging in banter with a drunken lout.

He started to laugh. "That's a good one." He pulled back on the chain saw and revved it a few times. Then he started toward me, the blades vibrating with menace. I stepped backwards a few paces and collided with someone.

Startled, I turned around and said, "Sorry," to the tall, solidly built woman dressed in a sleeveless blue work shirt, khaki shorts and hiking boots. Her long black hair was loosely held in a tortoiseshell clip at the back of her head, strands stuck out like straw. Her face and arms were covered in a confusion of freckles that made her pale skin look painful.

"Can I help you?" she shouted over the noise of the chain saw. She was watching the guy work on the tree, a worried look on her face.

I shook my head no and started to walk away across the cemetery toward the road where I'd parked my car.

"Wait up," she called, hurrying after me. I stopped.

"He didn't say anything, um, upsetting to you?"

There was an earnestness about her question that made me want to temper my answer. "I've heard worse."

She glanced back over her shoulder where the guy was cutting through the thick tree. "Whatever he said, he doesn't mean anything by it. Sometimes he doesn't think before he talks."

Especially when he's had a few, I thought. I couldn't believe she couldn't smell the liquor oozing from his pores—or maybe she could. "Don't worry about it," I reassured her.

"Good, good. I'm Reverend Suzanne Likely, by the way." She held out her hand to me and smiled.

"Rose Caffrey," I said, grasping her hand and smiling back.

Her whole face changed. "You're Karen's sister. Oh, my gosh, Dan Yeager told me about you. I was so sorry to hear about Karen."

"Was she a member of your church?" I didn't think Karen was religious, but I was discovering a lot of things about Karen I didn't know. Each discovery like a bandage ripped off revealing a wound underneath.

"Not for lack of trying on my part."

"Nice meeting you," I said and started to walk away again.

"Hold up."

I turned around.

"You look like you could use a cold drink, and my housekeeper left me a pitcher of lemonade. It's the least I can do to make up for Jimmy's rudeness."

"Jimmy?"

"Yeah, Jimmy Braun. His family used to own the old farmhouse Karen bought."

"Sit, please," Reverend Likely demanded, as she handed me one of the frosted glasses of lemonade. Her authoritarian tone surprised me.

Dutifully, I sat on the small floral sofa and she sat down next to me a little too close for my comfort, adding to the rectory office's cave-like feeling with its dark paneling and heavily draped windows. The only light, an overhead, cast a spotlight on the gray-speckled linoleum.

"So, that was Jimmy Braun," I began, sipping the homemade lemonade and glancing at her black liturgical robe carelessly thrown across her messy desk piled with papers and books. "Dan Yeager told me Karen had him evicted and that he'd been dealing drugs out of the house." I was still miffed at the guy's blatant hostility and perplexed by Reverend Likely's defensiveness.

"That's all in the past," she said, waving her hand as if swatting at flies. "He's working to turn his life around. Attends AA meetings regularly and works here as a caretaker in exchange for room and board. As to the drugs that was a rumor."

"I guess you'd know." She seemed so adamant about his reform; I knew it would be useless to mention the alcohol I smelled on him.

She took a big gulp of her lemonade and then placed the glass firmly on a side table. "When I first saw you walking around in the churchyard with your camera, I thought you might be another curiosity seeker looking for the unmarked graves. Ever since that article came out about the graves, we've had people stomping around the cemetery as if it were Disneyland. But then I saw you over by the Braun graves."

"Unmarked graves?" I asked, wondering if she was trying to divert my attention from the loathsome Jimmy Braun. "What unmarked graves?"

"You don't know about them?" She cocked her head in surprise.

"Should I?" I didn't have a clue what she was talking about.

"I just thought because you're Karen's sister. She might have told you."

"We really weren't that close," I said, to cover the hurt I was trying to push down.

"I'm sorry. Her death must have been particularly hard on you. And I'm babbling on about the graves."

Her sympathetic expression made me wince. I shifted in my seat. "I don't understand."

"Because now it's too late to fix it. I see this all the time in my line of work. 'Figure out what regrets you can live with,' I tell people. If you can't live with them, do something about it."

If she'd wanted to sucker punch me, she had. I felt the bitter taste of lemons in my mouth.

"So what's my sister's connection to the graves?" I coaxed her, desperate to change the subject.

"She's the one who's behind the search for the unmarked graves—or she was. She's also the driving force behind the Union County Trail of Tears Organization." She was still looking at me with that sympathetic expression.

"You do know about the Trail of Tears and the Cherokee who

were forced by the feds to relocate to Oklahoma in eighteen thirty-eight and eighteen thirty-nine?"

"Only that some of the Cherokee came through here on the northern route." I remembered Alex's theory that the portraits of the woman and child in the one mural might be Cherokee who'd walked the trail.

"Yeah, much of Route One Forty-Six follows the trail the Cherokee walked from the Ohio River west to the Mississippi River that awful winter."

"So you're saying the unmarked graves are of the Cherokee who died during that march?"

"That's what we're trying to find out. Lawrence Grey—he's a geology professor from the university and a board member of the UCTOT. He's been searching the cemetery with this ground-penetrating radar. But all he's been able to find so far are areas where the soil layers were disturbed. Which could mean the presence of graves." She picked up her drink and took another sip. "But we can't dig up those areas because if there are graves, it would be a desecration. So whether the Cherokee are buried there or early settlers, who knows?"

"How many graves are we talking about?" I asked. The cemetery wasn't that large.

"The radar couldn't tell how many, but the site's been witched about six times and we found fifteen graves."

"Witched?"

"It's a method old-timers use, similar to dousing for water sources. Where you use two rods of a particular metal and when you walk over a grave, the ends of the rod cross. Very unscientific."

My mind drifted back again to the Native American portraits in the one mural. "Were there any written records of who died?"

She let out a tight laugh. "You're kidding, right? You've got three detachments of Cherokee coming through southern Illinois in the hardest winter in memory. They don't have shoes, food, shelter, blankets or warm clothing." She ticked off the list on her fingers. Her fingernails were painted a shocking electric blue.

"They're sleeping on mud and ice. Then to make matters worse, they're trapped for a month between the frozen Ohio River and ice-packed Mississippi. Do you think anyone who lost a loved one along the trail put up a marker? And the soldiers sure as hell weren't going to be keeping records of such misery." Her voice was sharp with anger. "Not a great moment in American history, huh?"

The picture of devastation she'd painted was souring my stomach. "Didn't anybody help them?"

"Some farmers let them camp and hunt on their land at various stops along the trail. Some took in one or two young children. There's a story that the Cherokee offered their daughters in marriage to the locals, which as the legend goes, they accepted."

I saw the blaze of passion in her flushed cheeks.

"Sorry. I get pretty worked up when I talk about it. That's why we formed the UCTOT. To make people aware that the Cherokee came through here and what happened to them."

She ran her hands up and down her long legs. "I'm really surprised Karen never mentioned any of this to you. Your sister's the one who fought to have the church grounds certified as a historic site. And she convinced Lawrence to get involved. We're really going to miss her."

"Me, too," I said lamely. While I'd been pursuing an artistic career, my sister was fighting the good fight, bringing to light wrongs done to minorities in American history.

"Karen never said so, but I suspect that's why she bought the old Braun farmhouse." She downed the last of her lemonade.

"What do you mean?" Maybe I'd finally know the reason

behind Karen's uncharacteristic move.

"Edward Braun, the guy who built the farmhouse, allowed the Cherokee to camp and to bury their dead on his land, which eventually became the church cemetery. At least that's the story passed down in the Braun family. His son, Charles, was the first person buried in the cemetery. Edward must have had great sympathy for the Cherokee who were suffering bereavement just as he and his wife had the year before."

"So the church grounds and the cemetery were once owned by the Braun family," I said as if talking to myself. My mind circled back to the farmhouse mural, the ribbon road, the field scattered with blackbirds. I needed to get back to the farmhouse and study the mural more closely. And I needed to know more about the Braun family. "Just how much land did Edward Braun own?"

"It'd be easier if I showed you." She went over to a tall corner cabinet, opened a middle drawer from which she took an eleven-by-thirteen sheet of paper. Laying the sheet across her messy desk, she switched on the desk lamp and gestured me over. It was a plat survey map of Union country dated 1840.

"Maps are a hobby of mine," she explained as if I'd asked her. "Here is the Braun farm." She ran her finger over a large area of land. "Back then they owned about one hundred acres, from the farmhouse to Route One Forty-Six. In eighteen fifty-four, Edward deeded this ground to the church." She tapped the map with her electric-blue fingernail. "The rest got sold off through the years until what you have now."

It was a vast piece of land that included all the land that the church and the cemetery occupied.

She straightened up and said, "So, Dan tells me you're selling the house."

"Yeah, but he wasn't very encouraging. Karen died before she could finish the exterior renovations." I didn't know why, but I held back telling her about the mural room or Alex Hague, though probably Dan had already clued her in. Maybe I was smarting from her remark about regrets. "Soon as I clear out my sister's personal effects, I'm heading back to Chicago."

"I wish the UCTOT could buy the property, but we just don't have the funds. I know we could get it listed as a national historic site and open it to the public. Any chance you'd like to go that route, maybe deed the property to the association and get a huge tax write-off?"

"I wish I could, but I need the money. I'm selling it well under market value," I said encouragingly.

"Maybe I should have said, 'We don't have any funds.' We rely pretty much on pro bono for everything."

For an uncomfortable moment, I listened to the air conditioner click on and the cool air whoosh through the vents. "You know anything else about the Brauns? Where they came from, who they were, that kinda thing?"

"Sounds like you're smitten with the house."

I felt my face go hot. "Thought I'd include some history on the listing sheet to pique interest. What about Jimmy Braun? Would he know anything?"

She crossed her freckled arms over her chest. "No, I don't think he'd be any help to you."

Says you, I thought. "Any chance I can have a copy of this?"

Her large blue eyes disappeared with her broad smile. "Like I said, you're smitten. Sure I'll copy it for you. Only take a minute. You know you should check out the Morris University Library for archival material related to southern Illinois and the Braun family during that time period. I know when I was putting together the Trail of Tears Symposium last year, they were a big help. Come to think of it, I'll give you a copy of the symposium panels and my presentation, 'Trapped in Union County Between Two Rivers.'"

When she returned, she handed me a large brown envelope.

"You find out anything about the Brauns, let me know, or about the Cherokee who came through here. I want to get the truth out there about what the Cherokee went through that brutal winter. We can't change the past, but, as the old saying goes, if we don't learn from it, we're doomed to repeat it." She let out a laugh as if embarrassed by her own enthusiasm.

"Thanks for your help," I said.

"If there's anything else you need, come by. Even if you just want to talk."

"Like I said, once I clear out my sister's things, I'm heading back home to Chicago."

She extended her hand. "Nice meeting you, Rose."

As I took her hand, she put her other hand over mine. It almost felt like an embrace.

The grass shimmered in the afternoon heat as I walked across the cemetery grounds to my car musing on what I'd learned from Reverend Likely about Edward Braun, the Cherokee, and the Trail of Tears.

When I reached my car, I turned around, sensing someone watching me. Near the Braun graves stood Jimmy Braun. Very gradually as if in slow motion, he raised his fist and then released his middle finger, all the time a grin smeared across his face.

All in the past, huh? I thought, opening my car door and getting in.

Chapter Five

From Anna, it took me about forty minutes to reach Morris University in Carbondale. The campus was a sprawling blend of brick and concrete surrounded by forest, fields and lakes.

I pulled into the parking lot behind the library, turned off the engine, but didn't get out of the car. Instead I stared at the library building, a wonder of soaring glass and dusty red brick, questioning what I was doing here.

Shifting through old dusty papers was Karen's thing. Mine was tearing at the edges of art and beauty on stage, in galleries, and in public places. Making people think, making them uncomfortable in their own skins. Mainly because I was so uncomfortable in my own skin.

A string of crows squawked and rippled across the shifting blue afternoon, harsh and lovely, making me gaze up and watch until they'd shimmered past.

It's just an afternoon, not the rest of your life, I reasoned. Who knows? Maybe you'll find out if Karen bought the old house because of the graves and their connection to the Brauns.

I got out of the car, slammed the door and walked to the front entrance.

At the information desk, a thirty-something man with slender fingers and an attitude directed me to the rare books room on the first floor. "Just like it says here," he said impatiently, handing me an information sheet.

Once inside the glass doors, I was struck by the sleek modernism of the space, not at all how I would have envisioned a rare books room.

Behind the muted steel information counter sat a spiky-haired platinum blonde, who seemed to echo the modernity of the space. Her makeup was hardcore, her one eyebrow sported a silver hoop, and a snake's tail tattoo coiled round her neck.

"Can I help you?" she asked in a high-pitched, childish voice, which was at odds with her tough-chick look.

"I'm doing research on a house built in eighteen thirty-five in Anna. I want to know about the original owners of the house. Their name was Braun. Do you have any stuff like that?" I was trying not to sound too much like a novice.

"You're going to want archival letters and diaries dated around that time. Also, you can check census records for that period online. I can show you how to do that, if you like." Her jewelry-free eyebrow went up.

"I'll start with the letters and diaries." I was already regretting my decision.

She handed me a yellow card and said, "Put what you want in the request section. And I'll need two forms of ID, one a photo ID."

I took out my driver's license and my Chicago Artists Coalition membership card and handed them to her.

While I filled out the card, she photocopied my IDs. After I handed her the completed card, she stapled the photocopied IDs to the back of my request card and gave me back my documents.

"Chicago, huh?" She typed information into the computer at the front desk while she talked, then jotted something on another yellow card. "We don't get many researchers from Chicago down here. Chicago has such amazing university libraries, and, of course, the Newberry Library." She said *down here* as if the words were a judgment.

I forced a smile in response. All those weekends Karen had spent at the Newberry Library, and she'd never once let me know she was in the city.

"If you'll wait in that room over there, I'll bring you the documents. By the way, my name's Holly."

I went into the glass-enclosed room and sat at one of the long stainless tables. On a hot day like today, the cool surface was like a dip in a swimming pool.

After about ten minutes Holly returned.

"There isn't a lot, but here's what I found. We're still cataloguing a lot of this material. Ever since that Trail of Tears Symposium last fall, people have been donating like crazy. Most of the stuff is of dubious historical value. But we still have to go through it all." She plopped a handful of folders down on the table. "When you're looking at the material, try not to handle it too much. Just turn the pages as if they were in a book. If you need anything else, I'll be in the back storage room resorting the undergrads' idea of filing. There's a call button at the front desk. But don't take the archival material out of this room. You gotta love undergrads, always in a big hurry."

After she shuffled out of the room, I stared at the folders and groaned. This was going to take forever. After about an hour, I'd scanned all of the letters, none of which were to or from the Braun family.

I gathered up the folders, left them on the table, and went looking for Holly. She wasn't at the front desk, so I pressed the call button.

"Did you find what you were looking for?" she asked, when she reached the front desk.

"No. But thanks, anyway." I started for the door.

"You might try the period prior and the period after. Sometimes things get put in the wrong folders," she offered.

"You're kidding," I said sarcastically.

"You can always come back tomorrow."

"That's okay. Might as well get this over with."

"Research can be bitch, can't it? I'll bring the archival material to you in the documents room. You can fill out the yellow cards while you wait."

When she returned, she was carrying a banker's box. "Here's what we have. *Bon appétit.*"

Reluctantly, I opened the box and pulled out about ten folders, groaning louder this time. Like the others, each tab gave the time period of the documents contained inside. Though the time periods, as Holly explained, were earlier and later than the period I was looking for, I decided to check inside each folder anyway in case something had been misplaced.

About halfway into the pile I opened a folder labeled: Business Ledger, General Store, 1846–1861. Inside was one item—a brown leather binder, cracked and worn, holding yellowing papers. As I opened the leather binder to the front page, the hairs on the back of my neck tingled.

Written in an eloquent flourish, as if every letter was a work of art, were the words: "Diary of Mrs. Emily Lord Braun, wife of Edward Braun."

Below her name she'd written: January 1, 1838 to December 31, 1839.

My hand was trembling as I turned the first few pages and saw that each entry was dated. Though I wanted to scan the pages quickly, I resisted the urge, remembering what Karen had once said about her research.

"Research is like a house's foundation. Without it, the house wouldn't stand."

I turned to the first entry and started reading. Maybe here I'd find the answer to who had painted the murals. My grumblings had vanished and been replaced by curiosity and excitement.

The Lost Artist

From Emily Braun's entries, I was able to flesh out this pioneering woman who had left her home in Ohio to travel west with her husband, Edward Braun, and their son, Charlie, to southern Illinois, where Edward's wanderlust could be sated. He was the kind of man who saw opportunity around the next bend. I was so taken with the narrative of the Brauns' struggle to settle into the community, Edward's attempts at farming and running a small law practice, that when I read the first sentence of the September 13, 1838, entry I turned back a few pages thinking I'd skipped something. No, I hadn't.

> *September 13, 1838*
> *My beloved son Charlie died this morning around dawn. I write these words as if I am in a nightmare from which I will awake soon. Yesterday, he complained of a headache and was running a fever. Edward said it was an ague that would pass in a few days. Edward was wrong.*

The ink blurred with the last few words, and the rest of the page stood as a silent testament to her loss.
The next entry's date was: January 10, 1839.

> *Today, Edward attended to the sick Indians camping at the campgrounds. The weather has been dreadful. I don't know which is worst, the brutal cold or the ice and snow. I did not want my husband to go, but as his wife I cannot prevent him. Sometimes I wonder if Edward's grief over Charlie's death does not make him foolhardy. I have my faith, but Edward has lost his.*
>
> *My husband did not return until the next morning. That night the temperature dropped sharply and I feared for him. When he finally returned, he*

I turned to the next page; it was blank. The paper was the

same, yellowy and jagged, but nothing was written on it. And there were no more pages. Where were the rest of the pages? Emily had dated her diary from January 1, 1838, to December 31, 1839. I straightened the pages and closed the folder. Clearly this folder had been mislabeled. Maybe the pages had fallen out of the folder and were inside another folder. Quickly, I went through the remaining folders, not finding any diary pages written by Emily Braun.

I picked up the folder containing the diary and studied the mislabeled tab closely. It was thicker than the other tabs. With my fingernail, I push up on the edge. Underneath was another tab. Carefully, I pulled away the blank tab. The covered tab was dated: January 1, 1838, to December 31, 1839. Which meant that the entire diary had been here.

Someone had removed the rest of the diary entries and tried to cover it up.

Who had done this and why? What was contained in the missing pages?

I closed the diary and took it and the folder with me as I walked down the long hall to the archival storage room where Holly was still sitting sorting through files, boxes and papers. She looked up, startled, about to reprimand me for my breach in library protocol.

"Holly, I think we have a problem."

Holly stood and dusted off her jeans. "What kind of a problem?"

In answer I held the diary open to the last page, then showed her the tab and the remnants of the other tab, explaining what I'd found.

"Why would someone do that?" she asked. "If they wanted what was on those pages all they had to do was request copies. We do that all the time."

"Can you check to see who was the last person before me to

access these particular folders?"

"Sure. We keep the yellow cards filed according to the material requested. This way we can keep track of who requests what. Let's check out the request file drawers and see what we can find."

I followed her to a room marked Office two doors down. "Like I said before, we file these cards according to the documents requested. But because the folder was mislabeled, we might not find what we're looking for."

She pulled out a drawer and extracted a yellow card. "Okay, this is bizarre. Karen Caffrey, a professor at this university, requested the archival material dated eighteen thirty-eight through eighteen thirty-nine, Emily Lord Braun diary on June fifteen. So it must have been in the correctly labeled folder and box originally, but then was filed in the wrong box." She looked up, her eyes boring into mine. "Do you know her?"

I shrugged. "Caffrey's a fairly common name. Just a weird coincidence, I guess." I smiled innocently, inside wondering why I'd lied. Why was I feeling guilty as if I had done something wrong? "Anyway, who requested the folder before this Professor Caffrey?" My heart was thudding in my chest. Karen was the last person to request this folder. Had she been the person who'd removed the pages or had someone else done it prior?

Holly pulled out another card slowly, her forehead wrinkling in disbelief. "March ninth. Karen Caffrey again." She flipped through the section before and after the Braun document section. "Those are the only two requests. This is really strange."

"What do you mean?" I asked, afraid that she was referring to our shared name.

"Well, usually there's information in the section about when the item was first catalogued. But there's nothing here. Let me check online."

She left the room for a few minutes and went to the front

desk. I ran my hand back and forth over my stubbly head, not sure what to do. Was she going for the cops? I went to the door. Too late. Holly was bounding down the hallway.

When she came into the room, she was biting the side of her mouth. "It's listed in our online catalogue as Braun family papers but there's no information on when they were given to the library or by whom."

"Is that unusual?" I asked, relieved to see that she was alone.

"It happens. Sometimes the stuff is found in boxes in closets and nobody remembers how it got here." She bit the side of her mouth again. "I've called campus security. So you're going to have to wait until they get here."

Damn. I looked at my watch and let out an exasperated sigh of annoyance. "Look, I have another appointment I'm already late for." A feeling of panic was tightening my chest. For some inexplicable reason, police made my palms itch.

"They said you're not to leave. I told them about the theft, about Karen Caffrey having taken out the items." Suddenly Holly, the nonconformist, sounded like a cop.

"But I don't know anything. I'm the one who told you about the missing pages. You wouldn't have even known they were missing if it wasn't for me." I wanted out of there before security descended with their questions. I needed to think through what I'd discovered. Figure out Karen's connection to the missing diary pages.

"If they want to talk to me, here's my cell-phone number." I wrote my number on the back of my business card.

"You can't leave," she said as I started for the door. "I told them your name was Caffrey. They want to talk to you."

As I walked through the front doors of the library, I saw a security guard heading for the rare books room. I forced myself to walk at a normal pace. Not until I was inside my car did I let out a deep sigh of relief.

Why had I run? I could explain why I was researching the Braun archives. I hadn't done anything wrong. But maybe Karen had.

If so, why had she taken the pages? Something in those pages had turned my law-abiding sister into a thief.

But why not copy the pages, as Holly said? Why risk her academic reputation?

The only reason I could think of was she didn't want anyone else to read those pages. That would also explain why the diary folder was relabeled and misfiled. She didn't want to make it easy to find. But why didn't she take the entire diary? Because she knew it was listed in the online catalogue. None of this made sense.

When had Karen purchased the house? I dug through the mess of papers on my backseat and extracted the realty folder Dan Yeager had given me containing the comps.

April 21. That was the closing date. And the dates on the library request cards were March 9 and June 15.

Thinking through the chronology, I watched a guy wearing a red baseball cap bob through the parking lot, his head moving to the music from his earbuds, oblivious to everything.

Karen had purchased the house after discovering the diary. Something in Emily Braun's diary had made her buy that house. Was that something the murals or the unmarked graves or both?

And finding the murals hadn't happened as she'd told Alex Hague. She hadn't been removing wallpaper and inadvertently found the tracing of a mural. She knew the murals were there from the start. Maybe she'd torn a piece away from the wall to be sure. Who had painted them, and why were they so important? That was what I had to find out.

My cell phone's shrill ring startled me. I dug it out of my purse and checked the screen: MU Campus Security. I let it ring itself into silence, and then I turned my phone off.

Chapter Six

It was past four o'clock when I pulled up in front of the farmhouse. The sun's throbbing heat glazed the house in a harsh light—every defect on display for potential buyers to see—tilted chimney, peeling clapboards, sagging porch. Alex's car was still there in the very same spot where he'd parked it this morning. The guy was determined, if nothing else.

I exited the car and stood in the weedy grass, fighting my urge to tell him about the diary and the missing pages. Maybe he could help me find them. After all, he was an expert in historical research.

But I wasn't sure if I trusted him or, precisely, I didn't trust myself to know if he was trustworthy. When it came to men, I was almost always wrong. Two failed marriages and a string of lovers had taught me I didn't have a clue about men.

My first husband, Rick, who I'd married at nineteen, had been a struggling painter whose oeuvre was clown motifs. I'd been attracted to his ability to piss off my parents and my sister. It wasn't until he'd hit me a few times that I realized love shouldn't leave a mark. As if I had no long-term memory, I married Sam—by day an accountant, by night a gamer. He never hit me. In fact, he'd left no mark on me at all, and that was the problem. Nick was my only lasting male relationship.

No, this time I was going to do this alone.

Once inside, I paused at the foot of the stairs, holding the crammed envelope to my chest, listening to the sound of creaking floorboards overhead.

Good, he's still working. I crept up the stairs, down the hall and into Karen's study, hoping he wouldn't see me. I knew if he did, I'd end up blabbing everything like an insecure teenager in need of validation.

First things first—what was the date on that check to Alex? I rummaged in the box beside Karen's desk where I'd thrown her files, daybook and checkbook in my hurt and anger. The checkbook fell open to the page where Karen had recorded the check. Again, I gritted my teeth at the amount. The check was dated June sixteenth. That was the day after she'd accessed Emily Braun's diary for the last time and probably stolen the pages.

Quickly, I jotted down a timeline:

March 9—finds E. Braun's diary—MU Library

April 21—closes on Braun house

June 15—accesses E. Braun's diary for last time—MU Library

June 16—hires Alex Hague to restore murals

I rocked back in the chair and stared out the back window at the hill at the rear of the property where a stand of trees burnished in the late afternoon sun. If she'd stolen the diary pages, she'd done it before she'd hired Hague.

Maybe she'd stored information in her computer files about the house, the murals, the Brauns and/or the diary. I waited for her computer to power up.

Damn, I whispered. Her files were password protected. Okay, think: what password would she use? After trying family birthdays, the street in Chicago where we'd grown up, Kenmore, and every other personal reference, I was about to give up when I remembered Baby, the feral cat Karen had cared for when she was fourteen, until it was hit by a car.

To my utter astonishment, it worked. I was in.

Clever, Karen, very clever. Only four people knew about Baby, and two of them were dead. Now three.

I searched her hard drive and document files, did multiple searches via Finder. There was no information related to murals, the Brauns, or nineteenth-century painters. I clicked on her Bookmarks. Bingo. Her bookmarked research files were a potpourri of sites about the Trail of Tears, the Cherokee people, nineteenth-century mural painters, including Rufus Porter, and Alex Hague's Web site. I clicked on his Web site and scanned through it. His credentials were impeccable. Karen had chosen wisely.

After powering down the computer, I pushed back on the chair and stood up, rubbing the ache in my lower back, dreading what I needed to do next—search through hundreds of books for the missing diary pages. Karen might have hidden the pages in plain sight, so to speak, inside one of the books. That would be so Karen.

Though there had to be over five hundred books filling the floor-to-ceiling bookcases that lined the three walls, the task went fairly quickly, a matter of holding the books upside down and shaking them to dislodge any loose pages.

When I reached the last wall of books, the one Karen had fallen from, I went through the bottom shelves first. Nothing. Before tackling the upper shelves, I checked the books that had tumbled to the floor with Karen and were pushed against the wall. One novel entitled *Obsessed* and five books of poetry, hardly the kinds of books I'd expect Karen to be reading. Maybe that was why she'd stowed them on the top shelf. Nothing inside any of them. Might as well put them back on the shelf. I rested the ladder against the bookcase, jiggling it a few times to steady it.

With the books in my arms, I climbed up the ladder, which shimmied with every step. When I reached the second step near the top, I placed the books on the top step of the ladder. From here I could reach the top shelf, but Karen, who was four inches shorter than me at five feet one, would have had to stand on the very top step to reach the top shelf, a hazardous position on a shaky ladder. Why would she do that? The diary pages weren't hidden in the books. I tried to remember if I'd seen any loose pages when I'd found Karen. All I could conjure up was the horror of her dead body.

After putting the books back on the shelf, I very gingerly placed one foot on the top step, and then the other foot. The ladder swayed wildly. I threw my hands forward and clutched at the bookcase until the ladder stopped swaying. This was how Karen was standing when she fell, her head near the ceiling, with only the bookcase to steady herself. Thinking about it, a wave of vertigo washed through me.

I inched one foot down to the next step and started to put my other foot down when the creaking of the floorboards startled me and I missed the step, losing my balance. I pitched forward, grabbing for the bookcase, sending books flying. For a moment, the ladder wobbled and then it steadied.

"Didn't mean to scare you," Alex said. He was holding the ladder.

As I climbed down, pain radiated from my bruised shins.

"What were you doing up there, anyway?" he asked.

Rubbing at my shins, which were already turning blue, I said, "Putting books back." I resisted the urge to tell him I was searching for missing diary pages.

"Is that where Karen was when she fell?"

I hadn't told Alex anything about Karen's death except that she died from a fall.

"Do you need something?" I asked, as I started to gather up the fallen books.

"Thought you might like to see what I've got so far before I call it quits for today."

"Does it involve ladders?"

"Afraid so."

I followed him across the hall into the mural room, adrenaline still coursing through my body.

One long twelve-inch wide strip of the last mural revealed the faint blue of an ancient sky, wisps of clouds, a continuation of the smoky plume from the adjacent mural. Again, there was an enormous tree dominating the foreground. But there were blank spots where there was no paint, especially along the edge.

"What's happened here?" I asked.

"For some reason I'm having more trouble with this wall. When you remove old wallpaper that's been covered over with layers of paint, you can expect to see some loss in the paint layer. I didn't have this much trouble with the other walls. So I'm not sure what's going on."

"How much loss?"

He let out an annoyed sigh. "Look, I'm doing everything I can to restore this mural." As if a switch had been flipped, his whole demeanor changed, which made me wonder who the real Alex was: the charming and patient man who explained the intricacies of the mural restoration process or the annoyed, flushed man standing in front of me, the one who'd showed up angry on my doorstep this morning.

He must have read the confused look on my face, because his tone softened. "But the good news is, just like the other murals, this one sat under wallpaper and paint layers, and that means it was untouched by restoration. No one's messed with the original artist's intent. That also means it was protected from the smoke from kerosene lamps, which would have darkened it."

I crossed my arms over my chest as if needing to protect myself.

"Then it's going to take longer then you thought."

"Maybe not. Tomorrow it could move much quicker. You just

never know."

Tomorrow was Sunday. I'd be on my way back to Chicago with Karen's ashes and a few personal items. The house swept clean of her, as if she'd never been here.

"You like Mexican food?" he asked, pushing a lock of dark hair off his forehead. "There's a place near my motel that's pretty good."

Why not? I told myself. What could one dinner hurt? "Let me shower first and I'll meet you there."

The air-conditioning was nonexistent. And even with the front door propped open and the overhead fans whirling, the restaurant was uncomfortably warm with the heavy smell of fried onions and chilies. We sat at a back booth, munching on corn chips and salsa, a pitcher of margaritas half empty. Alex had ordered chicken mole and I'd ordered ceviche and one bean burrito.

"Performance artist, huh? What kind of performance art do you do?" He hadn't shaved, and his dark stubble gave him a roughish appearance.

"The kind that doesn't pay very well," I joked. Explaining my tortured view on the commodification of art was a buzz kill.

He laughed. "Why performance art?"

He wasn't giving up easily. "I like the immediacy." I licked the salt from the edge of my glass, then sipped at my drink. I was being purposely flippant, wanting to shift focus off me. "What about you?"

He took a long swallow of his drink before he answered. "You know, I never thought about it that way, but I guess I like the immediacy, too. Though it works differently for me. The immediacy comes from the vicarious thrill of entering into the artist's head through the art. When I'm doing a restoration, I become that artist in order to understand the art. I develop a kinship with that particular artist that reaches across time. I see into the artist's world, where the artist did this or that. I start to think like the artist." His green eyes had that faraway look, as if he were in another time and place. A time and place I knew and hungered after, because I could escape the burden of myself. I wondered if that was the allure of art for him as well.

"Has that happened with the murals?"

"Not yet. But I haven't gotten to the actual restoration part. But I am seeing what the artist was thinking when he made certain decisions, like using stencils for the farmhouse, drawing the tree freehand, placing the ribbon in the mural."

"And what does that tell you about our mysterious unknown artist?" I really wanted to know.

The waitress brought our food and asked if we needed anything else. He looked at the nearly empty pitcher. "You want another?"

"I'm good. You can walk home. I gotta drive."

He waited until the waitress left before continuing.

"I'd say our mysterious artist was mostly self-taught, had some formal training, but not enough to stand in his way. And he was gifted and resourceful." He shoved a piece of chicken mole into his mouth. "And melancholy."

I speared a shrimp and popped it into my mouth, the tart, briny taste like a cool explosion. "Why? Because of the somber colors and the figures of the Native American woman and child in separate windows?"

"That and the blackbird perched in the tree in the farmhouse mural."

"You mean how it's caught between leaving and staying."

"Yeah, the bird might be a symbol for something in the artist's life. Someone the artist lost, but can't let go of. So through the blackbird, the artist clings to that moment before the loss."

The image of the blurred ink on Emily Braun's diary page and her grief over the sudden death of her son Charlie came flooding back to me with a jolt.

I put my fork down, wiped my mouth with the paper napkin. "How come you never mentioned Karen's connection to the Union County Trail of Tears?" Ever since Reverend Likely told me about the UCTOT, I'd wondered about that. Now unsure how much I should confide in Alex about the missing diary pages, I needed an answer to that question.

He kept eating, not bothering to look up. "Because I thought you knew that. After all, you were sisters. Are you accusing me of something?"

His answer made sense, regardless of whether I bought it or not.

Maybe it was the margaritas or maybe it was his casual nonchalance. Whatever the reason, I decided to tell him. "I found Emily Braun's diary today." If I'd wanted to shock him, I'd succeeded. His jaw dropped and his eyes widened. "She was Edward Braun's first wife, the guy who built the farmhouse."

"Where did you find it, in the house?"

"At the MU library. But before you get too excited, a chunk of it is missing. Stolen, actually."

"Wait, back up." He placed his warm hand over mine momentarily.

As I explained my foray at the Union County Church grounds and how Reverend Likely suggested I research the archives at the MU library—leaving out the hostile Jimmy Braun and my dodging campus security—the warmth of his hand, like a slight burn, lingered.

"The thing is Karen was the last person to access the diary." I stared into his eyes, searching for reassurance that I'd been right to trust him with this information. "It looks like she stole the pages, which I'm having trouble believing. Karen wouldn't even break the spine of a book, let alone steal an archival document. But, then again, since I've been poking around in her life, I'm wondering if I ever really knew my sister."

"No mention of the murals or the artist in the diary, then." It was a rhetorical question.

I shook my head no. "I'm only telling you this because I'm leaving for Chicago tomorrow. Just thought you'd like that bit of information, in case you plan on doing any research at the MU archives." I took in a deep breath, still not sure what he knew or didn't know. "Unless you've already researched the archives."

Instead of answering, he cocked his head as if he hadn't heard me right, then he grinned. "You sure you can't stick around a few more days to see what's on the other wall?"

I wasn't sure. But I was starting to feel like the house was exerting a gravitational pull on me that I was finding harder and harder to resist. Reverend Likely was right; I was smitten with the house. Rose Theresa Caffrey, who thought material possessions were a trap cementing people into lives of drudgery, chasing the next sparkly thing. I had owned nothing. But, now, thanks to Karen, I did. And somehow the ownership felt ripe with possibility, which made me squirm.

"I've got to get back. I may be mounting a new show. You know how it is." I shifted in my seat as my cell phone vibrated in my jeans pocket. "E-mail me the digital photos of your progress."

"Will do." He put down his fork and crossed his arms on the table. "I wanted to double-check this tomorrow, but since you're taking off I might as well tell you."

By the downturn of his mouth, it wasn't good news. "It's nothing I can prove. But someone might have tampered with that last mural while I was away."

"Tampered? What do you mean?"

"Well, I document everything I do. Digital images and color slide film. When I started working this morning, the edges didn't look right to me. So I checked them against my digital images, and, sure enough, the edges were curled up about an inch, as if someone was trying to look underneath them."

"Couldn't humidity have curled the edges? That house is like a sweat lodge. Or maybe Karen did it."

"Not likely Karen would mess with the mural, since she'd hired me to restore it. And I don't think it was humidity. When I removed that twelve-inch wide section of wallpaper, there was a line of very faint gouge marks. That's where you saw most of the paint loss."

"Why didn't you tell me this when you showed me the mural?"

"Like I said, I wanted to check it out again. And you looked so frazzled."

He was lying. I could tell by the shift of his eyes. But why tell me at all? "Who would do that and why?"

"I don't know." He looked down at his plate for a second and then at me.

"And there's something else. Someone might be watching the house."

A surge of adrenaline shot up my spine.

"I saw the same car slow down, stop and then drive off."

"Maybe they're interested in buying the house."

"The car came by at least three times that I know of and at different times of the day. I heard it idling out front so I checked it out."

I thought back to the smoke smell and my sense that someone had been in the house last night. Jimmy Braun had been smoking a cigarette today at the cemetery. Was it he who had been in the house, trying to scare me like he scared Karen? If so, why? It wasn't like I was sticking around.

My appetite was gone. I pushed my plate away, picked up the pitcher, and poured the last of the margaritas into my glass. "Did you get a look at the driver?"

"The windows were tinted. It was one of those nondescript black sedans like government types drive."

Again, I didn't know if I believed him. But what would be the point of scaring me, especially since he knew I was leaving?

When the waitress brought the check, Alex insisted on picking up the tab. This wasn't a date, nor did I want him to think it was. I handed him a ten, my last ten, then drove him to his motel. He looked as tired as I felt.

After he got out of the car, he leaned in the passenger-side window, a cockeyed grin on his face. "What time you taking off tomorrow?"

"Maybe around eight A.M."

"Is six too early for me to get started?"

"Yeah, but come anyway. I'll give you a key to the house then."

As he disappeared through the lobby's sliding glass doors, I flipped open my cell phone, which had started vibrating again. MU Campus Security had left me three messages, each one more threatening than the last.

"Rose Caffrey, you need to call us ASAP regarding the theft of archival materials. If you don't return this call, we will have to take this matter to the local police."

I threw the phone on the passenger seat and pulled out onto Route 146. The sun had set and the unreasonable heat was gone. I left the car windows down and breathed in the still warm air.

A black sedan, stolen diary pages, the mural tampered with—I craved the noisy familiarity of Halsted Street, my studio apartment above the Greek restaurant Acropolis, the steady throb of neon lights, the lurch of traffic where night never seemed to quiet. Here in southern Illinois the dark was absolute and impossible to see into.

It wasn't until I turned onto Campground Road that I noticed the glare of headlights behind me coming fast. I sped up and the car fell back. As I followed the road's gentle curve left, I slowed down and suddenly the glaring lights were back. What's this jerk's problem?

I pushed the gas pedal down too hard, and my car swerved left off the road onto the grassy shoulder. Quickly I wrenched the steering wheel right and jumped back on the road. Glancing in the rearview mirror, I saw the car had fallen back. Whoever it was, was playing with me, trying to scare me. And succeeding. Was this the person who had driven by the house today?

Again, I checked the rearview mirror. The car was looming closer and closer.

I didn't think I could outrun this idiot, and heading for the deserted farmhouse wasn't a viable option. Maybe I should turn around and head back to Route 146? Pull into the stop 'n shop or one of the many fast-food joints. No, too far.

Wait. Around the next curve was the Union County Church. At least there I would be safe. That is, if I made it there.

I shoved the pedal to the floor, took the curve too fast, and went off the road for a moment. Just as I regained the road, I saw the entrance road to the church, turned wildly right and bumped down the long gravel road to the parking lot at the rear of the church. Coming to a stop, I switched off my headlights and waited, trying to still my breathing.

Sitting in the dark parking lot, I had a clear view of the road, which was illuminated by two streetlights.

Where was the car? Had the idiot given up? As if in answer, I saw the slow sweep of headlights. The car must have shot past the entrance road and was now turning around and heading in my direction.

Okay, don't panic. The lights are on in the rectory; if the car starts down the entrance road, you can make a run for it.

My heart pounded as I watched in a kind of awful amazement the car creep ever so slowly up the road. Then it stopped at the church entrance road and sat idling.

Under the streetlight I saw the car clearly, a red sedan, rusted and dented. Then the two front doors swung open and two guys jumped out, beer cans in their hands. They staggered around, then threw the beer cans at the stone markers, laughing, the liquid flashing a sick yellow in the glare. Then they jumped back into the red car, the tires screeching as they tore away back toward Route 146.

My hands were shaking as I crept down Old Cutoff Road toward the farmhouse. Drunken idiots, I thought, as I parked my car in front of the dark house.

As soon as I pushed open the front door, the pungent odor of cigarette smoke engulfed me. Someone had been inside. For a moment I stood in the dark hallway, with the door open, the key in my hand, not sure what I should do. Every instinct screamed *leave*. I glanced up the stairs, half expecting Karen to be standing there in the dark, telling me what to do next. Just like she'd always done growing up—the eternal big sister who resented and loved in equal portions. But the darkness held only the thin shadows of moonlight flickering through the windows.

The soft rumble of an engine made me turn away. A car idled on the road in front of the house like a threat aimed at me. I stared at the car, afraid to move, afraid to give myself away, clutching the key so hard it dug into my flesh.

Then just as stealthily the car crept down the gravel road as if it had intended nothing. It was the car Alex had described: dark sedan with tinted windows. I closed the door behind me, bolted the lock and went up the stairs, knowing there'd be no rest until

I was out of this house.

When I got to the mural room, I opened the envelope crammed with papers and dumped the contents on the floor. I shuffled through the papers until I found the 1840 plat survey map of Union County. Picking up the map, I walked to the farmhouse mural and placed it next to the farmhouse.

With my finger I traced the Braun property and then the mural of the Braun house and land. The scale was off, but the details corresponded. With the map in my hand, I stepped back a few paces, comparing the mural to the map. From the first the blackbirds sitting in the field in rows had bothered me, the presentation somehow off.

Now I saw the reason. Where the artist had drawn blackbirds in a field, on the map the field was the Campground Cemetery. They weren't blackbirds. They were graves. Rows of graves. Could they represent the unmarked graves of the Cherokee? And the artist had felt compelled to mark their passing in some way, here on this wall in this farmhouse.

But why?

I counted the blackbirds. There were sixteen. Reverend Likely said about fifteen graves were located by witching the site. Not exact, but pretty darned close.

Then I remembered that Charles Braun, the son of Emily and Edward, had died in 1838. If I added his grave to the fifteen witched graves, that would equal sixteen.

I knelt down and started to gather up the contents of the envelope. When I picked up the flyer on the Trail of Tears Symposium that Reverend Likely had given me, I stopped.

The last presentation of the day had been "Removing the Cherokees, a Soldier's Story: A Reenactment," by Daniel Yeager, member of the UCTOT Organization. Why hadn't he mentioned his connection to the UCTOT? Maybe as Alex had said tonight, "I thought you'd know that. After all, you were sisters."

I sat back on my heels, peering across the hallway to Karen's study. In the dim light, I saw the books still scattered on the floor from my near fall, a sick feeling gnawing at my gut. Had Karen's fall been an accident?

The warm night air drifted in the windows, ruffling the papers, scattering my thoughts. Tomorrow I'd be in Chicago, and maybe then this house would dissolve into memory.

Chapter Seven:
Litchfield, Connecticut, 1831
Wolcott Female Academy

Emily Lord wanted the plank floor to open up and swallow her; she wanted to sprout wings and fly into the morning snow; she wanted to be anywhere but standing in a classroom on a raised platform in front of forty girls delivering her first lesson as an assistant teacher at the Wolcott Female Academy.

The second hand on the clock inched toward the quarter hour and the bell rang, pulling Emily's gaze from the wintry window toward the sea of faces staring up at her in anticipation.

This is like my nightmare, she thought, suppressing the urge to laugh nervously. Only I'd been dressed in my chemise, and Miss Wolcott had the face of a cat.

Instead of laughing, she swallowed and whispered, "Um," her eyes rolling up toward the plaster ceiling as if her lesson floated there. Her stomach was knotted, her mind blank as the snow. She thought she might faint.

"Um," she repeated, looking down at her shaking hands, her mind frantically trying to remember some fragment of her lesson on early Roman history, but all she could remember were the words *"Et tu, Brute"* and the violence of Caesar's death.

"Augustus Caesar," she said, putting her hand to her chest, where the letter sat like a stone over her heart. She pulled her hand away quickly as if burned.

The academy's mistress, Miss Wolcott, who was seated in the first row of benches, tapped her cane twice on the pine floor with impatience. "Your journal, Miss Lord, where is it?"

Emily saw it plainly, lying open on Abigail Dunham's bedside table, where she'd left it last night when she jumped up to cut the stitch because Dr. Clayton's hands shook so badly.

"I don't know," she said, chewing on her lower lip.

Even as she'd said it, she knew it was a mistake not to tell the truth about her missing journal. By now Mrs. Dunham must had found it, maybe placed it on her foyer table, anticipating Emily retrieving it, or maybe she'd given it to Mrs. Clayton.

But her answer would lead to another question and finally to the question she couldn't answer, not standing in front of a roomful of girls. What was she doing in Abigail Dunham's bedroom past curfew?

Her eyes fixed on her friend, Lucy Nash, who coughed and then smiled slyly up at Emily, reminding her of their joke about Miss Wolcott, "She can't eat you, at least not uncooked."

Without meaning to, she laughed and quickly put her hand over her mouth. Miss Wolcott let out an exasperated sigh as she struggled to her feet. Once upright, she hobbled onto the classroom platform, every movement a torture.

Emily watched her in fascination. Frail and bent with age, wearing a mended black bombazine dress with an uneven hem, she radiated an unbreachable aura of authority. What must she have been like in her youth? thought Emily, half admiring the woman, half fearing her.

Miss Wolcott hit her cane on the platform once for attention, then began. "Who was the first emperor of Rome?" Her loud, strong voice belied her fragile appearance.

Emily moved to leave the platform, but Miss Wolcott stopped her with her cane. "You will stand here until I am finished," she commanded. "Then we will talk in my office about your punishment."

"But shouldn't I be transcribing?" Emily protested, not wanting to stand for two hours in front of the class, shamed.

"In what? Your lost journal?" Miss Wolcott seemed to look through her with those filmy blue eyes that saw nothing and everything. "And pull those shoulders back. You Ohio farm girls are near to hopeless."

Just because I'm a farm girl from Ohio doesn't make me hopeless, Emily fumed to herself.

By the second hour, Emily's back was throbbing from the fall she'd taken last night on the icy path as she'd left the Dunham house. She desperately wanted to rub at the pain, but she didn't want to draw more ire from Miss Wolcott.

To distract herself, her eyes roamed the room. The fringe on Maryanne Sebor's shawl was frayed and looked like blue hair; Alice Reeve's sleeves were too short, revealing wrists as delicate as hickory twigs; and Lucy's yellow ringlets bounced as she coughed into her hand.

Suddenly a shiver of sunlight flickered at the icy window, making a lacy pattern on the platform desk. Emily turned her head sideways as the light deepened then burst, blazing the window golden.

"Emily," Miss Wolcott said loudly. "Recite back to me the last question and its answer."

She felt the heat of embarrassment rise to her face. "Sorry, Mistress, I don't know."

The girls stirred in their seats, some smiling, others looking uncomfortable.

"Seems there's many things you don't know this morning."

Emily bit back her answer: I know how to paint light on water.

"Yes, Miss Wolcott," she said instead, just as the bell rang.

A commotion broke out as the students began talking and gathering up their things.

"Girls, girls." Miss Wolcott clapped her hands. "You will recite this morning's lesson back to me on Friday. Understood?"

"Yes, Mistress," the girls answered in unison.

"Now, you may leave."

Then she turned to Emily. "My office, if you please."

The office was so cold, Emily could see her breath. She sat in the rigid chair, her hands folded in her lap, her eyes downcast, her mind searching for a way to explain her missing journal.

"May I light a fire for you, Mistress?" Emily asked, hoping to mitigate her punishment.

"No need. We won't be here long." Miss Wolcott's demeanor was as severe as the chilly room, whose only ornamentation was a hair memorial, which hung on a wall adjacent to Miss Wolcott's desk. It was dedicated to Sally and dated 1793. Embroidered around the woven brown hair ring were the words: "She sparkled, exhaled, and went to heaven." Sally was the first student to die at the Wolcott Female Academy, when classes were held in Miss Wolcott's parlor on North Street, not the present white clapboard two-story building. Emily had often wondered if the rumors were true that Miss Wolcott had made the hair memorial.

"So, Miss Lord, what punishment do you think I should give you this time, since clearly the debit marks are having no effect?"

How was she to answer? Emily thought, nervously folding and unfolding her skirt as if she could refashion it, as if the fabric were her own skin.

"I don't think that's for me to say, Mistress."

Miss Wolcott pursed her thin lips in an ironic smile. "Is your intent to be dismissed from this school? Because I can find no other excuse for your constant tardiness, being unprepared, not completing your lessons."

Emily looked above the woman's small-bonneted head toward the window where snow was flying past in whirls and ripples as if it were being flung. Did she want to be dismissed? No, that would mean going home. Home held nothing for her anymore. It was just that she couldn't follow all these rules, which felt to her like a noose around her neck.

"Tell me, Emily." Now her voice had risen and was a wave crashing on the shore. "What am I to write your brother?"

At the mention of her brother Thomas, a spark of anger shot through Emily. "I would say I tried my best and I should do better the next time." She stared at a knot in the pine floor. In truth, she mused, I would not write him about anything. I have not written him since I arrived here last fall.

"And you think that is sufficient?" Miss Wolcott's hands rested on her desk, as if in prayer, a familiar pose that Emily knew meant she was being scrutinized and found wanting, as if only divine intervention could save her.

"Do you not say God considers us all works in progress, that we must strive every day for self-improvement?" Emily kept her head down, so Miss Wolcott would not see the smile playing around her mouth.

"Your cleverness would best be used in the classroom, young lady." She opened the middle drawer of her desk and pulled out a stack of envelopes tied with a ribbon. Emily's stomach contracted at the sight of Thomas's tight, even handwriting. Could he not leave her in peace, even here? Had she not done as he wanted against her own desires? And with what consequences? Elizabeth, her only surviving sister, had died while Emily had traveled by stagecoach to Litchfield. Thomas's letter had arrived weeks after Elizabeth's death. Now they were all gone, lost to fever. And only she and he remained.

"Your brother has been writing me most regularly, asking me to advise you in all things as if you were my own. He is most anxious about your progress as a teacher. I have been assuring him that you are progressing as expected, stretching the truth a little. Have I been wrong to do that?"

Emily stared into Miss Wolcott's milky blue eyes, searching them for some flicker of compassion. "You are a wonderful teacher. You truly are. But I am not suited to be a teacher." There, she'd said it.

There was no trace of the compassion she hoped to find. Miss Wolcott shook her head and struggled to her feet as if she needed distance from Emily. Standing with her back to her, she gazed out the window for what seemed to Emily a long time. When she turned around, her ironic smile was replaced by a hard line of determination.

"It is of no consequence whether you are suited to be a teacher or not. Mr. Lord has paid for you to receive a diploma from this school and intends for you to earn your way as a teacher. You should be grateful and appreciative that he has made such a financial sacrifice to educate you. A woman's worth in this world is measured by her usefulness, not by her wants and desires."

Emily had heard Miss Wolcott say these very words many times at school assemblies—how the girls needed to be more appreciative, to try harder, to be models of Christian womanhood. Even homesickness was a breach punishable by debit marks, as was complaining about the weather, wasting time, not sitting up straight—everything was subject to marks. Most of the time, Emily felt like she could barely breathe.

Bitterness rose up into Emily's throat. "My brother only wants to rid himself of me so he can marry. That is why I am here, Miss Wolcott. He can't afford to marry and support me. I am an encumbrance."

Miss Wolcott eased herself down into her chair. "That is his right."

Emily was desperate to break through the woman's carapace to reach the person who had woven the hair memorial, who cared that much about a student. "Miss Wolcott, did you know from the start that you wanted to be a teacher?"

"It was the best I could do for my family."

"But what of yourself?"

"Have you learned nothing from me this past year, Miss Lord?" She clicked her tongue.

It was useless. Emily was cold and tired; her back throbbed with pain. "I will try harder," she said, not meaning a word of it.

"Then we will consider today a new beginning." Miss Wolcott took a sheet of paper from her desk, dipped the quill into her inkwell and began writing. "I want you to give this letter to Dr. Clayton. I am instructing Doctor and Mrs. Clayton to monitor your studies more closely."

"Please don't do that. I said, 'I will try harder.'" Panic rose up into Emily's chest, her heart thudding.

"Is there something you're not telling me? Something that will explain your growing list of infractions?"

How could she tell her the truth without breaking her agreement? "It will be our little secret," Mrs. Clayton had said. "Miss Wolcott need not know."

"No, nothing."

"And your duties for the Claytons are not too taxing? I hear you sometimes accompany the doctor on his calls."

She froze in fear. "Mostly, I fetch him." How easily the lies come, Emily thought, when the reason is just.

"Hmm," Miss Wolcott tapped the quill against her chin. "I am also suggesting they make other arrangements in the matter of fetching Dr. Clayton past your curfew."

She continued to talk as she scratched at the paper, sealing Emily's fate with every stroke of her pen.

"And you are continuing to heed my instruction in the matter of your drawing? There is to be no more of it. Or do I need to add that to my letter?"

"I am." She glanced away from Miss Wolcott's penetrating gaze, Mrs. Clayton's words coming back to her: "I don't see what the fuss is about your drawing, anyway. A young lady should be accomplished in the ornamental arts."

"All that drawing is a distraction to your mind," the woman prattled on, "making it more difficult for you to concentrate on your scholarship. I'll add a reminder to the Claytons." She rocked the blotter back and forth over the letter, folded it and sealed it in an envelope.

"You will be given thirty debit marks. And I want you to write a ten-page essay on 'The Government of Our Passions,' which I will collect from you tomorrow morning, along with your mysteriously lost journal. If only you would harness yourself to your academic studies. No school will hire you based solely on your needlework, drawing ability and botany studies. Then where will you be?"

Not here, not in a place such as this, Emily thought. Devoting my time to the drudgery of communicating the basics to a few girls. But even as she rebelled, she knew the futility of it. To an unmarried woman, teaching was the only acceptable option.

"Yes, Mistress," she answered. Then she left Miss Wolcott's cold office where their breath had danced in the air between them.

She trudged down the wide plank stairs, her slender shoulders slumped, her footfalls as heavy as her thoughts.

It had all started so innocently. Mrs. Clayton sending her to fetch Dr. Clayton from the Town Tavern. "Mrs. Reeve has taken a bad turn," was all she'd said. "Fetch him at once." She'd hesitated, and then added, "And go with him to the Reeve house, Emily. It's getting dark." Emily had understood.

He wasn't intoxicated, but his hands were shaking slightly, always worse as night fell. She'd accompanied him to the house, up the stairs to the bedroom, where the sheets were blotted with blood and Mrs. Reeve was screaming with each pain. It had been she, Emily, who'd taken the knife and cut the cord round the infant's neck, shielded by the modest drapery. The baby had lived and Mrs. Reeve had healed and something in Emily had lightened. After all the death, first her father, then her mother, followed by her two sisters—the cholera had swept through her family with certainty.

I could destroy the letter, but Miss Wolcott expects an answer. I could beg Doctor and Mrs. Clayton to ignore the letter's instructions, which they would never do. I could . . . She'd reached the first floor and could think of nothing else she could do. The letter would end their unspoken bargain. There was no way around it. No more nightly calls with Dr. Clayton; no more drawing.

As quietly as possible, she entered Mr. Brady's Latin class, slid into the last bench next to Lucy, and took out paper from her worn satchel. Mr. Brady was declining the verb, to love. *Amo, amas, amat,* she wrote, her hand moving, her mind wandering.

Glancing at Lucy, who sat diligently writing, Emily reached inside her dress bodice and took out the letter, unfolding it on her lap under the desk and reading it again, as if it were written in a foreign language needing careful deciphering, each word, the sentences, the connotations and denotations.

Most of Edward's letter meandered, lost in its usual thicket of weather reports, books she should read and his struggles as a new lawyer. Then, near the end, like an afterthought, he proposed their engagement.

When she'd first read his proposal, she'd thought she'd misread it and reread the entire letter again. She could hear the steady and sure cadence of his deep gravelly voice.

I have asked your brother Thomas for permission to court

you. He has given his consent. I hope we are of like minds. I have thought long and hard about this. Our walks along the river last summer and our shared interests in education have led me to believe that you would make a fine wife and mother. When you return home in the summer, I will make our engagement proper with the seal of a ring.

Fondly,
Edward Braun, Esquire

P.S. In anticipation of your response, I recommend you read Benjamin Franklin's essay, "Reflections on Courtship and Marriage." It is very instructive and suited to your quick mind.

No, she hadn't misread the proposal. Sitting in her attic bedroom, Emily had folded the letter, put it back into its envelope, and pressed the flap down with the palm of her hand, as if by doing so she could erase the letter from her mind, knowing no matter her indifference toward Edward, his would be a hard proposal to dismiss. Although she was already nineteen, no man had showed the least interest in her, except as a friend. To know why, she had only to look in a mirror at her prominent nose, her small brown eyes, and her mouth that seemed to hold too many teeth.

The image of Edward's hands rose up, their tufts of hair so profuse they made her sick. Those hands would own her, would touch her, and would be the rest of her life. If she accepted his proposal, her life would change forever and she would have little to say about it.

Soon there would be another letter from Thomas to Miss Wolcott telling of the courtship and possible nuptials. She could refuse Edward—and what? Be a teacher? This would be her last semester at the school. Thomas would be free to marry.

"Latin is considered a dead language," Mr. Brady's instruction interrupted her thoughts. "Meaning it is no longer spoken. But, for young ladies such as yourselves, studying Latin is paramount for your education."

Emily folded the letter and slipped it into her satchel.

"Who has written you, Emily?" Lucy whispered.

"A friend," Emily answered, not wanting to confide in Lucy, who couldn't keep a secret to save her life.

She turned her paper over and began sketching the shadowy light as it fell on Mr. Brady's sleek hair and robust shoulders, too big, really, for a man so short.

Lucy peeked at the drawing. "Oh, Emmy," she whispered, "it's so like him."

Chapter Eight

"Why are you so late?" Mrs. Clayton asked as Emily dropped her satchel beneath the coatrack.

"Has something happened?" Emily saw her journal on the foyer table, wondering how it had gotten there. Mrs. Clayton had her cloak on, and her gray eyes were sharp with concern.

"You have to go now. Fetch the doctor from Mother Barnes's Tavern. Abigail Dunham will not wake. I was about to go myself when I saw you walking up the street."

"Why is he at Mother Barnes's?" Emily wanted to reach up and tuck the wisps of gray hair escaping Mrs. Clayton's bonnet. So like her mother's hair.

"It's the middle daughter," she tsked, shaking her head in pity. "She has female trouble. Now, hurry." She practically pushed Emily out the door, closing it behind her as if she were a peddler.

Her boots were soaked through to her stockings; her feet were wet and cold from walking from the academy. It was past six o'clock, and the street was lit only by the whiteness of the vast mountainous snow.

Emily wrapped her wool scarf around her neck, shoved her gloved hands inside her coat pocket, and started the two-mile hike to Mother Barnes's Tavern on Goshen Road, pondering what female trouble needed the ministering of Dr. Clayton.

Well, she'd soon know.

When she reached Goshen Road, she saw the two-storied

red-brick tavern in the distance, its yellow blocks of light staining the snow. She stood shivering on the snowy path, unsure of herself, listening to the weathered tavern sign creaking in the wind as if it were a warning. She'd never gone to the tavern alone, only on sleigh rides with other academy girls and boys from the Litchfield Law School.

She looked up at the full moon, which cast its cold light over the frozen landscape, afraid to enter the tavern's common room. The door opened directly into the common room where women weren't allowed except for Mother Barnes's oldest daughter Muriel, who was the barkeeper. Usually she and the other academy girls would be ushered by the law students down a long hallway into one of the back rooms reserved for their party. But Abigail Dunham was ill, and Dr. Clayton was inside.

With more determination than she felt, she shoved her hands deeper into her pockets and trudged forward. Miss Wolcott's words echoed in her head: "Be bold, ladies. Nothing is accomplished by feeble acts."

As Emily neared the tavern, the front door swung open suddenly, spilling out two men, making her step back into the shadows.

"I say you cheated," accused the short hatless man. He raised his fists and bounced on his toes in front of the larger man, taunting him.

"You're drunk," slurred the large man. "This be no fight, then."

The smaller man scrunched low and bobbed back and forth, his fists still raised. Then he punched the man in the face hard enough to knock his head back.

"C'mon, c'mon, you cheatin' son of a bitch."

The blow came so quickly Emily didn't realize the small man had been hit until she saw him splayed in the snow.

"Damn you, Jack. Now look what you done." The large man

hoisted the unconscious man over his shoulder and strode back into the tavern, the door slamming behind him.

For a moment, Emily stood in the shadows, her teeth chattering with cold and fear. Then she breathed in the frigid night air and stepped out of the dark shadows, pulled open the heavy door and entered the common room.

The tavern was alive with warmth, which emanated from the blazing hearths, candles, and the crush of men. A haze redolent of unwashed bodies and peat fires hung over the smoky room. The sharp odors of fish-oil and tallow, the fumes of tobacco and the scent of rum and whiskey assaulted Emily as she stood just inside the door not sure what to do.

Muriel stood behind the long plank bar joking with a group of ruddy-faced teamsters. Emily tried to catch her eye, but the woman wouldn't look her way, though she'd seen Emily enter the room.

Her brown hair was piled atop her head like a mound of dirt, her checks the color of beets, and her bosom swelled against her tight bodice. She was the comeliest of Mother Barnes's three daughters and the one with the foulest temper. Emily knew she despised the academy girls.

"Stuck up is what you lot is," Muriel had sniped at Emily when she'd asked for a clean fork. Muriel had taken the soiled fork spat on it and polished it on her dirty apron. "Clean enough for you."

"Well, there's nothing for it," Emily told herself, straightening her back as she wound her way through the ruckus of men toward the bar, the eyes of the men boring into her. One of the teamsters whispered something in Muriel's ear. She threw her head back and laughed, exposing two missing lower teeth.

"That's a ripe one, Sully," Muriel said. "Best not let my mother hear, though."

"Can I buy you a drink, miss?" one of the men asked Emily

as she stood behind the group.

"Females in the back," barked out Muriel. "You know the rules."

Emily swallowed and said, "I'm looking for Dr. Clayton. I have an urgent message for him."

Muriel narrowed her green eyes at her. "What makes you think he's here?"

Emily was tired and hungry. The day had been impossibly long and trying. "He's tending to your sister, Carrie, who has female *troubles.*" She stressed the word troubles. "Now, where are they?"

"Whoa," one of the men said. "This one's got grass."

Muriel leaned forward on the bar, as if she were going to reach across and throttle Emily, exposing more of her ample breasts. "Down the hallway, past the dance hall, and up the back stairs." She jerked her thumb toward the hallway.

"Thank you," Emily said, turning on her heel and hurrying out of the congested room, her wet skirt and boots trailing the floor with melting snow and mud. Her heart was fluttering in her chest like a captured bird.

Not for the first time, she considered what it must be like to stand in the common room, telling tales of the road in a language that would make her blush. As crude and uneducated as those men were, they could choose the course of their lives. She picked up her soggy skirt and hurried, suddenly not caring who saw her pantaloons.

As she approached the dance hall, she heard the sound of fiddle music and stopped a minute to peek into the room. The tables were teeming with students from the Litchfield Law School and the Wolcott Female Academy. Some were dancing the garland dance, some were eating and drinking, and amid the riotous noise were Mother Barnes and Lizzie, her youngest daughter, serving suppers of stew and slabs of hard bread and tankards of ale.

But what held her transfixed was the room's transformation. What had been plain whitewashed plaster walls now was a Garden of Eden. Almost every wall surface bloomed with fantastical trees, elms and evergreens, large and small, in glorious colors of forest green, yellow ocher, cadmium. There were gently sloping hills and a surprising volcano flanked by a palm tree. On a side wall was a harbor scene totally out of place, yet compelling with its plume of smoke and a man in a stovepipe hat in the foreground. Several ships were harbored: two clippers with sails like billowing sheets, a primitive sailboat, and, most unusual, a three-masted galleon.

"What can I do for you, miss?" Mother Barnes was balancing a tray of empty plates. Her bulging stomach and round flushed face seemed to give off heat.

As Emily's eyes roved the walls, all thoughts of what had sent her to the tavern were momentarily forgotten. "Who painted these?" she asked, pointing toward the walls.

"Pretty ain't they. That young man who's fiddling done 'um."

Emily stared at the sandy-haired man working the fiddle with unbridled enthusiasm. He was rail thin with a beaky nose and eyes so deep-set they were barely visible.

"His name's Painter. Jacob Painter. The name suits him. Seeing he's a traveling painter. He tells me he's making his way from Maine down to Virginia with not a penny in his pocket. Imagine that. Shows up at my door and says he'll paint the tavern walls upstairs and down for food and lodging and throws in the fiddling for free. Would you be wanting a supper? 'Cause we're about to run out."

"No, I'm here for Dr. Clayton."

Her face closed. "He can't leave yet," she pleaded. "She's in a terrible way. Them powders he gave her ain't bringing her around. Doc had me brew up some ginger tea. He says that should fix her."

Emily put her head down to hide her embarrassment at Mother Barnes's frankness and hurried toward the stairs. So Carrie's female troubles were a blockage. Now she understood why Mrs. Clayton had cloaked her words. Carrie was with child and out of wedlock.

When she reached the landing she heard a low, anguished moaning and Dr. Clayton's raised voice. "Stop your thrashing," he demanded.

Even before she stepped into the sparsely furnished room, she smelled the vomit. Once inside she saw two pails beside the bed; one contained vomit, the other was empty.

Dr. Clayton was leaning over Carrie, his thickly veined hands vigorously kneading her midsection, a sheen of sweat on the top of his balding head. With every pressure of his hands, Carrie groaned in pain, protesting.

"This is what comes of lying, girl," he said cruelly.

Carrie's head jerked back and forth on the pillow like a crazed metronome. "I told you true. I took them powders just as you told me."

"Dr. Clayton," Emily called out sternly, unable to bear Carrie's groans or the harshest of his words and actions.

He stopped kneading and turned toward her, a quizzical look on his sweaty face. "Emily, what are you doing here?"

"Mrs. Clayton sent me. Abigail Dunham won't wake. You are to go at once."

"Yes, yes," he mumbled to himself, wiping his bloodstained hands on the bedsheet. "How long since consciousness?" He began packing up his bag.

"Mrs. Clayton didn't say," Emily responded.

Suddenly, Carrie screamed, "Make it stop," as another wave of cramps seized her and she thrashed with pain, curling into a tight ball of agony. When the pain subsided, her body uncurled and she rolled over onto her back, staring up at the smoke-stained ceiling.

Emily watched in horror as the sheet and the bottom of Carrie's night shift turned a sickly red, the metallic smell of blood filling the room.

Dr. Clayton leaned over the prone Carrie and put his ear to her chest. Then held her hand, feeling for a pulse.

"Is she gone?" Emily asked.

His hands shook as he let Carrie's hand fall to the bed. "Her heart beats faintly."

He struggled into his coat, grabbed his black bag and turned to Emily. "There's nothing else to do now. She's lost too much blood. I'll let the mother know. Be a good girl and clean up the sheets and change her night shift. And be quick about it. No need for the mother to see that. And don't forget to empty the pail."

"But," Emily began, then stopped. She was at his mercy.

As he made for the door, he put his trembling hand on her shoulder. "Mark the hour as well, will you?" With that he left the room.

Emily followed him out into the hallway. "But how am I to get home?"

"Mother Barnes will see to it."

When Emily walked back into the room Carrie still lay on her back, her eyes riveted to the ceiling, whispering as if in prayer, "No, no more. I told you true. I told you true." A trickle of blood ran from her nose. Emily picked up the rag floating in the bowl, rang out the excess water, and gently wiped the blood away.

For a moment she felt powerless to do anything but sit and dab at the thick blood oozing from her nose. When it lessened, she rose from the chair, found another sheet and thin blanket in the chest under the drafty window.

With as much tenderness as possible, she rolled Carrie's body from one side of the bed to the other, pulling out the blood-drenched sheet where a tiny thing lay glistening inside the bloody sack. Her stomach roiled at the sight. Quickly, she balled up the sheet and shoved it into the empty pail. Her hands were sticky with the blood, and she wiped them on the rag. Then she put a clean sheet on the bed.

Since she couldn't find another night shift, she could do nothing about the soiled one. So she found a thin blanket in the chest and placed it over Carrie, whose bleeding was slowing.

Holding her breath, Emily picked up the two pails, clattered down the back stairs and out the rear door, to the privy where she shoved the balled sheet into the hole. Then she emptied the vomit pail beside the privy, kicking snow over the awful contents. Bending over she cleaned the two pails with snow and then went back up the stairs into the sickroom to wait for Mother Barnes.

When she sat down again beside the bed, that's when she noticed the phial and the cup on the night table.

In his haste to leave, Dr. Clayton had left the phial that must have contained the medicine to bring on the menses. She sniffed at the traces of the oily mixture coating the glass. The strong scent of juniper berry prickled her nose. Surely, Dr. Clayton would want to reuse the bottle. She slipped it into her dress pocket.

The cup stained with tea and an oily substance she thought might be witch hazel, she left on the bedside table.

Satisfied with the room, she took Carrie's hand, which felt cool and light, as if it were dissolving beneath her fingers, and held it.

The blood had stopped trickling from her nose, but there were flecks of vomit on her parched lips. With the wet rag, Emily wiped away the flecks, then sat silently smoothing her dark hair, which seemed blacker against her sickly white skin.

For a moment Carrie opened her eyes and stared fiercely at Emily as if she hated her, opening her mouth wide.

And then one long breath rattled from her into a silence broken only by the fiddler's music downstairs. He was playing "Home Sweet Home." Emily looked at the tiny clock on the fireplace mantel: twelve twenty-five.

When Mother Barnes came into the room, Emily was still holding Carrie's hand, whose slender warmth ebbed.

"Has she passed?" the woman asked, her voice rich with resignation.

"Just now," Emily said, placing Carrie's hand gently on the blanket and standing.

"Well, there's nothing for it now." Tears ran down Mother Barnes's florid face. Staring at Emily as if she dared her to disagree, she said, "She was a good girl. I don't care what anyone says. Too gentle by far."

Emily nodded her head yes. She knew nothing of Carrie Barnes, except sometimes she put extra bread on your plate and had a way of dipping her chin as if expecting a blow.

"Was she in much pain?" Mother Barnes asked, her voice hopeful.

"She passed quietly." Emily glanced away from the woman's probing. No need to tell her of Carrie's thrashing agony.

"Tell Muriel to fetch the stable boy. He'll see you home."

A slit of light shone under Dr. Clayton's study. As Emily crept past the door, Dr. Clayton called out, "Is that you Emily?"

It was after one in the morning, and Emily longed for the comfort and solitude of her attic room and her bed. Her hands and feet were blocks of ice from the sleigh ride home. The stable boy, silent and swift, probably wanting the warmth of his own bed, had whipped the horse hard, flinging up snow. Even the buffalo robe had done little to shield her from the bone-cutting cold.

She eased the door open. Dr. Clayton sat behind the ornately carved desk, rubbing at his eyes, his old books surrounding him like another wall. Even in the dim kerosene light, she saw smudges of blood on his shirt cuff. His balding pate glistened and his eyes were deeply circled. His spectacles lay facedown on the desk as if they'd fallen from his nose.

"Come, come." He gestured Emily into the room, barely looking at her as she took the chair nearest the sputtering fire.

"Did you note the time?" His voice was hollow with exhaustion.

"Twelve twenty-five."

"And the sheet and pail? You saw to them?"

"Everything, except her night shift."

"Good, good." He drummed his fingers on the desk.

There was something on his mind, and he was struggling to find a way to broach the subject. How like her father he was, Emily thought. Not in appearance but in demeanor. That same halting sharpness that hid a tenderness he found burdensome. She wanted to tell him that with her there was no need to hide. But she held her tongue, listening to the slow tick of the carriage clock.

Finally, she said, "Is there something else?"

"Did you happen to find a phial when you were cleaning up?"

She reached into her dress pocket for the phial, and placed it on his desk.

"Good, girl." He held up the phial, turning it in the firelight. Then he slipped it into his coat pocket. "At the end, did she say anything?"

"All she said was, 'No, no more,' and, 'I told you true.' " Emily felt a prick of unease creeping up her spine. She wanted to ask what truth Carrie had been attesting to, but she knew it was not her place to ask.

"Unpredictable business if they lie." He pursed his mouth, deepening the creases.

Emily stared at her hands folded on her lap, not knowing what to say. Was he blaming Carrie for her own death? What had she lied to him about? Or was he absolving himself of her death? "I'm sure there was nothing else you could do for her."

"Of course, of course. To bed with you, now. Don't want Miss Wolcott writing me more letters, do we?" He smiled wearily.

At the mention of letters, Emily felt that sick dread again.

She said good night and walked down the long hallway where she'd dropped her satchel hours ago, which now seemed like days. As she neared the silver tray on the hall table, she pulled out Miss Wolcott's letter and put it on the tray as if it were a flower soon to wither and die, thinking of Mother Barnes's words, "Well, there's nothing for it now."

The attic room was cold. Moonlight like snow whitened the narrow bed, and Emily didn't even undress except to loosen her corset. As tired as she was, she couldn't sleep. That look of fierce anger on Carrie's face stayed with her, as did the blood and the vomit.

The winds of cholera that had swept through her family, taking them as if they were so many leaves fallen, brightly colored and feverish; and, at the end, her sister Ann had looked at her with that same fierce rage—as if to say, not now, not me. Sometimes she thought she'd said, "Why not you?"

Finally, Emily fell into a troubled sleep, rampant with dreams, where walls grew vines and cities and oceans and every color knew her by name, calling to her in voices like breath, and under it all were the angry faces of the dead.

Chapter Nine

When Emily rose at six, the letter was gone and so was Dr. Clayton.

"Poor man," Mrs. Clayton tsked over breakfast, picking at her biscuit as if she were a bird. "Noah Cole's wife has taken to her bed."

Emily smiled fondly at Mrs. Clayton, who had a peculiar habit of not saying a woman's name when she was laboring to deliver a child.

If Dr. Clayton reminded her of her father in behavior, Mrs. Clayton held no resemblance to her mother in behavior or appearance, except for the gray hair. Emily's mother had been a broad-shouldered woman with a toughness learned on her family's Ohio farm as the oldest of seven girls. Her shock of gray hair had come at thirty, and with it a directness that her father found impossible to purge.

"Perhaps since it is the third child, it will be quick," Emily offered, as if to say, "You don't need to protect me."

Mrs. Clayton's sallow face flushed slightly. "Won't you be late for your first class? It's nearly eight-twenty?"

"Miss Wolcott understands my duties," she lied, wanting to see if Mrs. Clayton had read the letter.

"You are a Godsend," Mrs. Clayton beamed at her. "What would we do without you?"

"As you and Dr. Clayton are to me," Emily answered, downing the last of her tea.

Standing in the foyer, buttoning her wool coat, she realized that something had shifted inside her last night with Carrie's death, as if she were an ocean floor where islands formed and rose overnight.

As she trudged down the pathway in the rutted footsteps toward the school, she wondered if Miss Wolcott, with her strange watery blue eyes, would see the shift. Then as the first bell echoed, instead of hurrying, she slowed her pace. Miss Wolcott might see, but she would never understand.

Just as she reached North Street and the school, she heard the slow crunching of wheels moving down the snowy road, and she saw Mr. Murphy's dray. As he came closer, he touched the brim of his hat.

"Good morning, miss," he said.

As if she'd planned it, the words tumbled out. "By any chance are you heading toward Goshen Road?" she asked.

"My next delivery be the tavern."

"Could I ask a ride?"

Mr. Murphy pulled her up onto the seat and flicked the horse's rein. "Sad, that," he said. "About Carrie."

"Sad," Emily repeated, shuddering, her face inside the collar of her coat as if afraid to be seen when she was only cold.

A yew wreath tied with black ribbons hung from the tavern door, its ends fluttering in the cold morning. Emily glanced up at the second story, where all the curtains were drawn. The place felt empty and abandoned, except for the rhythmic hammering coming from the barn, where Emily knew the coffin was being constructed. As she stood shivering in the cold, holding her worn school satchel, she questioned her rashness in coming. What could she do? Would they want her help? Was that why she was here?

By now Miss Wolcott would have noted her absence, another

debit mark, black and ugly beside her name. Another letter written to Dr. Clayton; maybe to Thomas as well.

With a heavy sigh, Emily pushed open the door and stepped into the common room, prepared to see Carrie's body laid out on one of the long tables. Instead the room, hazy with muted light and smoke, was scattered with chairs, the floor dirty, the long bar strewn with tankards, the hearth cold. The chaos death left was all too familiar a sight.

For a long moment Emily stood paralyzed by memory. That last day as her mother became a shadow on the bed, the crockery buzzed with flies, every surface dust-choked, and the cows moaned outside, their udders full.

Later, as Thomas readied the mourning room, she wouldn't allow him to light the candles, slapping his hand away.

"No," she'd cried, expecting at any moment for her mother's eyes to open. "You will not do that to her."

Emily shook herself free of the memory and strode down the hallway, her boots clattering on the wood with their own rhythm. She'd watched Carrie's spirit leave; it was her duty, if not her right, to be here. She touched the gold locket she'd put around her neck this morning. It held the small black-and-white picture of the weeping woman beneath the willow trees, its weight an obligation.

Before she reached the dance hall, she smelled the candles and knew where Carrie was laid out. Unlike the common room, the dance hall wavered with morning light, the curtains open, the floor swept clean, the tables and chairs orderly. And there in the middle of the room, lying on a long table, was Carrie's body. And sitting beside her with his back to the door was the itinerant painter Jacob Painter, holding a crude wooden palette and a paintbrush.

Of course, Emily thought. Mother Barnes would ask him to do a mourning portrait. Her daughter was dead, and this would be a fitting memorial to her.

If he knew she was there, he didn't acknowledge her presence, continuing to paint, stopping and starting, dabbing and staring. Her fingers itched to dig out her sketchbook from her satchel. Instead she watched, marveling at the incongruity of the scene: Carrie's lifeless body, the fiddler-painter resurrecting her likeness, and surrounding it all, this veritable Garden of Eden, rampant with colors and textures and thoughts she could only imagine.

She'd seen the work of other itinerant painters at the Wolcott and Beecher homes on North Street. But none matched the sheer boldness of color and composition of these walls. Even the windows, which were framed with overarching trees, leading the eye to the view outside, showed his cleverness. Around their edges ran rose friezes. The roses were vividly red, as if they had bloomed minutes ago.

Emily flushed with the realization that she'd come to the tavern not just for Carrie, but to see the murals again, by chance to meet Jacob Painter.

Stepping over the threshold, she walked to where the painter worked as if pulled by an invisible thread. Even after she came up beside him, he continued to paint, not even glancing to see who stood there.

Emily studied the portrait. Carrie appeared as in life, sitting up in a chair, wearing a blue cotton dress with a lace collar, her black hair held back with a matching ribbon, her blue eyes startling with that stare, one hand holding a red rose, its stem broken—a life cut short. She was so lifelike, it was hard to reconcile the portrait with the dead girl's body lying on the wood table, clad in the same dress, the same ribbon round her hair. It was as if Carrie had merged with the murals' world of trees and ships.

Finally, Jacob Painter stopped painting, and turned toward

her. "Are you kin?" His eyes were dark as night taking her in, making her put her hand over her heart in self-consciousness.

"I'm Emily Lord," she answered, standing straighter as if she could dislodge his stare.

"That mean you're kin? 'Cause if so, Mother Barnes is in the kitchen. And I need to get this done."

"I was with her. Carrie," she began. "When she passed." Something about him made her want to confide in him. "Not that you should change the sea," she added, "but the waters would be stormy." Behind Carrie was a window giving a view of water where a boat rested on a flat sea.

Now he did put down the paintbrush and rested the palette on his knee. "That was a kindness you did, telling Mother Barnes she passed quiet. What do you think of the likeness?"

He seemed to genuinely want her opinion. "It's as if she still lives." She paused, not sure if she should continue. "Except you wouldn't see it unless you moved her hair ever so much. But Carrie has a tiny mole, here." She pushed her own hair back near her temple.

"Didn't see it," he answered defensively. "And don't particularly like touching dead bodies."

"Let me show you." She walked around the table and gently moved Carrie's hair. "See."

He'd come around the table and was standing so close to her, she could feel his warmth.

"Carrie always wore her hair pulled back so you saw it. Not like it is now."

He ran his long, paint-smudged hands through his sandy hair, staring at her, and then walked back to his chair. He wiped the paintbrush on a dirty rag, dipped the tip into the black paint and with a sure hand touched the tip to the canvas.

Emily came back to the portrait. "Yes, that's right. Can you show me how you do all this?"

"What? Portraits?" He gestured toward the portrait.

"No, the murals."

"Look, miss, I don't know what your game is, but I don't need any trouble with females. Like I said, Mother Barnes is in the kitchen."

"I'm a student at the Wolcott Female Academy. I'm training to be a teacher."

"That's all very interesting, but I don't see what that has to do with my murals."

Emily reached into her satchel and pulled out one of her sketches, a depiction of the town from Chestnut Hill. A native woman draped in a sarong and wearing a necklace and bracelet made of dogteeth stood on the hill. After attending Mrs. Thurston's lecture on the Sandwich Islands where she'd served as a missionary, Emily had drawn the native woman on the hill. The drawing was nonsensical to everyone but her.

She held it out to him.

He studied the sketch, then said, "You drew this?"

"I know it seems silly and the colors are off. But . . ."

He held up his hand to stop her. "You're right about the colors. The rest, well . . ." He shrugged his shoulders. "Nothing I can teach you. It's all there."

"What do you mean?"

"The skill. It's raw, but it's now a matter of doing. Just keep at it. You'll make a good teacher."

She was about to explain that she wasn't asking about her skill as a teacher, she was asking about her skill as an artist, but then Muriel came into the room.

"What are you doing in here?" she demanded in a derisive tone.

Emily felt her face go hot. "I came to see if I could help."

"You and that doctor done enough. What he'd give her last

night, huh?" She accused. " 'Cause last time she had no trouble."

"I'm sure he did his best."

She let out a mean laugh. "He saves that for those on North Street, missy. Now, get out of here. We don't need anything from you."

Mortified, Emily hurried from the dance hall, holding her satchel against her chest like a shield. Now she couldn't ask Jacob Painter how he mixed his colors or why he'd painted a volcano and a galleon in his murals—one out of place, the other out of time and place. Did they have a meaning to him? They seemed to belong and not to belong. Were they like the native woman in her sketch, a figment of herself? If she could, she would wear dogteeth ornaments and wrapped garments.

Once outside in the cold, she realized she'd left her sketch with Jacob Painter. There was no going back. Walking around the back of the tavern, she saw that Mr. Murphy's dray was gone.

It would be a long walk back. As she started up the road through the snow, she heard someone shouting from behind her. It was Mother Barnes. She waited for the woman to catch up to her.

"I'm so glad I caught you." She was panting heavily. "Muriel said you were here. I want you to have these." She held out her hand to Emily. There were two silver spoons, the sight of which made her cringe.

"I can't take those," Emily said, not wanting the coffin spoons.

"You eased her into the hereafter. You have to take them."

Reluctantly, Emily took the coffin spoons from the woman, not wanting to upset her by refusing her disturbing gift.

"One day when you have a babe, hang these over the cradle for the teething and think of me and Carrie." She shook her head sadly. "I just don't understand why the doc's powders didn't fix her like before."

So the rumors about Carrie's weakness with men were true. "I wouldn't know, Mother Barnes," Emily said. "You might want to ask the doctor."

"That's what Muriel says. Well, best be on your way. It looks like more snow coming."

Another burden, Emily thought, as she trudged the long way back.

As she reached the academy, she stopped to gaze at the white building, a blank against the snow and the white sky. Only the dark elm trees surrounding the school with their skeletal branches seemed real.

If she went in now, her absence might be explained. "I felt ill this morning. But now I'm feeling better."

She didn't have the strength to lie. Better to go home.

"Emily, is that you?" Mrs. Clayton called from the parlor as Emily closed the front door.

She unlaced her boots, shrugged out of her coat, and came to the parlor doorway. "I'm not well," she said.

Mrs. Clayton put down her needlework and said, "Oh, dear. I hope it's not the ague that's going around."

Emily put her hand to her forehead. "I don't think I have a fever, just a stomach upset." She turned to leave.

"Come see how your drawing has inspired me," said Mrs. Clayton, beckoning to her and holding the silk-embroidered picture out to Emily.

Emily walked slowly toward Mrs. Clayton, not wanting to look at anything reminiscent of her home. She'd reluctantly sketched the scene of her family's farm as a favor to Mrs. Clayton, who found great pleasure in her needlework.

"What do you think?"

There was her family farm with the barn, fence and rows of trees she knew so well. All planted by her grandfather and father. The deep greens of the orchard, the red barn and white fence, the trees brown barked and green leaved, as if summer were eternal. Only a small section of the orchard was left to complete.

"It's beautiful," Emily managed to say, overcome with homesickness so severe that her stomach churned.

Mrs. Clayton looked up at her, then picked up her needle and pulled another green stitch through the silk.

"Since you're not well, maybe it can wait," she said, continuing to ply her needle through the delicate silk fabric.

Emily had no idea what the woman was talking about. Mrs. Clayton must have caught the puzzled look on her face.

"He's read Miss Wolcott's letter and wants to speak to you tonight. I'll do what I can, but you know how he is about these matters."

Emily trudged up the stairs to her attic bedroom, now really sick to her stomach.

She sat at the table in her bedroom, finishing the composition Miss Wolcott had assigned her as punishment, when she heard Dr. Clayton's raised voice coming from his study below, which made her stop for a moment, trying to make out the words.

But all she could hear were muffled sounds, Dr. Clayton loud and demanding, Mrs. Clayton low and soothing, their voices rising and falling as if they were tidal. A quiver went through her. She put down her pen, smudging the last word she'd written and rubbed at her forehead. Listening to Dr. Clayton's angry tones, Emily knew Mrs. Clayton had not been able to intercede for her in regards to Miss Wolcott's letter. Sick or not, she would be called to his study.

She heard quick footsteps on the stairs. The door opened a crack, casting Mrs. Clayton in a halo of candlelight. "He wants to see you now." Mrs. Clayton's face was blotchy, her eyes red. "Say nothing counter. I could do nothing for you."

She patted Emily's arm before they descended the stairs.

"Sit, sit." Dr. Clayton gruffly gestured Emily toward a chair.

He stood with his back to the hearth, his hands behind him, staring down at his shoes, lost in thought. The heavy curtains were drawn, and the kerosene lamp cast strange shadows round the room.

Emily averted her eyes from the letter, which lay open on the massive desk, anxious for the whole ordeal to be over, knowing its inevitable outcome.

Finally he went to his desk, sat down, picked up his spectacles and slipped the loops over his ears, peering at her as if he'd never seen her before.

When she couldn't stand the silence any longer, she said, "Please, if you will let me explain."

He put his hand up to stop her. "You know I think of you as if you were my daughter."

Hadn't Miss Wolcott said the same thing and then punished her anyway?

"And your help has been"—he paused and licked his thin lips as if the next word was on his tongue—"most helpful." There were hollowed circles under his eyes, and his ring of gray hair hung lanky.

"But I'm afraid I have not been dutiful toward you." He tapped the letter with his finger repeatedly, each tapping increasing in tempo. "You are to be prepared for your lessons. Miss Wolcott says here you forgot your journal."

"I have it now," Emily defended herself.

"Where was it?"

"Abigail Dunham's bedroom."

"Humph," he replied. "How did you come to leave it there?"

Did he not remember her jumping up to cut the thread when his hand shook? She searched his face for some realization but saw none.

"Dr. Clayton, I helped with the stitching up of her head," she said, trying to jolt his memory.

"No excuse for this journal business. Miss Wolcott is very concerned about your studies. We can't have this. I have a duty to the community and to your family in your regard."

He rubbed at his forehead as if that could bring back the memory. "You'll not accompany me on calls after curfew. In fact, I think it best you confine yourself to household tasks."

"Is that all?" she asked, just wanting to leave. He'd said nothing about her drawing.

He leaned forward and put his head in his hands as if he couldn't hold it any longer, his voice weary. "At the next public fault-telling session, you will confess your lies. And, I, not my wife, will prepare the certificate for Miss Wolcott so there will be no misunderstanding."

"My lies?" Emily's hand went to her throat at the thought of the public sessions.

"You told Miss Wolcott that you didn't know where your journal was. And now you tell me you do. I will write in the certificate that you were lying about that."

"If I lied, it was for you," she said emphatically.

"Now, now, young lady, no need for that. You lied for yourself. And now Mrs. Clayton tells me you're still drawing after Miss Wolcott said you were not to draw. All must be admitted to."

"I did not mean to lie. Please don't write that in the certificate. I promise I will stop all drawing; I will concentrate on my lessons. I will strive to be an excellent teacher." Her face beat with blood. She would promise him anything rather than stand in front of the community like a common criminal and admit to being a liar.

"It seems you do not mean many things."

"Dr. Clayton, I don't know to what you refer. Is there something else I have done wrong?"

He closed his eyes and sat back. "You would be much happier in life if you would accept your circumstances."

"What circumstances?" Emily blurted out, unable to control her emotions.

"Of your sex. Now, go. I am tired."

From the window at the top of the stairs the full moon was ablaze with cold light. Emily climbed toward it, the doctor's words rumbling inside her. How could he accuse her of not accepting her sex? She had not asked to go on calls. It was he who could not accept whatever caused his hands to shake and befuddle his mind.

Chapter Ten

The schoolroom felt like a courtroom, the bench a punishment, and the snow blowing past the windows countless accusations.

Emily sat in the second row, watching eight-year-old Clarissa Bacon throw back her head and confess her petty faults as if they were lines in a play. Clarissa was a sturdy girl, squat and auburn haired with a piggish nose and a fondness for stray animals.

"I complained of the cold and talked in class."

Sitting directly behind Miss Wolcott, Emily saw her head nod in approval, heard the crinkling of the boarder's certificate in her hands, which sounded like applause.

"Is that all your faults for this week, then, Clarissa?"

"Um," Clarissa pondered, her eyes rolling upward. "Oh, I forgot." She pushed her broad shoulders back. "Slouching." A large grin occupied her face.

"What else?" Miss Wolcott coaxed. She was always gentlest with the younger girls.

"I snuck a sickly dog into the boardinghouse?" she asked.

"And?"

"And kept it in my room for a week until it died."

"And why was this a fault?"

"Because it smelled bad?"

A titter of laughter rippled through the audience. Emily peered over her shoulder. The room had filled to capacity since the session began two hours ago, making her stomach knot.

"No, Clarissa, because it broke the boardinghouse rules."

She colored and put her head down. "Am I excused?"

"Very good," Miss Wolcott said in lieu of an answer.

Clarissa curtsied, then skipped down from the platform.

"Lucy Nash," Miss Wolcott called. She never went in alphabetical order, preferring instead to leave the worst infractions until the last. Emily was the only student besides Lucy who hadn't yet taken the platform.

Why was I last? she questioned. Surely lying, drawing, and being unprepared were no worse infractions than keeping a sick dog in the boardinghouse.

And no one knows I went to the tavern the morning after Carrie's death, she reassured herself, except Mr. Murphy, Jacob Painter, Mother Barnes, and Muriel. What interest would Painter have in town meetings? And Mother Barnes and Muriel never attended the fault-telling sessions. Mr. Murphy only occasionally.

She took in a deep breath, trying to quell her nervous stomach, remembering how concerned Mrs. Clayton had been about her health, insisting she rest the remainder of the week.

When she'd claimed she was well enough to help Mrs. Clayton with household chores, Mrs. Clayton had said, "Best to concentrate on your studies." Now she suspected something else had been behind her solicitousness about her health and her studies. But what?

Lucy's coughing drew Emily's attention back to the platform where Lucy struggled to talk.

"Take your time, dear," Miss Wolcott encouraged.

Emily heard the restlessness of the audience, the rustle of dresses, the clearing of throats, and the whispering.

Lucy stood taller and said, "It's a small thing really, and I didn't know its seriousness."

Why isn't she looking at me, Emily wondered? Whenever one

or the other had to mount the platform and confess, they kept their eyes focused on the other to get through it. Emily tried to catch Lucy's eye, but she refused to meet her gaze.

"I know I should have been paying attention to the lesson, but I was so homesick and Emily wasn't there. And, well, I looked out the window, and, as if I wished it, there was Emily walking past. So I excused myself on the pretense of being ill, got my coat and ran outside. But she was on Mr. Murphy's dray and I tried to call to her, but she was too far away. I know I shouldn't have lied. That's all."

Emily felt a cold sweat break out all over her body. Her face was hot and she put her cold hands up to it as if they could cool her flaming cheeks.

"Is there anything else, Lucy?" Miss Wolcott was already shuffling through her papers.

"No, Mistress."

Lucy walked quickly past the row of benches where Emily sat with her head down, her eyes straight ahead.

"Emily Lord, if you please," Miss Wolcott called.

She can't make me go up there, Emily told herself. I'll just sit here and she'll give up when she sees I'm not budging.

Miss Wolcott turned around and stared at Emily, those large blue eyes filmy with purpose. "Courage," she whispered, "it'll be over quickly." Then she turned back around in her seat.

"Emily Lord," Miss Wolcott repeated only louder.

As Emily stood, her knees wobbled and she thought she might faint. She wanted to run from the schoolroom, out into the cold morning, and then what?

As she took the platform, her eyes roved the packed assembly. Doctor and Mrs. Clayton were sitting on the aisle near the back of the room. Mrs. Clayton smiled up at her reassuringly. Like Lucy, Dr. Clayton would not meet her eye. Mr. Murphy was there as well.

Scattered throughout the room were students she recognized from the law school. The room was so crowded that there were people standing in the back and along the walls. She could barely breathe.

Miss Wolcott rose to her feet, leaning on her cane, a certificate paper in her one hand. "Where were you going on Tuesday morning at nine o'clock with Mr. Murphy?" Miss Wolcott inquired, a crisp accusatory tone punctuating her words.

Emily kept her eyes focused on the wood floor, afraid to look up and meet the glaring stare of the community. "To Mother Barnes's Tavern." Her words came out as a croak.

Miss Wolcott didn't seem at all surprised at her revelation. "For what purpose were you going to the tavern on a Tuesday morning when you were expected at school?"

She didn't need to look at Miss Wolcott; she knew the woman so well, had listened to her lessons and lectures for nearly a year. She recognized the subtle shift in her tone from accusatory to questioning.

"I had not planned to go there. But . . ." Now she hesitated. How could she tell this crowd her innermost feelings?

"Yes, and what? Mr. Murphy suggested you go?"

"No."

"Then what?"

"You see, Carrie Barnes had died the night before." She lifted her head and stared out into the assembled crowd. They were glaring at her, poised for her answer. "And it was like watching my sister Ann die all over again. The way she looked at me. It was horrible. And I thought I would go there and be of help to the family. Since I'd been with her at her end. Then maybe I wouldn't feel so sad." Her voice trailed off.

The silence was absolute. The only sound the crackling of wood in the hearth.

"Well, Emily, it seems this becomes a lie covering a lie." Miss

Wolcott held out the certificate from Dr. Clayton. "You told Mrs. Clayton you had gone to school and came home because you were ill."

"I lied."

"And why were you with Carrie Barnes? Had you gone to the tavern that night for a sleigh party?" Miss Wolcott was suggesting a way out. But how could she take it?

Dr. Clayton still would not meet her eye, and Mrs. Clayton kept smiling at her. How silly the woman looked, Emily thought suddenly, like a deranged witch.

"I was sent to fetch Dr. Clayton, who was attending to Carrie. Abigail Dunham would not wake and the doctor was needed. He told me to stay with Carrie and note the time of her passing. She was near to dying."

"Well, we don't like our girls at taverns unaccompanied, but since you were sent on a mission of mercy, sometimes rules must be bent. Is there anything else you need to confess?" Miss Wolcott glanced over her shoulder as she spoke for the benefit of the townspeople.

There was her drawing, but no one knew of it except Doctor and Mrs. Clayton. And besides, she hadn't drawn all week.

"No, Mistress."

"Then you may leave."

Emily started to walk across the platform when a shout came from the back of the room.

"She lies."

Miss Wolcott turned sharply. "Who is that?" She thrust her small head forward squinting.

Muriel Barnes emerged from the crowd and walked to the center aisle. "She's a liar. Ask her where I found her when she should have been at this school?"

"Emily, what does she mean?" Miss Wolcott demanded.

Emily just shook her head from side to side, fighting back tears.

"She, miss academy girl, was cozying up to the painter, Jacob. I caught them in the mourning room, close as can be, right there in front of my dead sister's body." She jabbed her finger in Emily's direction.

A communal gasp filled the room.

"Emily, is this true?"

"No!" she cried. "No."

"Oh, it's true. I saw her with my own two eyes."

"It wasn't like that," Emily defended herself. "I was admiring his mourning portrait of Carrie. That's all."

Miss Wolcott's face had gone ashen, and she was staring at Emily as if she were an exotic insect. "Miss Wolcott, please," Emily begged.

The woman turned away, addressing the assembly in a stern voice, "Be assured, Miss Lord will be taken to task."

"You have to believe me," Emily whispered. "You have to." Even as she said the words, she knew they had no power to sway the woman whose obligation to the community outweighed her obligation to a wayward student.

With shoulders slumped, Emily stumbled from the platform and hurried down the aisle, pushing past Muriel, who stood smirking at her.

Once outside, she ran down North Street through the piles of snow, as if a pack of wild dogs were chasing her, her only thought: I have to get away from here. As she slogged through the deep snow, she held her wool skirt up, slipping and sliding, her corset stays digging into her sides, oblivious to the cold. When she reached the Clayton house, she was sweating and panting so hard, she had to stop and lean against the house to catch her breath.

For a moment she breathed in the cold air, wondering what

to do. She would be dismissed from the academy; of that she was sure, sent home with a scathing letter to Thomas outlining her infractions.

"No!" she cried aloud, her stomach revolting at the thought of Thomas's disdain.

Quickly she hurried to the barn where the two horses were stabled. She threw a saddle on the brown roan, fastened the halter and reins, and then mounted the horse. Not sure where she was going, just that she had to leave this place.

As she tore down the snow-packed streets of Litchfield past the large hulking houses, the gnarled elms, the law school, the female academy, her skirts flew up, revealing her white pantaloons, a wildness coursing through her. She welcomed the wind that scoured her face, numbing everything.

When she reached Goshen Road, she whipped the horse harder, the tavern looming ahead as a crazy idea flashed into her brain. If Jacob Painter was still there, she'd beg him to take her with him.

The place was still shuttered, the yew wreath brittle, a sign read *Closed for family death*. She tied the horse up and walked around the back of the tavern.

He had to be there. He had to be.

A yellow light blazed in an upstairs window. The back door was unlocked. She pulled it open and went inside.

Momentarily, she stood in the dim hallway listening for him. The upstairs floorboards creaked. She could smell the heavy scent of paint. He was still here.

She hiked up her wet skirts and went up the back stairs and found him in Carrie's room painting the walls. If death had recently been here, life had come again. The bold trees, the summer fields, a few cows, the tavern beside a lone tree.

She didn't wait for him to acknowledge her presence, but

walked into the room with a confidence that was quickly waning.

"When do you leave?" she demanded her hands fisted by her sides.

He put his paintbrush and palette on the stripped bed, a perplexed look on his face. "What are you doing here, miss?"

"You have to take me with you. I have nowhere else to go." She'd meant to ease into her request, but the sight of him took her words away.

He took a few steps toward her. "What has happened?"

"It's done. I've done it. Even the Mistress has turned her back to me. And all because I stood in the mourning room that day with you."

"You're shivering," he said, putting his arms around her, pulling her close and holding her until she stopped shaking. His arms felt lean and muscular, and his smell was smoky; she heard the low steady beat of his heart.

"Miss, you don't even know me," he whispered into her hair. "What kind of man I am." Even as he protested, she knew he could be persuaded. If only she could say the right reason, the one that would turn him forever toward her.

"But I do," she whispered back. "I see it on these walls and the ones downstairs. Your heart is wondrous, like mine. Magical, my mother called me."

"Stop." His arms fell away.

"I won't." She rose up on her toes, put her arms around his neck and kissed his mouth hard, the way Edward had kissed hers by the river last summer. A bruising kiss she now understood.

When he finally pulled away, she saw the waver in his dark eyes. He had not expected this of her.

"You'll take me, then? I can help with the drawing and painting. You've seen what I can do. No one need know I am a woman. I'll cut my hair, wear men's clothes. And, at night, I'll be a woman again."

He was considering it, she could tell. "Surely you've had an offer of marriage."

It was as if he had slapped her. She put her hand over her mouth. "Am I that repulsive to you?"

He moved away toward the window. "I can't take you with me. Nor do I want to. What I do, I do alone. That's the way I am."

She heard the back door slam shut and someone moving around downstairs. She sat down on the bed, all the fight gone from her.

"You'll regret this." She wanted to hurt him.

"Probably, but this has nothing to do with me."

He was right. Her wanting to go with him had nothing to do with him. He was a way to escape herself. "What am I going to do now?" She wanted to cry, but she couldn't.

He reached into his kit bag and took out a battered-looking book. "I've about memorized it. So why don't you take it? My uncle wrote it."

The book was *Curious Arts,* by Rufus Porter. "In exchange for your drawing of the town with the native woman. I'd like to keep it."

He placed the book in her lap.

"There's two drawings folded up inside I picked up during my travels. You can have them, too."

She took the book and stood up. "Can I tell you something that's been weighing on my conscience?" she asked.

He hesitated then said, "Sure."

"I think Dr. Clayton killed Carrie." There. She'd said it. The words filled the room as if they were embodied.

"Killed her?" He stepped back and looked at her suspiciously.

"Not on purpose. But killed her just the same. It all came

rushing back to me when I walked into this room, the bottle, what he said, what Mother Barnes said. I think he gave her too much of the medicine. I didn't want to see it, because he was so like my father. And he gets confused and shaky at night."

Painter looked over her head toward the doorway where Muriel stood listening.

Emily turned and saw her. "There's nothing you can do about it," she said to the woman with spite. "I'll deny I ever said it."

Then she turned back to Painter, seeking his answer. He put up his hands. "I'm about through here. Be gone by the afternoon."

As she walked past Muriel, she said, "See? Sometimes the truth doesn't make a difference."

All the way back to the house, she let the horse find its way slowly, running her fingers through its reddish mane, which was so like her sister Ann's hair.

When she entered the house, Mrs. Clayton clucked at her. "I was so worried about you. Everyone was so shocked the way you ran out of there."

She didn't wait to hear the rest. Instead, she climbed the steep steps to her attic bedroom, pulled out her trunk, and packed. When she was finished, she sat at the narrow table and began to write.

Dear Edward,
 It is with great joy that I accept your proposal of marriage. I will be returning home soon and will explain everything.

She stopped and loosened the ribbon from her braid and shook her hair free, then wrapped the ribbon around her finger, tightening it until the tip of her finger was numb. Then she let it uncurl and finished the letter.

Chapter Eleven: Chicago, Illinois, Present Day

Sitting in the dark theater, the homeless woman's words washed over me, her voice as flat and lifeless as the stark stage, as flat and lifeless as I felt. I didn't want to be there. Even with Nick's raucous rants, it was taking all my energy to stay awake. Since returning to Chicago, I still hadn't gotten a good night's sleep. Dreams of Karen and the old house plagued me.

But Nick had insisted I attend a run-through. He was having problems with the cast and he wanted my feedback. Without him I'd be on the streets, so I'd agreed.

"Besides, it'll get your mind off everything that's happened," he'd said over breakfast, his grayish-blue eyes full of concern. Though in his middle forties, Nick appeared ten years younger. Maybe it was his blond hair or his short but trim body, or maybe that optimism he wore like a dare.

"But I was planning on clearing out Karen's stuff at the Newberry Library today and maybe do some research." I'd gone through Karen's daybook again yesterday and found a letter from the Newberry stuffed in the back flap. She was a Newberry Fellow. When I called the library, I was connected to the Curator of Special Collections and Maps, Dr. Peter Morant, who said to bring a photo ID and a death certificate, and I could collect her things.

"Do you really think those murals are worth anything? Sounds like wishful thinking to me, RT." He poured more cream in his coffee and mixed it with his finger.

I'd explained about the house and the murals and their possible value, leaving out Karen's supposed theft and my evasion of the campus police, who I'd yet to call back. Let them try and find me, I thought.

"I don't know. But Karen did." I hadn't confided my suspicion that Karen's death hadn't been accidental. What proof did I have, except a gut feeling?

"Just one run-through," he pleaded, licking his finger. "You'll be outta there by one, two at the latest. By the way, I like how your hair's growing out kinda Mitzi Gaynor, *South Pacific*, or Jean Seberg, *Joan of Arc*."

"Both blondes, not me," I laughed at his fifties' movie reference, staring up at the poster of Jean Harlow with her platinum-blonde hair, pencil-thin eyebrows, and come-hither look. Nick was a connoisseur of films from the thirties, forties, and fifties. His loft was strewn with movie posters.

Now, watching his production of *Homeless, In Their Own Words*, I wondered if he had another motive.

"It's not like you can't have Nikes or a pair of Reeboks," said Joanne, a plump disheveled woman whose husband had left her with three kids and an insurmountable debt. "It means"—the thundering of the el train made her pause—"you, you, uh, you can't have shoes. You have to wear the same shoes with the holes in them every day."

"Stop, stop," Nick shouted from the audience for the tenth time. Because of Nick's constant interruptions, the woman had yet to make it through her monologue once.

Joanne walked to the stage's apron and peered out into the darkness. "You keep stopping me like that, and I'm going to lose my rhythm. I lose my rhythm, and I lose my words."

Nick leaned over and whispered, "Do you believe her? Those are *her* damned words. How can she lose them?" He turned his red face toward me. "You're practically homeless. I should have you do the part."

He'd already replaced two of the homeless women who'd backed out at the last minute with professional actors, shattering his dream of having an all formerly homeless cast.

"If you want me to move out, just say so," I answered back, wanting no part of the production. Early in my performance career, I'd tried acting and failed miserably. It was impossible for me to inhabit anyone's skin but my own, no matter how uncomfortable that skin was.

He got up from his seat, trudged down the center aisle and jumped up on the stage. "Darling," he began, putting his arm around the woman. "Where's the passion? Where's the anger?"

The woman shrugged off his arm. "I can't do this. Between the el and you, I can't concentrate."

"You can do this, and you will. Think of your kids."

"You leave my kids out of this. They don't deserve seeing me up here talking about wanting to die." With that she stormed off the stage.

"Joanne, come back. Your kids don't even have to be here."

The slam of the back door echoed through the theater.

Margaret, one of the homeless mothers who had no problem accessing her anger, emerged from the wings. "She's gone, Nick. What we gonna do now?"

"RT, get up here."

It was almost four o'clock when we broke for the day. Before I left, I made Nick swear he'd find another actor before opening night on Friday. But the way he asked "Would I do that to you?" made me question his sincerity.

The Newberry Library closed at five, not leaving me much time to clear out Karen's workstation, let alone do any research on the Brauns. At least I could pack up her books and papers and check out her Newberry account. Maybe, in Karen's carrel,

I'd find something related to the murals.

Luck was on my side. An el train was pulling up just as I reached the platform, and it started to rain. By four-fifteen, I was inside the glass doors of the Newberry Library on West Walton Street, basking in the icy air-conditioning as I handed the guard my ID and asked to see Dr. Morant.

The guard looked me up and down as if I were on the FBI's Most Wanted List. His eyes resting briefly on the purple bandanna I'd tied around my head to cover my stubbly head. Even I was getting tired of the covert stares.

"If you're with the event, you're supposed to come in the back entrance and take the freight elevator. And you can't bring that in here." The guard pointed to the backpack hanging from my shoulder. "There are lockers behind that wall where you can check it."

"I'm not here about an event. Just call Dr. Morant. He's expecting me. It's about my deceased sister, Karen Caffrey. She's a fellow, or was a fellow here. I'm here to collect her books and papers." Why was I explaining my personal life to this guy?

He picked up the phone on his podium and punched in a few numbers.

"There's a Rose Caffrey says you're expecting her. Yes, okay." He hung up the phone and handed me back my ID. "He'll be right down. Have a seat over there. Make sure you check your backpack."

After checking my backpack, I plopped down on one of the marble benches adjacent to Ulysses S. Grant's portrait, tapping my foot in annoyance. I'll bet if I'd dressed in one of Karen's ubiquitous suits, he'd let me in, backpack and all.

As I waited for Dr. Morant, I saw that the railing leading up to the second floor was interlaced with white tulle and tiny tea lights. On the landing was a tree strewn with lights, and two tall glass hurricane candleholders decorated the window ledge. I wondered what event the library was hosting.

"Rose Caffrey?" I was so lost in thought, I hadn't noticed the man approach.

Dr. Morant looked nothing like he sounded on the phone. Based on his clipped, almost-British accent, I'd anticipated a man in a dark suit and tie with a face as pinched as his vowels. Instead, he was dressed in jeans and a short-sleeved, pale-green shirt. His resemblance to a young Mick Jagger was uncanny, right down to those full lips and shaggy brown hair.

He shook my hand and said, "Peter Morant. I didn't know Karen very well, but I've heard her make presentations. Excellent mind. The fellows' carrels are on the fourth floor."

I followed him up the white marble stairs to the first floor where we caught the elevator. As we rode up to the fourth floor, he said, "Here's her password." He handed me a Post-it note with Karen's password. "You should have enough time to pack up her things and access her Newberry account. There's a computer at the back of the room. But if you don't have enough time, just come to my office on the third floor at the east end of the hall—name's on the door—and I'll let Frank know. We're hosting a benefit tonight in Main Hall, so security's pretty tight. Nobody gets past Frank without an invitation."

No kidding.

Once we exited the elevator, he led me to the first room on the right across from the stairs. The Center for the History of Cartography/Center for Renaissance Studies was crammed with rows and rows of modular carrels, a veritable warren of cubbyholes.

"Karen's carrel is over here on the left against the wall."

A small white card tacked to the outside wall identified the carrel's occupant and project: Karen Caffrey, Morris University,

"Challenging the State: American Indians and the Trail of Tears."

He pulled one of the books from the shelf and explained, "Many of these books belong to the Newberry. You can tell by the reserve slips sticking out of the books." He opened the book and showed me the salmon-colored slip. "The rest are Karen's. Oh, I almost forgot." He dug a key out of his shirt pocket. "At the back of the room is a file cabinet with Karen's name on it. You'll want to clear that out as well. I'll leave you to it."

I slipped the key in the same pocket with the Post-it note.

After he left, I stood for a few minutes taking in Karen's workstation. It was as if she'd merely stepped away and would return shortly: her black sweater draped the back of the chair, a pen rested beside a pile of books and a flip calendar displayed the month of June and a quote from the Japanese poet Basho, 1644–1694: "The glare of lightning/through the darkness travels/the night heron's scream." My stomach clutched with emotions I didn't want to feel about regrets and missed opportunities.

Tentatively I sat down and started searching through the various books for the missing diary pages, separating Karen's books from the library's books as I searched. Nothing. Stacking Karen's books on the desk, I looked around for something to carry them in. In the trash basket, I found a plastic bag. I put Karen's books in the bag and tied her sweater around my waist. There was nothing written on the calendar, so I threw it in the trash.

Pushing back on the chair and about to leave, I then remembered the file cabinet and Karen's Newberry account. When I'd called Dr. Morant, he informed me that the library would be shutting down Karen's account, but that I might want to look at her files and print up her research. I dug the key and Post-it note from my jeans pocket, then glanced at my watch. It was four forty-five P.M.

I picked up the heavy bag of books and walked to the back of the room where Morant said the file cabinets and communal computer were.

Inside Karen's file cabinet were six notebooks. I flipped through those—no diary pages. When I was back at Nick's apartment, I'd go through them and see if there was anything relevant to the murals. I managed to fit the notebooks in the plastic bag along with the books.

It didn't take long to access Karen's account.

Sure enough, there was Karen's research on the Trail of Tears, the Cherokee, nineteenth-century mural painters, including Rufus Porter, pretty much what she'd bookmarked in her computer at home. I decided there was too much to print in fifteen minutes, so I opened her e-mail account, intending to send the files as an attachment to my laptop, when I noticed an unopened e-mail. It was dated July third, the day Karen died. The subject was Baby. It was from Karen to Karen.

My heart was pounding as I opened the e-mail.

There was no text, only an attachment. I opened the attachment and read the first entry.

March 9: Found Emily Braun's diary at the MU Library while doing research for the Trail of Tears Organization. It was like finding gold in a clear stream. Drove out to the farmhouse holding my breath all the way, afraid it was gone, like so many other old farmhouses. But there it was, falling apart, yet still standing. The For Sale sign looked as battered as the house. An old beat-up truck was parked in front, so someone is still living there. I left a message with Dan. If only the murals haven't been destroyed. It would be like stepping back in time. And to think that Emily Braun, a nineteenth-century woman, an indirect disciple of Rufus Porter, was the artist. Her descriptions of the murals are so vivid. If only the murals come close to her descriptions. And then there's her extraordinary life. More research to be done.

"Wow," I said aloud. There was the answer I'd been looking for—the identity of the mural artist, Emily Braun.

Not an itinerant male painter as Alex had thought. I reread Karen's e-mail. "An indirect disciple of Rufus Porter." What did she mean by indirect?

Like a cool breeze, the trickling notes of a piano invaded the room, quickly joined by the warmer tones of a cello. The musicians must be warming up. I checked my watch again; it was after five P.M. I'd better get moving.

Suddenly an explosion of thunder sounded overhead, followed by the gush of rain hitting the windows lining the back of the room. Great, I'd be drenched by the time I reached the el station.

Quickly, I forwarded the e-mail and Karen's research files to my e-mail address. After shutting down the computer, I bent to retrieve the plastic bag, when the room went dark.

Oh, no. I should have told Morant I was still here. Frank, Mr. Friendly Guard, probably turned off the lights. I was about to stand and leave, when I heard someone moving around in the room; slow measured footsteps heading down the aisle toward the back of the room, toward me.

The guard wouldn't be walking around in a dark room, would he? Why would anyone be creeping around the fellows' carrels in the dark? I could think of no legitimate reason. Maybe I should just stand up and announce myself and end the suspense. No. Something was off. Why would someone turn off the lights, then lurk about in the room?

There was nowhere for me to run, since the only exit was the one I'd entered, and whoever was in the room would see me. All I could do was wait until the person left. Quietly, I crawled under the computer-station table and pulled the chair in front of me.

Now the musicians were playing "Georgia on My Mind," and thunder was repeating as if in accompaniment. I strained to listen for footsteps. Very faintly I heard them coming closer and closer to where I was hiding. As the song ended, the room went quiet. All I could hear was my heart beating too loudly and the rain hitting the windows.

Then the footsteps resumed, this time growing fainter and fainter. The person was leaving. I let out a long deep breath, realizing I hadn't been breathing. I waited a few more minutes, listening for any sounds, but all I heard was the whoosh of the air-conditioning, then the upbeat of "When the Saints Go Marching In."

I eased the chair forward, crawled out from under the table, picked up the bag and started down the aisle toward the exit. Walking through the double glass doors into the dimly lit hallway, I looked right and left, debating whether to take the elevator and decided on the open staircase, which seemed safer than a closed elevator car.

As I shuffled down the stairs toting the heavy bag, I hummed along with the music, "My Kind of Town," picturing the women decked out in gowns, the men in tuxedos milling around on the first floor, maybe holding flutes of champagne.

Just as I reached the second floor, I paused to shift the bag's weight to my left arm before opening the door when I sensed someone moving quickly behind me. I started to turn. Then an arm was around my throat, choking me, my body lifted off the ground as I was yanked backwards. I thrashed against my attacker, dropping the bag as I clawed at his arm with both hands and kicked at his legs. But the more I thrashed the tighter his grasp on my throat.

He was dragging me farther and farther down the dim

hallway away from the stairs, away from any help. Everything was beginning to blur as I gasped for air. As I slumped against him, I felt my body surrender. Whatever he wanted from me, he was going to get. And there was nothing I could do. Just as I was losing consciousness, he eased up on his grip and I took in a long ragged breath.

"This is your only warning," he whispered in my ear, his breath warm and intimate like a lover's.

I tried to speak but his arm tightened again and my throat closed. Blood was pounding in my head; this time I was going to pass out. I prayed not to die.

Then he shoved me away so hard I fell against the window ledge, hitting my head and collapsing on the marble floor. The sound of his retreating footsteps moved away.

Stunned, grasping for breath I lay there afraid to get up—afraid he was still nearby hiding, playing some sick game with me. Nauseated, my head spinning, I rolled over on my side and curled into a ball, waiting for the nausea to pass, the marble floor like a cool river pulling me back.

Then I eased myself up on one elbow and looked down the long dark hallway. He was gone. And so were Karen's books and notebooks. All that was left was her sweater lying in a black heap on the floor. I got up slowly. My legs were trembling as I walked up to the third floor clutching Karen's sweater to my chest like a security blanket.

When I got to Morant's office, he was putting on his tuxedo jacket. I swallowed hard and tried to talk but nothing came out but a squeak.

He looked up in surprise. "Rose, are you okay?"

Now I was shaking so hard I could barely stand. "I thought he was going to kill me," I whispered, rubbing at my throat.

He came around his desk and guided me to a chair.

"What are you talking about? Who was going to kill you?"

I managed to tell him in a whispery voice what happened.

His forehead was creased with worry. "Look, I've got to alert security. You can rest here in my office until the EMTs arrive. I'll lock the door."

My voice came out in a croak. "I'm fine. No EMTs."

It was after seven o'clock when I left the Newberry Library, the event well under way, with men in tuxes and women in an array of silky gowns holding champagne flutes just as I'd imagined. The attacker and the bag were nowhere to be found. This time I'd told the police everything, from Karen's death to the attacker's warning. I was scared.

"He must have been following me," I explained. "He wanted Karen's notebooks. He couldn't get them without a key." I was convinced that the attack was connected to the murals.

The two cops exchanged glances as if to say *you gotta be kidding*.

The older cop with the overhanging belly said, "Probably some drug head, who snuck in with the catering people through the back door. Decided to take a look around, saw you, and grabbed that bag of yours, thinking there was something he could sell for drug money."

"I'm telling you, it wasn't a drug head," I whispered. My throat was sore as hell. The knot on my head pulsed. "He said it was my only warning. He knew me."

"Ma'am, drug heads say crazy things. You can't take that personally."

If I could have managed to shout, I would have. But all I could produce was an exasperated, wispy, "You're wrong."

They ended the interview saying, "We'll let you know if your items show up."

Now, walking down Southport to Nick's loft apartment, the city's gritty haze clung to my skin like an infection. The rain had stopped, leaving behind humidity dense with exhaust. My every breath was labored as if it were my last. Cars lined the street bumper to bumper, ready for combat. The city exhaled raw hostility.

I kept looking over my shoulder, expecting at any moment to see the attacker lunge at me from an alley or step out of a bar doorway. Even if he were there waiting, I wouldn't recognize him. I never saw him. All I had were sensory images—a minty coffee smell, medium build, jeans, running shoes. That could be anybody.

There was no doubt in my mind that he knew who I was and what I was doing at the library. Now he had all Karen's notebooks and books. I didn't even know what was in the notebooks. But at least I had her files.

My suspicion that Karen's death hadn't been accidental was looking less and less like a suspicion. If Karen had been murdered, what about the murals and the diary were worth killing for?

Nearing the narrow walkway between the two buildings that led to the coach house, I flipped open my cell phone and turned it on, quickening my pace. There were two messages both from Alex Hague.

"Rose, a cop showed up here this morning looking for you. I told him you were in Chicago. He wouldn't tell me what he wanted. Why are the police looking for you?"

The second message came in around six P.M. "I e-mailed you some digital photos. Call me after you look at them. I think I know who our mystery artist is."

I punched in his number as I emerged into the open courtyard and the fading summer light. Rick and Josh, Nick's downstairs neighbors, were sitting in the courtyard sipping wine, their tabby cat beside them. I waved and kept walking. They waved back, lifting their wine glasses in a casual salute.

"Alex," I began, when he picked up.

"You saw the initials, ELB," he interrupted, his voice edgy with excitement. "I uncovered them today. It has to be Emily Braun. Her maiden name was Lord."

"I know." Had I told him Emily's middle name? No, but he could have seen it on her gravestone.

"What do you mean you know?" He sounded irritated.

"I found Karen's files at the Newberry Library. It's all there. She kept a journal of sorts. I haven't had time to read through all of it yet. But the first entry names Emily as the artist."

"I can barely hear you. Do you have a cold?"

"I was attacked today at the Newberry."

"What are you talking about?"

"I haven't figured it out yet. But there's something in those murals that's dangerous." Not until I said the words aloud did they seem real to me.

When I reached the coach-house steps, I sat down and related what had happened. After I finished, he let out a long whistle. "Maybe the cops are right. The attack could have been random."

All the fight had gone out of me. "His arm was around my throat. It wasn't random. How close are you to finishing that last mural?"

"By the weekend it should be done."

"You haven't told anyone about the murals, have you?"

"Only the lab in Boston."

"Keep it that way. I'll be down there Sunday." I realized I'd said *down there* with the same derisive inflection as Holly.

I walked up the steps and went inside the small vestibule. The piled-up flyers and newspapers, the smell of cat urine and dampness was like a tonic. I unlocked the entry door and started up the stairway. Finally the tension in my body started to ease.

Chapter Twelve

When Nick walked into the loft, I was sitting at the glass kitchen table, which was smudged with fingerprints and water rings, staring at Alex's digital photos. Just as he said, Emily's initials were in the corner of the last mural, ELB.

"What's this look like to you?" I'd been pondering the incongruent last mural, which seemed to have no connection to the other three murals.

He threw down his messenger bag on the black leather sectional, sending up a puff of dust. The coach-house loft was totally open with skylights and banks of windows on three sides. The only private areas were at the back, two small bedrooms and a bathroom. The bamboo floors and steel countertops gave the place a clean, functional look even when it was dusty and dirty, as it was most of the time.

"I swear those women are going to be the death of me," he said as he walked over. "Jane, you know the one who had four kids by four different men? She refuses to go on last. Something about making her too nervous. Remind me, why did I think this was a good idea."

Nick leaned over my shoulder. "Is that one of the murals?" I caught the sandalwood scent of his expensive shampoo. His only vanity was his hair, blond and curly; he wore it longish and tousled as if he'd just gotten out of bed.

"Yeah, the last one to be uncovered. See those initials at the bottom. That's our mysterious artist—Emily Lord Braun."

"A woman, huh? I'd have never figured that from those brushstrokes."

"What?" I turned and gave him a nasty look.

"I'm not being sexist, but the brushstrokes seem broad and determined, you know, masculine."

He tilted his head sideways. "But they could also be angry brushstrokes. Is that an altar on top of that hill? And what's that on the altar?" He pulled up a chair beside me and turned the computer screen toward him. "That's a kid. Damn, that's brutal."

"Or biblical. I think it's the sacrifice of Isaac by his father Abraham. See that woman on her knees crying? That's probably Sarah. The clothes look biblical. What do you make of the landscape?"

"Palm trees, the open water. It's tropical. What's a tropical scene doing in a nineteenth-century southern Illinois farmhouse?"

"That's what I've been wondering." I turned the screen back to me and brought up the mural to the right of this one and turned the screen again. "Check this out."

"A volcano spewing smoke right into that tropical mural. This chick had some imagination."

"And some awesome artistic talent."

"What's with your voice?" Nick asked. "You sound all raspy. Are you trying to get out of Friday's performance?"

Before I could answer, he looked at my neck. "How'd you get that bruise?"

I got up and walked into the living-room area to calm the tremor coursing through my body.

"RT, what happened?" He followed me and grabbed me by the shoulders to stop me from pacing.

"Let go of me." I hadn't meant to shout. Nick dropped his hands as if they'd been burned.

"Sorry," I said. "How about we have a beer and I'll tell you about it."

After I'd stopped sobbing, Nick said, "What are you going to do now?"

"I don't know. Read through Karen's files, and try to make sense of what is happening." I blew my nose, then wadded the tissue into a tight ball in my fist. "Did you find a replacement for Joanne?" I asked, wanting to change the subject.

"Still working on it." He ran his finger through his hair nervously.

"Then I guess I'd better learn my lines before Friday." I'd probably stink playing Joanne, whose lyrical mantra, "I'll tell you what it's like," packed an honesty I feared accessing. Who knows? Maybe her words would tap the increasing guilt I felt over Karen's death. If I'd showed up at her house the day before she died, like she'd asked me, maybe she'd still be alive.

"You don't have to do this. I can cut the part. Though your whiskey voice will add to your characterization." He slid his hand over mine. "RT, you should let this go. That guy's restoring the murals. You're selling the house. What more can you do?"

"I can't." I held my hand very still. "She was my sister. I need to finish what she started." I didn't add, *I think she was murdered.*

Light poured into the loft, that soft Chicago summer light burdened with smog. It was barely six A.M.; Nick was still asleep. All night, sleep had been elusive, filled with nightmares of a man chasing me into breathlessness.

I'd been up since four A.M. poring over Karen's files. Ten pages of a legal pad were filled with my notes, and my stomach was sour with the three cups of coffee I'd had.

Though I now knew the minute details of the Trail of Tears

horror, the complete and long life of Rufus Porter and his male students, understood nineteenth-century mural techniques, farmhouse buildings, and the mores of nineteenth-century rural Americans, I was no closer to understanding how or why Emily Braun painted those murals.

Something about the immediacy of my sister's words had kept me from starting with her personal diary. I kept seeing her broken body sprawled across the floor, my guilt like another self.

You owe her this, I told myself as I closed the research files and opened Karen's journal.

Before reading the entries, I scrolled through the document. The dates were chronological but not daily. Okay, stop stalling.

March 18: It took him long enough, but Dan finally got back to me. I can see the house tomorrow. His excuse? A recalcitrant son who's living there, though he's not the legal owner. Honestly, what did I ever see in Dan?

So she had been involved with Dan Yeager. Well, that explained her lacy underwear. Though I was still having trouble picturing Karen with him.

March 19: While Dan was checking out wiring in the cellar, my ruse, I dragged a chair to the bedroom doorway and used the palette knife I'd hidden in my purse to lift a tiny section of the painted layers of wallpaper. I couldn't see much, but there's definitely a painting underneath. Using a dab of paste, also hidden in my purse, along the edge, I pressed the layers back in place. My hands were shaking so badly I got a gob of paste on my blouse. Thank you, Emily, for telling me which room the murals were in. It's like you're here guiding me.

April 1: Eureka! The house is mine. Braun, Sr., accepted my offer today.

The date only adds to my elation. April from the Latin Aperire, meaning to open—the season when trees and flowers begin to open. Now my life will open. It's not too late to start over. It's not. Lenny Fish and his cohorts will wish they'd given me tenure when my stunning book on Emily Braun and the Trail of Tears erupts. To think of her genius. Another woman unsung. But I will sing her.

I stared unseeing at the computer screen. Karen had lied about why she'd left the university in Chicago and taken the job in southern Illinois. It hadn't been because she was tired of living in Chicago. She'd been sent packing. What a blow that must have been to her self-esteem. After all those years. How many? Ten years, then to be denied the pay off—tenure.

There were only a handful of entries left. The next few dealt with her research and the restoration of the farmhouse's interior. Then another surprise.

June 6: I think I've found the "perfect" art restorer for the murals, Alex Hague. The once-prestigious Alex Hague, senior restoration artist of the Boston Museum of Fine Arts. Now disgraced restoration artist. The newspaper article stated that there was no direct proof he'd stolen the statue of the head of Christ, but it was under his guardianship when it mysteriously disappeared. He'd resigned quietly. Like me, he lost everything. He'll understand what I'm about to do. Whether he stole the head or not, he'll be on my side.

My mind reeling, I stood up and walked over to the large kitchen window overlooking the adjacent duplex. A toddler dressed in Spiderman pajamas was playing on the deck, riding around and around in a circle on his three-wheeler.

Alex Hague might be a thief. And Karen had hired him because of that possibility.

I returned to the computer.

June 15: The secret is now safe.

June 16: Hired Hague. He tried to act like he was fitting me into his busy schedule, but I could tell he was elated with my most generous and hard-to-refuse offer.

June 21: The first mural revealed today. The Braun farmhouse complete with the unmarked graves of the Cherokee disguised as blackbirds. Oh, Emily, how I admire your cleverness and your talent. How I wish I'd known you. After Hague left for the day, I stood in front of the mural and with my fingers traced your painterly thoughts as if I could conjure you.

July 3: Emily Braun's grave is empty. Lawrence claims the oak tree tumbled over and exposed the empty grave. What happened to Emily?

My hand went to my chest as if a bullet had suddenly lodged there. Emily's grave was empty? That's why the gravesite looked disturbed. Someone had put the dirt back. Why hadn't Reverend Likely said anything to me about it? And what, as Karen asked, had happened to Emily?

Lawrence? Where had I see his name before? I rummaged through the brown envelope and found the Trail of Tears Symposium flyer. There he was: Lawrence Grey gave a PowerPoint presentation on remote sensing at the Campground Church Cemetery. He was a professor at MU.

Quickly I Googled remote sensing.

"What are you doing up so early?" Nick asked, stumbling into the kitchen in his gray T-shirt and shorts, his blondish hair sticking up all over his head in loose curls.

"Couldn't sleep."

He went over to the coffeemaker and poured himself the last of the coffee.

"Listen, I've got to go back to southern Illinois."

"Have it your way," he grumbled.

He took his coffee and went back to his bedroom, slamming the door so hard the dishes clattered on the shelves.

I read the definition of remote sensing five times before it registered. Not that it was hard to understand—noninvasive ground-penetrating radar—pretty much as Likely had explained. What didn't register was that Nick was furious at me, and I didn't know what to do about it.

Chapter Thirteen

Opening night went off without a hitch. To a standing-room-only audience, the actors and remaining homeless women had delivered a powerful performance about loss. Just before curtain, Nick announced that I would be playing the part of Joanne and would be reading my lines. A quick study, I'd managed to memorize some of my lines and used a newspaper as a prop to hide the script.

For the first time, I didn't feel like I was trying to be a character in a play. I became Joanne, raging and sad, lonely and bereft. All the emotion from Karen's death was channeled into my portrayal.

"Nick, get your bony white ass over here," Margaret called to Nick across the crowded dance studio above the theater. "Your girl's coppin' out on us."

An unintelligible hip-hop song was blaring. Gyrating dancers scattered over the floor, some watching themselves in the mirrors, others oblivious to everything but the music.

I was tired, my nerves frayed, and all I wanted was to go back to Nick's loft and soak in a bubble bath. The thought of having the place to myself was irresistible. Bright and early tomorrow I was heading back to Anna, Illinois, and the Braun farmhouse. Maybe once I saw the last mural in context with the other murals, I'd be closer to solving the murals' secrets—the story Emily had painted on those walls so long ago.

Nick staggered over, that familiar drunken grin plastered on his face, all his cool anger of the past few days gone. The last time he'd been this angry with me was when I'd called it quits as lovers and bed buddies.

"I wouldn't mess with Margaret here, RT," he slurred. "She's a pretty tough lady. You saw those scars."

From her monologue, I knew about Margaret's toughness. At one point, she bares her arms to the audience and says, "I cut up and down. That's how much I loved that man." In the theater's spotlight, the scars looked like snakes under her skin.

"Rosie, girl, the party's just gettin' started. You gotta meet my oldest, Duane. He should be here soon. He the one I told you about. Turned his life around." She made a big circle with her hand. "Big-time security guard over at one of them big-time office buildings on Michigan Avenue."

"I really wish I could stay. But I'm taking off tomorrow really early, driving down to southern Illinois."

"That about your sister?"

I glared at Nick, who shrugged his shoulders and walked away toward the makeshift bar. Nick couldn't keep a secret to save his life. I wondered what else he'd told Margaret.

"I'll walk down with you. Maybe catch Duane on his way up."

Before I could protest, she was weaving her way through the throng of cast members, techs, family and friends. Nick, in his infinite wisdom, had invited several Chicago theater reviewers. I saw the reviewer from the *Chicago Times* with his arm around Nick's shoulder, deep in conversation. The way Nick was smiling, I knew it would be a good review.

When we reached the back exit door, I started to say, "Margaret, you hang in there."

But she pushed the door open and stepped into the alley. "I need some air, and you need for me to walk you to the el."

I grabbed her arm. "What's going on?" Had Nick told her

about the attack at the Newberry?

Margaret's face turned serious. "There's a guy following you. At first, I didn't think nothin' of it. But when I saw him again tonight, lurking around the theater, I figured I should tell you. Last night after rehearsal when I left, he was standing across the street. I was waiting on Duane out front and seen when you left, he left. Then tonight, you know I got here late, and there he was again."

My stomach knotted. Was my attacker still following me? If so, why? He'd gotten what he wanted—Karen's books and notebooks. Why follow me now? Did he think I had the diary pages? "What did he look like?"

"Lean and mean. Baseball cap pulled low over his face, jeans, black shirt with a collar like them golfers wear."

"Thanks. But it's probably nothing. Just a coincidence." I didn't want to involve Margaret and her son in my problems. They had enough of their own. Nick told me Margaret was about to be evicted again and would be moving in with her son.

"Listen, Rosie, I know the streets and I know bad. This guy was bad. Duane be here soon. You best wait on him. This guy after you? 'Cause Duane can see to him, if you know what I mean. He'll never bother you again."

I looked over her head and saw a yellow cab out front. "There's a cab. I'll be fine. Tell Duane I'm sorry I missed him." Before she could stop me, I hurried down the alley. When I reached the street, I got in the cab.

"Drop me at the nearest el station." I couldn't justify a twenty-dollar cab fare to the loft. All I needed was to throw this guy off my trail. Once sequestered in the loft, I'd be safe.

The cabdriver gave me an angry look in the rearview mirror, then yanked down the meter lever. As the cab pulled away, I peered out the window, looking for anyone matching Margaret's description. If he was there, I didn't see him.

Sitting near the door on the el train as it clattered north, Joanne's words rang in my head as if they were mine. "I don't have the luxury of a little nervous breakdown or a little time out. I have to keep pressing forwards at what I'm doing if I'm going to make it to the end of this. I need to keep running the race. So it means don't get sick, don't need a break, nothin'. Just continue until you drop."

She'd been talking about saving her children from a life of homelessness. I couldn't save Karen. It was too late for that. But I could see this through to the end, wherever it led. I could finish what my sister had started.

The bars were packed as I hurried down Southport toward the loft, my eyes alert to lean-and-mean-looking males, which could describe half the guys roaming Southport. Quinn's Irish Pub and Restaurant was so crowded, I had to walk in the street to get past it. I didn't see Michael Quinn with his shock of white hair anywhere, but I heard a lively Irish jig being played. No doubt, another one of Quinn's charity cases, personally sponsored by Quinn and brought over from the old country.

When I reached the alley, I peered into the dark passageway. Nothing. Just the coach house, like a beacon of safety, at the end. I took in a deep breath and ran toward it. Just as I entered the courtyard, I saw a man standing motionless in the shadows beside the coach house. His back was to me.

I dug into my purse and brought out the pepper spray I'd bought after the attack at the library. I pushed the lever open and held it up as I crept slowly toward the coach house. Just as I neared the steps, the guy turned abruptly around and I pressed down on the lever, aiming it at his face.

But missed. Startled by his open fly I pepper sprayed his chin.

"What the hell are you doing, you crazy bitch?" he slurred, swiping at the pepper spray burning his chin.

Clearly he wasn't my attacker. He was overweight and too tall.

Still I held the pepper spray up at him. "Get outta here, before I call the cops!" I yelled. "This isn't a urinal."

"Okay, okay," he said, zipping up his pants and running away down the alley. Not until I was sitting in a warm bubble bath nursing a beer did I stop shaking.

Chapter Fourteen

After seven hours of driving south on Interstate 57 past endless stretches of prairie and farmland, I reached the exit for Anna just as the sun was sliding toward the horizon, a big orange shimmering ball full of molten heat. About an hour south of Chicago, I'd stopped glancing at my rearview mirror.

If someone were tailing me, I'd spot him. There were few cars on the interstate, and the land stretched toward the horizon uninterrupted, except for the occasional farm, rest stop or oddity, like the corrugated-metal cross outside of Effingham that had to be four stories high.

As I turned onto Campground Road, I checked my car's temp gauge: ninety-nine degrees. From my one bathroom break near Marion, where the humidity was like a wall I had to walk through, I knew the humidity was probably worse here.

The road curved right, and I slowed my car as I passed the Campground Cemetery. The fallen oak tree had been removed, reminding me of the mental list of people I wanted to talk to, and Lawrence Grey was at the top of that list. What did he know about Emily Braun's empty grave? From the university's Web site, I'd discovered that he was teaching a summer class on Midwestern Earthquakes and the New Madrid Seismic Zone, and his office hours were: Monday nine to eleven A.M.

Turning left on Old Cutoff, my heart started to race. I took in a deep breath and let it out slowly. I wasn't sure how I was going to handle Alex Hague, the suspected thief. There'd been no proof that he'd stolen the statue, though it had never been recovered. But he'd been the person restoring it. And he'd resigned from the museum's restoration department, which was like an admission of guilt.

Yet Karen had hired him. "He'll understand what I'm about to do," she'd written in her journal. "Whether he stole the head or not, he'll be on my side."

Just ahead I saw the farmhouse rising against the fading sky like an ancient ship tossed on a dark green sea. Alex's rental car was parked in front and next to it stood another car. As I neared the house, I recognized the car. It was Dan Yeager's. What's he doing here?

Okay, maybe he's showing a potential buyer the house. Best to wait until they're done. I wasn't in the mood to answer a lot of buyer questions. I parked across the road from the house under the shade of a large maple tree, let the window down and shut the engine off.

All the windows in the farmhouse were open and the sound of raised voices wafted across the road, which made me doubt my theory of a house showing. But what could Alex and Dan be arguing about?

Suddenly Dan swung the front door open with such force, it crashed against the side of the house with a loud bang. He hurried down the front steps toward his car, with Alex right behind him.

"You'd better get control of yourself," Alex shouted at him.

As if he'd been hit, Dan turned around and said, "Keep you damned mouth shut. That's all I'm saying." He punctuated his words with his index finger directed at Alex's chest.

"Or what?" Alex slapped his hand away.

Instead of answering, Dan turned, jumped into his car, and spun out toward the road.

He drove right past me, but in his anger, I doubt that he saw me. He was pounding the steering wheel with one hand, still shouting.

I sat for a moment considering what I just witnessed. The intensity of their fight seemed personal. What had Alex said that had prompted Dan to tell him to keep his mouth shut? And what had Dan done that Alex had told him to get control of himself?

I started my car, letting it slowly creep up the road to the house, debating which question I'd ask Alex first.

When I opened the door to the kitchen, Alex was standing at the sink, looking out the window, drinking a beer. He glanced at me over his shoulder, then finished his beer before he turned and gave me a scowl that could melt paint.

"You gotta set that agent of yours straight," he said. He threw the can into the open trash bin and wiped his mouth with the back of his hand. His appearance matched his mood—stubbly beard, dirty jeans and T-shirt, his eyes darkly circled.

"Either he backs off, or I'm outta here."

There was that temper again.

"Well, hello to you, too," I said, opening the fridge and taking out the last beer. I put the cold beer to my forehead. "And could it be any hotter in here?"

I popped the top, pulled out a chair and sat down, kicking off my flip-flops.

That seemed to diffuse some of his anger. He joined me at the table.

"What's Dan done to get you so ticked off?" I rolled my shoulders, trying to dislodge the kinks from the weary hours of driving.

He ran his long fingers through his black hair. "I wouldn't let him show the house."

So that was what the argument was about, if I believed him.

Now it was my turn to lose it. "Did you forget we had a deal?"

His eyes slid sideways. "Look, I'm this close to being done." He held up his right hand with his thumb and index fingers almost touching. His hand was nicked and red-looking, as if he'd been doing hard labor, not restoring a mural. "I need to finish. Then you can do whatever you want."

"You got that right." I dug my cell phone out of my shorts pocket. "I'm telling Dan he can show the house."

Alex reached across the table, grabbed the cell phone from my hand and closed it. "You're making a mistake."

"Give me back my phone." Who did this guy think he was?

He placed it on the table between us, his hand still over it. "I'm at a critical phase in the restoration." He pushed back on his chair and stood up. Then he touched me lightly on my shoulder. "Come upstairs and see for yourself."

All but one twelve-by-twelve strip was uncovered. But what was uncovered was in stark contrast to the other murals. Where the other murals were a skillful blend of stencils and freehand drawing, this mural was the culmination of an artist, showing advanced perspective and a more artistic and detailed scene. No stencils; all painted freehand. The digital photos he'd e-mailed me didn't do it justice.

"There are the initials ELB." He motioned to the right corner. "Clever how she did that, weaving them into the vines." He studied me. "So Karen knew all along who the artist was."

I didn't want to talk to him about what Karen knew or didn't know.

"I wonder why Emily Braun chose to do a biblical scene for this mural. It doesn't fit the motif of the other murals," I questioned.

"Normally, I'd say it was a practice mural. But the artistry of this mural is superior to the others. And look at this." He picked up a large tattered book from the floor and opened it to a marked page. "That's a Rufus Porter mural done around eighteen forty-five in a Massachusetts house."

Taking the book from him, I compared the two murals. The two murals were very similar in design and theme with many of the same elements.

"This doesn't make sense. How can these two murals be so much alike? This one painted by Emily Braun around eighteen thirty-nine and the Porter one painted around eighteen forty-five."

He shook his head. "The only two explanations I have are either this mural had a third source, or Emily was one of Porter's students."

"How is that possible? Not just because she was female, but also because, as far as I know, the only places she ever lived were Ohio and Illinois. Do you know otherwise?" I was baiting him, trying to find out what he knew.

"What do you think? I'm holding out on you?" His question sounded like a threat.

I looked into his feverish green eyes, searching for a reason to trust him. "I don't know, Alex, are you? Were you ever going to tell me about the stolen statue?"

We stood facing each other in that room that seemed to breathe heat and fumes as if the past were layered in the air. Sweat was rivering down my back.

"How?" he started to ask then stopped. "So Karen did know and hired me anyway. I thought so. For what it's worth, I didn't take that statue. I don't know what happened to it. Yes, I was restoring it. But I wasn't the only one with access to it. Anyone in the restoration department could have taken it. And it's never turned up anywhere. So whoever took it either got rid of it on the black market or wanted it for himself."

I could feel myself being swayed, but then my gut kicked in—

or, rather, the memory of all the men I'd trusted who'd turned out to be untrustworthy.

"Murals aren't statues," I said. "I don't see you easily disposing of these. So I guess it doesn't really matter if you took the statue, does it? Just finish this job." My words were more to convince myself than him.

"Whatever you say. What else did you find in her files?"

"Not her files, her personal journal. She knew these murals were here before she bought the house. In fact, they're the reason she bought this heap." I still didn't trust him enough to tell him about Emily Braun's empty grave.

"That tells me she knew something about the murals, something important." He gestured toward the walls as if he could make the secret appear with the flourish of his arm.

"There's something we're not seeing," I answered. "And Karen discovered that something in Emily's diary."

"Have you found the missing pages?"

"No. I've gone through all of Karen's stuff. They weren't in the notebooks or the books the attacker stole from me at the Newberry Library."

"And there's nowhere else you can look? Did you search her campus office?"

I'd forgotten about her office. "She wouldn't hide the pages there. It would have been too risky," I said, already knowing I'd check it out first thing tomorrow.

"What are you going to do about Yeager?"

I turned slowly in a circle, letting the murals sing to me, their faded colors patchy with time. I thought about Emily Braun standing in this room with her paintbrush and palette, flowering the walls with her art. Her hair would be pinned up, her simple cotton dress too hot, yet she would continue painting, creating against the heat, the loss of her son, against the hard richness of her life.

Then I picked up a scrap of painted, layered wallpaper Alex had piled in a corner, thinking about what I wanted. I was no longer sure of anything, especially if Karen's death was accidental.

"Have you counted them, the wallpaper layers?" It was an idle question. I knew what I wanted. I'd known what I would do since the attacker had held my life in his hands.

"Seventeen," he answered.

What were a few more days, a week in the scheme of things? What was time, after all, but layers left behind?

"I'm not selling the house."

Chapter Fifteen

The next morning I'd called Dan Yeager on my way to Morris University in Carbondale. As I drove north on Route 51, under the rumpled blue sky heavy with dark clouds hugging the horizon, my head ached with tiredness. I'd spent another restless night on Karen's white settee, listening to the unfamiliar sounds of the old house, falling in and out of sleep. Somewhere in the night I thought I smelled cigarette smoke again.

After I told Dan to take the house off the market, he sputtered around and finally said, "You'll have to sign some papers. I can fax them to you or mail them."

"No need. I'll come by your office today. I'm down here clearing out the last of Karen's stuff." A necessary white lie.

He gave me directions to the office in a curt voice, probably envisioning his commission evaporating. "You know, this is a real shame, your deciding to do this. There was this young couple who contacted me. Thinking about relocating from Chicago to here. They wanted a fixer-upper with some history."

Why was I finding that hard to believe? A young couple relocating from Chicago to downstate Illinois where there was no industry to speak of, except the correctional center. I also hadn't forgotten about his relationship with Karen that he'd never mentioned.

"Why southern Illinois? Do they have family here?" I asked, incredulous.

"That I didn't ask."

Okay, he was lying. Any seasoned real-estate agent would ask why they were moving here.

I heard him riffling through some papers. "What changed your mind? I thought you needed the money?"

There was a sneer in his tone that surprised me. "It's complicated."

I hung up with the promise of signing the papers today. Glancing at the car's clock, I saw I had enough time to settle things with the police before heading over to the university. It would only be a matter of time before they found out I was back and came banging on my door.

The Union County Sheriff's Department was in Jonesboro right off Route 146. A two-story schoolhouse brick building that was bleached listless by the sun.

At the front desk, I asked to see Officer Dade, even though he wasn't the cop who'd come to the house. He'd seemed sympathetic the night of Karen's death. I was hoping to play on those same sympathies.

The receptionist eyed me over her bifocals. "What's this in relation to, ma'am?"

"I was asked to come in."

"Uh-huh," she said, picking up the phone. "And your name is?"

"Rose Caffrey."

"A Rose Caffrey is here. She said she was asked to come in. Sure thing." She placed the phone in its cradle and eyed me again over her bifocals. "He'll be right out."

By the grim look on his face, I knew I was in trouble. He led me to a back room with a large table and three chairs and an overhead light that cast a halo on the table.

"Have a seat." He sat down and opened the folder he'd been carrying. "That wasn't too smart, taking off like that."

"I'm sorry. I know it was stupid." I took in a deep breath. I could feel myself slipping into character. It wasn't that hard—grieving, confused sister, still in a state of shock.

I stared down at my hands, which were folded neatly on the table. I knew he was looking at my inch-long hair, probably thinking I was unstable.

When I looked up, his expression had softened. "We're going to have to search your sister's things for the missing diary pages."

"I already did that. They weren't there."

"You'll understand if I don't take your word for it."

"Look, Officer Dade, I think someone might have killed my sister for those diary pages. And someone attacked me in Chicago at the Newberry Library, stole all my sister's notebooks and books. If you don't believe me, you can call Dr. Morant at the Newberry. He was there."

Dade didn't betray any emotion, merely kept bending the edge of the folder back and forth between his thick fingers. "What's so important about these missing diary pages?"

"I'm not sure. But they're connected to the murals at her house." Though I knew how absurd it all sounded, I told him everything.

He leaned back in his chair and scratched his head. "You messing with me, Ms. Caffrey? 'Cause I hope you're not."

"I'm not messing with you. Ask yourself, why would I report the pages missing to the librarian if I had them?"

"Yeah, I see your point. So why did you run? Why didn't you wait for the campus police?"

"I was scared. I'd just found my sister dead, then I find out that she might have stolen these pages. I admit it was stupid. But I didn't take them."

He didn't say anything. "Give me your car keys. Here's what's going to happen. I'm going to search your vehicle and your sister's residence."

"Fine. My car's the green SUV out front. Here are the keys. Knock yourself out."

He was gone about thirty minutes. When he returned, he had dark stains under his arms and down his back. He placed the keys on the table.

"I'll be by the house at six tonight. Make sure you're there."

I got up and went to the door.

"For what it's worth," he said, "I know you had nothing to do with taking those pages."

The history department offices were on the third floor of University Hall, a long, narrow building with a grove of trees on the west side and a group of smaller buildings on the east. The building was a cool respite from the unrelenting heat and impending rain. As I reached the third floor, I saw the administrative office on the right. The door was open, and a plump middle-aged woman bundled in a white sweater sat at the main desk. The office was jammed with three large desks, a copy machine, a wall of faculty mailboxes and reams of stacked paper. Once inside, I understood why the woman was wearing a sweater on such a hot day. The office was frigidly cold.

"I'm Rose Caffrey, Karen Caffrey's sister."

She put her hand to her chest and said, "Oh, dear. I am so, so sorry. I still can't believe she's gone. We all thought the world of her. Such a smart woman, and so good to her students." She was breathless when she stopped talking.

"I was wondering if I could have access to her office to clear out her things."

Without answering, she stood up and went to a tall cabinet behind her desk. She pulled out a large box overflowing with books and papers and notebooks. "I'm so glad you came. I called the emergency number Professor Caffrey had given us, but it was disconnected. I wasn't sure what to do with her belongings."

She plopped the box on her desk. "Now, all I need is a form of ID, and you can take the professor's things. Not that I don't think you're her sister. I just need it for my records."

I showed her my driver's license, which she copied. My eyes raked over the box, and I wondered if the pages were there.

"What about her e-mail account and her computer?" I asked. "Can I access her e-mails and files?"

She gave me a perplexed look. "Oh, well. The e-mail account is closed, and her files were erased. I hope that's not a problem."

Wow, the department didn't waste any time moving on. "Is it okay if I see her office?"

She let out an annoyed sigh. "I assure you I boxed up everything."

"I'm not questioning that. I just want to see it, you know, sort of a closure thing."

She gave me another perplexed look. "Well, okay, I don't see any harm in that. Let me get a key."

As I took the key and the box and was about to leave, she said, "The department will be having a memorial service during the fall term. Is there a number where we can reach you? Maybe you'd like to say a few words."

I put the box down and handed her one of my business cards—a black card with my name, occupation, phone number and e-mail address in white lettering, all very stark and dramatic.

She stared at it as if it were written in another language, probably debating whether to ask about my occupation. "I'll call you when we have a date for the service. I sure hope you can come."

"So do I," I said, realizing I meant it.

Karen's office was on the other side of the building at the end of a long, dark hallway. The floor felt deserted, and the echo of my footsteps only added to that feeling. Even during the academic year, it would still feel that way. This would have suited Karen, I thought, as I unlocked her office door and went inside. The room smelled musty, and dust whirled in the shadowy light, which rippled the room as if it were under water.

Behind her desk was a large window, overlooking the green woods. I switched on the desk lamp and started searching through her desk drawers. Nothing.

Then I went through the tiny black metal closet along one wall. Nothing in there but two wire hangers. All the bookshelves were blank, smudged with dust. I even searched under her desk and all the chairs, half expecting to find some secret message from Karen.

Then I sat down in her chair and turned off the lamp. Her feet would just reach the floor. I could see her leaning forward, putting her elbows on the desk as she talked to students, that earnest expression on her face. On the other side of the desk were two chairs. How many students had sat there over the years seeking her counsel, impressed with her quick, critical mind? Though this was not where she'd wanted to be, she'd made a life for herself. Had she been happy? Why didn't I know that?

The sound of footsteps in the hallway interrupted my thoughts. As if a switch had been flipped, my senses went on high alert. Slowly, I slipped out of the chair and crouched behind the desk, the memory of the Newberry attack playing in my head. The footsteps were coming this way.

Then they stopped. I peeked around the desk and saw a large shadow darkening the door's opaque glass. It was a man. He didn't move, just stood there very quietly not moving. Then I heard the rattle of the doorknob. Had I locked it? Yes, I remembered turning the lock.

The doorknob rattled again.

Whoever it was wanted in.

He tried the doorknob a third time. Surely, he must know it was locked. And why was he trying to get into Karen's office? I watched in horror as he leaned close to the glass, putting his two hands against it, trying to see into the room.

Then, just as unexpectedly, he left. He must have taken the stairs because I didn't hear his footsteps going back down the hall, only the sound of a door closing.

It's not the same guy, I told myself, touching my throat. But how could I be sure? Could he have followed me to southern Illinois?

I stood up, went to the door and inched it open, peering down the long deserted hallway. It was empty. I grabbed the box of Karen's things, shut the door behind me, and ran down the hallway to the administrative office.

"Was there a man walking around up here a minute ago?" I said, trying to catch my breath.

The woman looked up from her computer. "Is something wrong?" she asked.

"There was a man trying to get into my sister's office."

"Well, I didn't see anyone. It was probably a lost student."

I could tell from her attitude that she'd decided I was someone who needed to be handled.

"No," I said defiantly. "It wasn't a student. He didn't knock. He just kept trying to turn the doorknob. You must have seen someone." I realized how hysterical I sounded.

"Couldn't have been the janitor. He has a key." She drummed her fingers on her computer keys. "Well, I wouldn't worry about it. You find what you were looking for?"

"I'm not sure," I said, still thinking about the man outside the door.

"It just takes time, dear." Then she went back to her computer.

When I got to my car, I went through Karen's stuff. Books,

old syllabi, grade books, nothing related to the house, the Brauns, and no diary pages. It was ten forty-five A.M.; I'd have to hurry to catch Lawrence Grey during his office hours, which ended at eleven A.M.

I stowed Karen's stuff in the hatch and headed east to Peterson Laboratory.

"I'd never guess you two were sisters," Lawrence Grey said as we walked from Peterson Laboratory to the parking lot. The fast-moving clouds had turned dark, and the air felt wet with impending rain.

"That's what people tell me." Besides our age difference, I often thought our radically different physical appearances added to our distant relationship: Karen, short, blonde with large breasts she tried to hide; me, tall and bony with long dangling legs and arms. We just didn't look like sisters.

I'd caught Larry, as he insisted I call him, just as he was leaving his office, told him who I was and that I'd seen his name on the Trail of Tears symposium flyer.

"I'm giving a paper in Springfield tonight on the New Madrid Seismic Zone, and I'm already late," he'd explained as he locked his office door. "So we'll have to talk as we walk."

Stubbly dark beard, with rimless glasses, jeans worn out in the knees and rear and a large brimmed canvas hat, he was exactly what I expected a geologist to look like. He wasn't a big man, but he gave the appearance of taking up space. Maybe it was his large hands, or maybe it was his confident exuberance.

"Karen left me her house, the old Braun farmhouse," I began. "I don't know how much you know about the Brauns or their house. But I'm fascinated with its history and I was wondering—" Before I could finish my question, he cut me off.

"Can't help you there. Geology is my game. I leave old houses and history to people like Karen."

"But you are a member of the TOT board and worked closely with Karen."

Again he interrupted me. "Look, Karen and I shared only one common interest, and that was the TOT, making sure that we got the word out and that the federal government funded the Interpretation Center. Though we were colleagues, we didn't socialize much, except the end of the year LAS party, where the drinks flowed freely."

Thunder rippled in the distance. "Looks like another rainy one." He started walking faster. "To be honest, we butted heads more often than not about how to accomplish our goals."

"What about the Campground Cemetery? The Brauns are buried there. And you've been doing research at the cemetery looking for the unmarked Cherokee graves."

He stopped suddenly and turned to face me, studying me as if I were under one of his microscopes. "You're going to find out anyway. And since you now own the house, you have a right to know."

He folded his arms across his chest. "The night Karen died, the committee members had a meeting at her house about my discovery. Karen was going to handle the press. But then she died. It had to do with Emily Braun."

If he'd wanted to grab my attention, he had it. I knew what he was going to say, but I wanted him to tell me about the empty grave.

"Using noninvasive geophysical methods, I'd been investigating whether there were unmarked graves at the cemetery. Preliminary results indicated that these subsurface imaging methods, especially the ground-penetrating radar, located unmarked graves at the church site, which may belong to the Trail of Tears time period." He took in a deep breath and blew it out through his mouth.

I wasn't about to tell him my theory that the blackbirds in

the farmhouse murals marked the graves of the Cherokee and the lone grave of Charlie Braun. Until I understood the murals, no one else could know about them.

"We've been getting a lot of rain this season. Well, the day before Karen died, I was working at the cemetery, when all of sudden there was this tremendous crash over by the Braun graves."

"You mean the oak tree? I saw where it fell over."

"Right. When the tree fell over, it took with it a lot of the soil from Emily Braun's grave. The roots must have grown down into the gravesite. Of course, I went over to see what happened. And, what I found was very surprising." He paused. "The grave was empty. No body."

"Could the body have been moved?" I'd been considering possible scenarios to explain the empty grave.

"Move the body but leave the coffin? Don't think so."

"Wait. There was a coffin, but no body?" Karen's journal hadn't said anything about a coffin. Had she used the word grave in its fullest meaning—a resting place?

"Yeah. The coffin had pretty much rotted away, but the coffin nails were still there, but no body."

"That doesn't make sense. What happened to Emily Braun's body?" I asked.

"I've been giving this a lot of thought, and I think the question should be: what happened to Emily Braun? If her body wasn't in that coffin, why wasn't it? Was she buried somewhere else? If so, why?"

A few drops of rain started to fall, big wet drops staining the concrete. He began walking again.

My mind was spinning with possibilities. "Maybe she wasn't dead."

He frowned at me. "Why would someone want to make

people think she was, then? And go to all the trouble of burying a coffin?"

"I don't know."

We'd reached his vehicle, a beat-up truck with buckets and toolboxes strewn around in the dirty bed. He opened the door and tossed his briefcase onto the seat.

"What was Karen's reaction when you told her about the empty grave or coffin?"

He said, "You would have thought I'd thrown a grenade at her. I've never seen such a look of shock. She didn't even want the board to release the news. She had some lame reason about it affecting the federal grant money. Of course, that was ridiculous. We all agreed, if anything, the empty grave would have no impact or might help our cause, drawing attention to the trail and all its mysteries. C'mon, what difference does it make in the scheme of things after all these years if an early settler's body is missing from her coffin? Even if foul play was involved, all the people are long dead."

What he said made sense. But his nonchalant attitude puzzled me. Sure, he wasn't a historian, but he was invested in finding the unmarked Cherokee graves. And Emily wasn't just some early settler; she was a witness to what the Cherokee endured.

He climbed up into the cab and rolled down the window. "I'll be back late tomorrow if you have any other questions. Sorry about Karen. I'll miss her. She kept me on my toes."

"One more thing," I said. "Who was at the meeting at Karen's house?"

"Besides me, Dan Yeager and Suzanne Likely."

The rain was coming down in sheets as I ran to my car. Just as I got inside, a loud crack of lightning hit nearby. An empty coffin, no trace of what happened to Emily Braun. If she hadn't died, why would someone want to make it look like she had?

I could think of only one reason: so she could disappear.

Chapter Sixteen

Driving to Dan Yeager's office along Route 146, I passed salvage yards, coin laundries, taverns, funeral homes, and in between the quick-fire towns that seemed on the brink of loss. Things falling apart, lost to their own purpose. A road sign near the correctional center read: *Do not pick up hitchhikers.* A warning? A threat?

I knew from Karen's exhaustive research on the area that it once thrived with verdant farms and prosperous small towns. With much of Route 146 as the main thoroughfare connecting two major waterways, the Ohio River and the Mississippi River, it had been one gateway to the west, to promise.

Dan Yeager's realty office was a quaint, restored train car next to a public park. The rain had slowed but not stopped. I dashed around a large puddle and up the wood steps. Dan was huddled under the air conditioner, the phone cradled in his left shoulder. He waved me inside and indicated I should sit down.

"Uh-huh, sure, can do," he said with the cheery tone that I'd found so pleasantly open and that now struck me as ingenuous. Business must be slow, because he was dressed in shorts and a golf shirt, and his golf clubs rested against the wall behind his desk.

Neither he nor Suzanne Likely had told me about the meeting at Karen's house the night she died or the purpose of that meeting—Emily Braun's empty coffin.

He hung up the phone and said, "Cats and dogs out there. I

was hoping to get a game of golf in today, but weatherman says rain straight through to tomorrow. I have to say I'm surprised at your decision." He rifled through the stacks of papers on his disorderly desk. "I never tell my clients what to do, but I think you should leave the house on the market."

He found the papers and shuffled them into a neat pile.

"You don't tell your clients a lot of things, Dan," I blurted out. "Like the meeting at Karen's house the night she died and the empty grave Lawrence Grey discovered."

It was as if I'd struck him. His face flushed and he cleared his throat.

"Gee, I'm sorry. I wasn't trying to hide anything. I didn't want to upset you more than you already were upset. You were pretty shook up over Karen's death. I didn't want to make it worse. And, to be honest, I didn't think it was relevant. I hope you don't think I was being purposely dishonest."

Now I was embarrassed. Lack of sleep was making me paranoid. "No, I don't think that. I just wondered why you didn't mention it."

"It's not like it's going to stay a secret much longer anyway. Larry Grey is writing a press release and then everyone will know. Are you ready for that?" He put his elbows on the desk and leaned toward me, a look of concern on his face.

"Ready for what?"

"The local paper will probably want to talk to you about the house. Larry's had some national coverage about his work at the cemetery, so the national papers might pick up on this. You know how it is. Everyone loves stories about missing bodies."

I hadn't thought about the publicity. "When's Larry releasing the story to the papers?"

"Why? Is there a problem?"

Yeah, there was a problem, four amazing murals that I didn't want anyone to know about yet. "No problem, just wondering. I really don't want the press traipsing around the property."

"Don't see how you can prevent that. They're going to want a picture for their story. Are you planning on sticking around or are you heading back to Chicago?"

Why did it feel like his question was fraught with undercurrents? "Haven't made up my mind yet."

"You're sure about taking the house off the market, then?"

The one thing I was sure of. "Yup."

"Wish I could change your mind. But I learned long ago not to argue with a client once their mind's made up."

He pushed the papers across the desk toward me. "Sign, initial and date where I've put x's."

When I was done I stood up to leave.

"You'll let me know if you decide to put it on the market again? Unless, of course, you want to go with another Realtor."

"If I decide to sell, you'll be the first to know."

He walked me to the door and shook my hand. "Don't let the house stand abandoned too long. Word gets out, and you'll have vagrants taking up residence or, worse, thieves stripping the place bare."

He stood under the train car's overhang watching me drive away. Like a sharp note, the smell of his lime cologne hung in the car's musty air. I cranked the AC to max and sped home, reassuring myself that once I understood the murals, I'd be through with the house. I could get back to my life. I could make art again.

When I reached the house, Alex's rental car wasn't there. It was after five o'clock; he must have called it quits for the day. Good. I wanted to be alone with the murals without him hovering. Emily's empty coffin, the ribbon road leading to the field scattered with blackbirds: what was Emily saying? I needed to look at the farmhouse mural as if I hadn't seen it before.

Walking toward the house, the rain-soaked grass sucked at my running shoes, seeping through to my feet. I glanced up at the sky, which was a fearsome tumult of low cumulous clouds, dark-edged and weighted; here and there anemic blue patches struggled through. Although the rain had stopped, it had brought no relief from the pounding heat and humidity. A fine mist was rising from the emerald weedy grass, making the house and the surrounding land appear dreamlike.

The front door was unlocked, which seemed needlessly careless, as if Alex had left in a hurry. I wasn't going to be caught off guard. If my attacker followed me from Chicago, I wanted to be ready for him. I positioned my car keys in my hand as a weapon, took in a deep breath, and went inside.

The house ticked with emptiness. No one was there; I could feel it—only the stink of chemicals and age remained.

Climbing the staircase, I kept my keys at the ready and headed for the mural room, checking each room along the way.

Stepping across the doorway into the room, I felt the murals transport me to another time and place. As if in a trance, I spotted a clean brush atop Alex's toolbox—tiny with a slender wood handle and fine bristles. I flicked the bristles across the palm of my hand. They felt sturdy yet delicate, capable of the most detailed work, like painting eyelashes or feathers.

Standing in front of the farmhouse mural, I let myself enter the painting, smelling the greenness of the grass, the warmth of the sun. I took the paintbrush and followed Emily's strokes as if I was learning her. In the cemetery the blackbirds were short, sad strokes full of darkness. The enormous maple tree was slender as rain, the farmhouse careful. When I came to the large blackbird, its outstretched wings were strongly stroked upward and felt joyous. Blackbirds—their wings were beating inside my head. My fingers let go of the brush, which fell to the floor quietly.

I stepped back out of the mural room as if I'd been pulled and went to Karen's study, quickly powering up her computer. I Googled Cherokee clans and waited.

There were seven: wolf, blue, long hair, paint, deer, wild potato and bird. The bird clan was the keeper of the sacred feathers and bird medicine. They were messengers and very skilled in using blowguns and snares for bird hunting. Their color was purple, and their wood was maple.

Why hadn't I made the connection before? The field of blackbirds, the large blackbird in the tree about to take wing, the enormous maple tree—were they meant to be Cherokee symbols?

I went back to the mural room, this time studying the house directly across the room from the Braun house, the one with the Native American boy and woman in the windows. Their feathers were purple.

Reverend Likely's words rang in my head.

Some took one or two young children, she'd answered when I asked if anyone had helped the Cherokee.

Had Emily and Edward Braun taken in a Cherokee child that winter? Was that what the large blackbird represented—this child? Edward Braun had let the Cherokee bury their dead on his land where his own son was buried. And after losing their son, surely a child would have been welcomed. But what had happened to that child? What had happened to Emily, for that matter?

And how did the other two murals figure in the story, the one with the municipal-looking buildings and houses set in a sprawling countryside, and the biblical mural of the sacrifice of Isaac by Abraham?

What story was Emily telling me? What secrets was she hiding?

The sound of a car door slamming shut startled me. I hurried down the stairs and looked through the parlor window. Alex was walking toward the house, carrying a pizza box and a brown bag in one hand and a twelve-pack of beer in the other.

Should I tell him about the empty coffin, the bird clan? I asked myself, swinging the front door open and smiling as he came up the steps.

"You read my mind," I said instead. There was a buoyancy, a lightness about him I didn't want to squelch.

"You gotta love college towns," he said. "You're not going to believe what I have in the bag. Hope you like sushi."

"What's not to like?"

"Oh, I let that cop, Dade, go through the house. He said you gave him permission."

"What did he say when he left?"

"Something about having a good evening."

We were camped out under the large oak tree on the knoll behind the house, sitting on rickety lawn chairs Alex had found in the cellar. The pizza had been satisfyingly gooey and rich, the sushi a little suspect. But I was so hungry I ate every last bite, resisting the urge to lick my plate. Alex had splurged on an expensive foreign beer that was light and frothy, as if it were defining summer.

We'd each downed two beers and were working on the third.

"You know what was the worst part of being accused of theft?" Alex asked, his long legs stretched out, slumped in the chair.

The question came out of nowhere. I sensed he wanted to unburden himself to me. I let him.

"Not losing my job, though that was bad enough. Those bastards didn't even give me a chance to clear myself. The suspicion was enough for them. No, the worst was losing my daughter."

I fought my desire to gawk at him. Instead I kept my eyes focused on the small valley below, the rolling softness of evening as if glazed by greenness.

"You have a daughter?"

"Grace. She's ten. Lives with her mother in London. That's where I was when Karen died, visiting Grace. I lost custody. Her mother, Jessica, is now a curator for the Tate Museum."

He took a long draw of his beer. "We met at the museum in Boston. We were both restoration artists."

"Was she working there when the statue went missing?"

"Yeah, but she had nothing to do with it."

Was he still in love with his wife? He was so quick to defend her.

A slight breeze stirred the leaves. Now I did stare at him, taking in the hawkish nose, the thick dark hair, the long lanky body, the wounded hands of a craftsman. His mood had turned.

"Alex," I said softly. "I've discovered something about the murals." I told him about Emily's body missing from the coffin, the meaning of the blackbirds, my hunch that the Brauns had taken in a Cherokee child.

His eyes were like the day's heat—simmering, full of exhausted intent. When I finished, he reached out and took my hand. His hand was strong and warm.

"There's more," he said. "So much more."

He pulled me up and led me down the knoll toward the house, not letting go of my hand until we were back inside the mural room. If we were lovers, I'd know where this was headed, but we weren't. We were lovers of another kind.

Shards of dying sunlight cascaded across the scarred wood floor. Alex positioned me before the biblical mural, one hand on my shoulder as if I needed to be steadied, and pointed to the image of Sarah. The line of her hair washed away to a different kind of hair, straighter, out of proportion to her drawn figure.

I'd noticed it, but thought Emily had done an earlier sketch and painted over it.

"Pentimento," I whispered as if we were in a sacred place.

"That's what I thought." His hand left my shoulder and he picked up a strange-looking light, plugged it into the wall socket, and then directed it toward the biblical mural. When he flipped the switch, the biblical mural disappeared and another appeared, an entirely different mural. I let out a gasp.

As he moved the light slowly over the wall, I wondered at the fantastical mural, full of tropical images and strange people—their bodies heavily tattooed, the women naked except for grassy skirts. Their fingernails looked like claws. But as arresting as the images were, the context of the mural was even more shocking. One woman carried a naked infant toward a woman who knelt before a stone altar gashed with strange marks. The kneeling woman appeared to be begging for the child's life—her hands were folded as if in prayer, her face bereft. Though she was dressed as the other woman, her features and coloring were clearly European, from her light wavy hair to her blue eyes. Behind the kneeling woman was a native man looking away from the scene; one hand on his hip, the other holding a long knife. In the foreground another native man sat, his arms folded, his expression fierce, his fingers more clawlike than the others, as if he were turning into a horrific bird of prey.

"You see it, don't you, the resemblance?"

"Yes, it's the same motif as the biblical mural painted over it—a scene of child sacrifice. But everything else is different." I stepped closer. "Could you direct the machine here? I thought I saw a word written along the bottom."

The word wasn't in English. *"Confesionario,"* I said. "It's Spanish, right?"

"Its literal meaning is confessional, like the confessional booth Roman Catholics use to confess their sins to a priest."

"Alex, what is going on here?"

"I don't know. This first mural shouldn't be here. It makes no historical sense."

"When did you find it?" Now my sensors were up.

"Today. I don't usually x-ray a mural. But when I saw the Pentimento, or what appeared to be Pentimento, I suspected there might be another mural underneath. I called around the university for an x-radiography and was able to get a hold of one this morning. No way was I prepared for what I found." He seemed genuinely perplexed.

"It's as if we peeled back the layers of time too far."

He switched the X-ray off.

"If only I had Emily's lost diary pages," I said. "Maybe they would explain this mural. It's nearly impossible to fathom how she could have painted this. The native people clearly aren't Cherokee. The terrain's all wrong. Not to mention the tattoos and talon-like nails, the hair—nothing fits. I poured over Karen's research on the Cherokee. These aren't Cherokee."

"That's why I took digital images of the mural and e-mailed the images to a colleague of mine at Boston University, Helene Ramirez Roundoak. She's an expert on Native American imagery and culture. I'm hoping she can identify the native people in the mural."

"And in the meantime?" I asked.

"That's up to you."

I wasn't sure what he was asking. He must have read my confusion.

"I can finish up the restoration of the other three murals. I recommend letting this one sit until we get more info on it. Or I can pack up my stuff and get out of your hair." He grinned at his lame joke.

"Karen would want you to finish the job." Coward, I told myself. Why couldn't I tell him it was what I wanted, too?

Because I didn't want him to know that my desire for his continued presence wasn't just about the murals.

"Are you heading back to Chicago?"

"Not yet. I have a few loose ends to tie up first."

"Like whether there's any truth to your hunch about the Brauns taking in a Cherokee child? How are you going to do that? After all this time and the lack of records, there's no way to find that out."

Why was he being so negative all of a sudden? Minutes before he'd been full of energy and optimism, shining his fancy light around the mural as if he were a kid in a toy store. Maybe he had to be the one shining the light.

"You'd be surprised what people remember and pass down through generations, just waiting for the right time to tell their story. I think it's the right time. I just have to find that person." Whether I believed that or not, I wasn't going to let Alex think he'd dampened my determination.

After he left I went back to the mural room. *Confesionario.* What a strange word to write on a mural depicting a native rite.

I studied the breach in the mural, Sarah's hair fading into the native woman's hair. Then it came to me, the derivation of the word Pentimento. As an art student, I'd found it provocative. In Italian it meant to repent.

Confesionario, repentance, both words about mistakes and misdeeds and the belief that atonement and forgiveness and second chances were possible if you were truly sorry.

A warm breeze wafted through the room, bringing with it the pungent dark smells of night. I looked away from the mural toward the windows where the moon sickled the sky as if it, too, were a breach.

Alex had shown me the hidden mural; he'd let me in. Then why was I feeling like he wished he hadn't?

Chapter Seventeen

"You could to talk to Emery Wallace. He owns Emery's Antiques. It's at the corner of Routes Forty-Five and One Forty-Six. You can't miss it. Brick, one-story building with lots of junk out front he calls antiques."

I'd phoned Reverend Likely and asked her if she knew if the Brauns had taken in a Cherokee child.

"What's Emery's connection to the Trail?" I sat at the kitchen table jotting down Wallace's name and address on the back of the symposium flyer.

"He claims one of his ancestors was taken in by one of the local families. He's not from around here, though. Showed up a few years ago and opened the antiques shop."

She paused. "Is there something you found in Karen's research that makes you think they did? 'Cause Karen never said anything to the committee about a Cherokee child being taken in by the Brauns." Her tone bordered on accusatory.

Though I'd anticipated that question, I hadn't anticipated her wariness. "It was more of an idea than a fact," I said, nervously shaking the pen between my two fingers. "She'd written a question in her notes asking if the Brauns took in a Cherokee child. Then she'd starred it twice. So I thought I'd check it out. You know, add to the ambiance of the house."

"Okay, well, Emery asked a lot of questions at the symposium about local families who took in Cherokee children. Maybe not so much questions as statements about his being a descendant of a child left with one of the local families. When Karen asked him if he had any proof, he said it was family lore. Afterward, she looked into it and said it was all anecdotal."

I could hear the skepticism in her voice. "So you think he made it up?" I asked, drawing a large question mark next to his name.

"Who knows? Generations ago his family lived here, but left. Now he's returned and wants to fit into the community. It couldn't hurt to talk to him. You know the old saw about the truth being somewhere in the middle."

Just as Reverend Likely had described, the sidewalk in front of Emery's antiques was littered with junk—a 1940s baby carriage, a dented zinc washtub, boxes of old books, postcards and photos. Parked along the curb was a Harley-Davidson complete with tasseled handlebars and side satchels.

The inside of the shop fared no better. A miscellany of items cluttered the large plank-floored room, spilling out in no particular order. In the middle of the room was an island of glass cases crammed with jewelry. A computer and a cash register rested inside the island on a long narrow wood counter.

The only saving grace of Emery's Antiques was the icy air of the AC that mitigated the pervading musty smell of age.

A large muscular man with a bleached-blond ponytail and dark roots wearing a muscle T and cut-off jean shorts was sitting on a tall stool behind the island. When I walked in, he said, "We have a special today. Everything out on the sidewalk is half off."

"I'll have to take a look before I leave," I answered as a way to ease into my questions. Even at half off, I wasn't interested. "I'm looking for Emery Wallace."

"You found him." He was in stark contrast to his name. I'd pictured a middle-aged balding man with thick glasses. This guy looked like a contender on World Wide Wrestling.

"You're here for the summer wine tasting, right? You have to spend at least thirty dollars to get a discount on the tickets." He pointed his finger as if putting a visual period at the end of his sentence.

"There are wineries here?" I had no idea what he was talking about. Wineries in southern Illinois sounded like an oxymoron. But what I knew about wine and wineries was close to nothing.

"Wow, I'm usually right on the money. You look edgy, very urban. What with the hair and the black *Be Present* T-shirt you got on. Someone who isn't afraid to explore outside her boundaries of comfort."

I felt my face go hot. No wonder he wasn't getting a lot of business. Who wants to be psychoanalyzed by some stranger?

"Hobby of mine," he explained, seeing my discomfort. "Psych major in college. I'm usually right."

"Actually, I'm here to ask you about one of your ancestors. The one you claim was a Cherokee child left with a local family."

"It's not a claim." His whole body tensed. "Who told you that?"

"Reverend Likely. She's one of the Trail of Tears committee members. She told me to talk to you about your family."

"You got to be shittin' me." He stood up and put his hands on his hips. "You know how many times I've contacted those people? And they shut me out every time. Told me I had to have verifiable proof. They're putting together a book for that Interpretive Center they hope to build. I thought my family's story should be in that book."

"Do you have verifiable proof?"

"What's your interest in all this?" He rested his elbows on the glass case.

"My sister was Karen Caffrey, the director of the committee.

She died recently and left me her house. It's the old Braun family farmhouse dating back to around eighteen thirty-five. I'm researching the family's history, and I think they might have taken in a Cherokee child."

"I know who you sister was." His tone was sharp and angry. "I'm sorry about her passing. But she came in here asking me a lot of questions about my great-great-great-grandmother. How old was she when the Reagan family took her in? Who did she marry? When did my family leave the area? Did I have any letters or documents about her? In the story passed down was there any mention of the Braun family? Building up my hopes.

"I thought for sure she was going to use the information. But then she tells me she can't because I don't have any letters or documents. 'Why did you waste my time, then?' I said to her. She was taking notes like she was on fire. You know what she answered? 'It doesn't mean it isn't true.' What the hell good is that?" He pushed away from the counter.

Had Karen known it was true because she'd read it in Emily's diary?

I could see he was still seething, feeling shut out of a community he felt he belonged in by a badge of suffering endured by his Cherokee ancestors. Shut out of a story that was his.

"You know how angry I was? I went and had my DNA tested. Yeah, and guess what? I have Native American blood. Not much, but it's there. Then you know what else I did? I wrote every last one of my family members on my mother's side, even remote cousins, asking them what they knew about this great-great-great-grandmother."

He stopped and stared at me. "Well, I got my verifiable proof."

"What was it?" I tried to keep the excitement out of my voice.

"How's that any of your business?"

"You're right, it's none of my business," I conceded, wanting to placate him and keep him talking.

It must have worked, because he continued. "I thought about going to that committee and showing them. But after they treated me like an idiot at that symposium of theirs, they can go hang themselves."

"Listen, all I want to know is if what you found mentions a child taken in by the Brauns? Can you at least tell me that?"

He put his large hands on the countertop, spreading his fingers wide. "How much is it worth to you?"

In his mind, he'd been dismissed and ignored. He wasn't going to be played again. This time he was going to get something in return.

I glanced around the shop, not seeing anything I wanted. Then I perused the glass case of jewelry. A gold-filigreed locket with a tarnished chain caught my eye. "This locket? How much?"

He opened the glass case, took out the locket and read the price tag on the back before placing it on the countertop in front of me. "Fifty, but for you one hundred."

"You're not messing with me, are you? There was definitely something about the Brauns taking in a child?" I wasn't sure if this guy wasn't playing me, getting back at my sister through me.

"Uh-huh."

I dug through my wallet—all I had left was sixty dollars. He watched me take out the money and put it on the counter. "This is all I have. Take it or leave it."

"You got a credit card," he answered.

My cards were almost maxed out, and the balance and interest were multiplying like rabbits in spring. But what choice did I have?

He swiped the card, wrapped up the locket in purple tissue paper and put it in a box.

Then he squared his bulky shoulders and began talking as if

delivering a lecture. "Before my Cherokee ancestor died, she wrote about her experiences on the trail and being trapped here when the rivers froze over. It's pretty brutal stuff. She lost her entire family except her father. He's the one who leaves her with the Reagan family. She was eleven years old and sick. They nursed her back to health and raised her as a kind of poor relation." He held up his large hand as if he were taking an oath. "And I can prove it."

He went to the back of the shop and disappeared behind a curtain hung over a doorway. When he returned, he was carrying a sheaf of Xeroxed papers. His pride over his discovery had overcome his need for revenge.

Though these weren't the original documents, you'd have thought they were, the way he delicately went through the pages until he came to the one he was looking for. I could see the flourish of the eloquent writing on the paper.

"Here it is. This is what she writes. 'There were many children left with the white families. But I was closest to one boy, William Silk or Talking Bird. Our mothers were of the bird clan. He was taken in by the family who owned the land where my mother and brother were buried. No one knows what happened to him. Some say he ran away. Some say he died. This was how it was for us. This never knowing.' "

When Emery looked up, there were tears in his eyes. He blinked them away.

"You should let the committee see this," I said. "You owe it to your great-great-great-grandmother."

For a moment, his face was washed clean of all anger and in its place was a terrible sadness.

"Did you know that until about thirty years ago, no one would admit being related to the Cherokee who were left here? Did you know that those Cherokee who came through here were better educated than the people living here? Did you know that the Christian Cherokee sang hymns along the way? Did you know that when they were ferried across the Ohio River and came ashore in Golconda, the locals spit on them?"

"I'm sorry," I said, knowing whatever I said would be inadequate.

"Yeah, I owe it to her. But I'm not letting that committee anywhere near this."

Carefully, he arranged the papers in a neat pile. "This is my family's story. And I'm going to be the one to tell it. Enjoy your locket. You made a good choice."

When I got back to my car, I took the locket out and opened it. Inside were two tintypes of a man and a woman circa 1885. The past was everywhere and nowhere.

I closed the locket and put it back in its box.

The Brauns had taken in a Cherokee child named William Silk or Talking Bird. Emily had painted a large bird in the maple tree, caught at the moment of leaving. I had no doubt: that bird represented this Cherokee boy from the bird clan. Had he died? Was that what she was saying?

I waited until a truck passed before pulling back onto Route 146.

Or could Talking Bird have run away, as Wallace's ancestor suggested? And if so, where would he have gone?

The sky had turned threatening and the winds were gusting, snapping small branches, and strewing them across Campground Road. My head throbbed with humidity.

As I neared the Campground Cemetery and the church, I saw a line of cars exiting the parking lot. Reverend Likely stood near the lot, waving good-bye to her parishioners. It wasn't Sunday, and I didn't see a bridal party, so there must have been some special prayer service. I waited near the church entrance road for the cars to disperse, then turned down the road and parked in the church parking lot. By the time I exited my car, Reverend Likely was headed for the rectory, her robes flapping in the wind like bat wings.

I hurried after her and shouted, "Reverend Likely," just as she was about to enter the rectory. She turned and waved me over.

"You have time for a cold one? It's got to be happy hour somewhere," she joked.

"Afraid I can't. But I saw Emery Wallace. He has proof of his claim."

Another gust swirled dust up at us. "You'd better come inside. Looks like it's about to pour."

I stepped inside the cool recess of the rectory. "I can't stay. I just wanted you to know what I found out."

"I'll tell the committee. We're going to want to see what he has." Her gaze was penetrating in the dark cool foyer. "If it's legit, we'll include it in the Interpretive Center's book."

I shook my head no. "He's not going to let you do that."

"And why not? That's what he's been wanting." I heard a steely resolve I hadn't expected.

"Because he's angry with the committee. In his mind, you treated him like an idiot. That was the word he used, idiot."

"Don't worry about it," she said, patting my shoulder. "I can be pretty persuasive when I want to be."

"Unless you're prepared to offer him money, he's not going to do it. The only way I found out anything about the Brauns was to overpay for a piece of jewelry. He's got a grudge against the committee. I think it goes deeper than your not showing him respect at the symposium."

"I appreciate your warning me, but, like I said, I can be pretty persuasive." She shrugged out of her robe and threw it over her arm as if she were shrugging out of a costume. "What did you find out about the Brauns? Did they take in a Cherokee child?"

"According to Emery's ancestor, they took in a boy."

"Did you find out his name?" She stepped into my personal space, making me back up. I was up against the wall.

Something was behind her questions, and it wasn't just friendly curiosity. Her closeness in the dim rectory foyer, with my back pressed to the wall and her size, seemed threatening. I was suddenly frightened of her. "No. Just that they took in a boy."

She stepped back. "Would have been more interesting to have a name . . . for the history of the house. No way to trace a nameless boy, though."

"Yeah," I said, moving toward the door. "No way."

Chapter Eighteen

Thunder rumbled in the distance, and the sky was the color of gray slate as I parked in front of the farmhouse. I was still trying to interpret my odd encounter with Reverend Likely. Nothing overt in her behavior or her words, but an undertone, not so much of menace, but of desperation. She had backed me into a corner, literally. Her eyes wildly pleading. But why? What did she care if the Brauns took in a Cherokee child and what his name was?

I was so lost in my musings, I didn't see him until he was right in front of me, blocking the porch, his arms crossed over his chest, his feet planted as if for a fight.

Startled, I dropped my keys.

"If I were you, I'd get outta here," Jimmy Braun spat at me. He reeked of alcohol and cigarettes. Behind his large, thick glasses, his eyes seemed to swim.

"What do you want?" I spat right back at him. In Chicago, you learned when to run and when to stand your ground. Jimmy was drunk or high or both—which was an obvious clue that I should run. But he was on my property, and I'd had enough of people getting in my grill today.

"This is my house and my land." He gestured toward the house. "I want you gone." He jabbed his dirty finger at my head.

"In case you don't remember, this is my house. You're the one who should be gone." I dug my cell phone out of my pocket.

"Don't make me call the cops."

He slapped the cell phone out of my hand. It landed with a splat in the muddy grass. "Your sister thought she could take what's mine. Look what happened to her."

He yanked his baseball cap off his head and squeezed the brim in his fist so hard I heard a crack.

"See what I can do?" He shoved the cap back on his head. Its broken brim formed a V. "Nothing here belongs to you. You got that? Everything in there is mine. Even those pretty paintings, you found. Mine, all mine. You can tell your boyfriend that, too." He pounded his chest as if he were a deranged ape.

He knew about the murals. How?

"What do you know about them?" I asked, now more curious than scared.

He threw his head back and let out an ugly laugh. He was missing a slew of teeth, and the rest looked broken down.

"Wouldn't you like to know?" he taunted.

Then he turned and stomped away, through the tall grass toward the dense woods near the house.

As I watched his retreat, a horrifying realization came over me. He'd been in the house? That was him I smelled that first night. That acrid scent of cigarettes hanging in the humid air like a deadly intention.

Now he was at the edge of the woods. In a minute he'd be gone, like a ghost still free to haunt me at night. I wasn't going to let him get away with it any longer. I ran after him.

When I reached the woods, I spotted him just ahead, moving slowly down a muddy, narrow path. The trees knitted out the light, the air was too heavy, the underbrush impossibly tangled with undergrowth.

"You've been sneaking into my house," I shouted after him. "I smelled you." I sounded like a crazy woman. But I didn't care. All common sense gone, my willfulness propelled me forward.

He paid no attention to me but kept stumbling deeper and deeper into the woods. And I kept following him. At the next curve in the path, suddenly I lost sight of him as if he'd evaporated into the thick miasma. A phantom I'd imagined.

I stood still for a moment listening, trying to hear him. No sounds except the call of a bird followed by thunder rumbling like waves crashing toward the shore, its violence full of meaning. Turn around and go home, it seemed to say, while you still can.

Then rain poured down on me as if a bucket had been upended. The dense tree cover helpless against the onslaught. I was drenched, rivulets of water running down my face and neck and arms, saturating my T-shirt, jeans, causing the muddy path to dissolve into a river. I wiped water out of my eyes, tasted its sourness on my tongue.

It was useless, and yet I slogged down the path, looking from right to left trying to catch a glimpse of him. Another roll of thunder, this time closer.

This was pure foolishness. Jimmy Braun was out of his head on some kind of substance. What did I think I was going to get out of him? He'd threatened me, not overtly, but indirectly. "Look what happened to her," he'd said about Karen. As if to say, "The same thing could happen to you." Had he caused Karen's death?

"I know you're here somewhere," I yelled above the rain and thunder. "So why don't you face me like a man." He knew something. I felt it; either about the murals or about Karen's death. In his drug-induced state, he might let something slip.

Even with the heat and humidity, I'd started to shiver. "Just tell what you know," I pleaded, holding my arms to stop the shivering. I wanted to cry; I wanted to rage. All the pain and hurt bubbled up inside me. I choked it down.

Another thunderous burst, this time directly overhead. I looked up into the dark sky. The thought of being struck by lightning made me turn around and start back down the path toward the farmhouse. Then I heard a snap behind me, and suddenly I was flying, catapulted forward. I put out my arms to break my fall, landing in the mud, all the air knocked out of me.

Breathless, I tried to get up, but was pushed down deeper into the mud. His foot was on my back, holding me down like a pinned insect. I turned sideways, spitting out mud, taking in short painful breaths.

"Who's the man now, bitch?" He pushed harder on my back.

I stopped struggling. "Did you kill my sister?" I demanded, my anger back.

His foot eased off. "This is your last warning."

Then he was gone.

Gingerly, I eased myself up, sitting back on my heels for a moment. My back ached with shooting pains where he'd stomped on it. I rubbed at my hurt muscles. In a few hours the muscles would tighten and then I'd be in real pain. I got up slowly, wiped the mud from my face and took a step forward. With the carefulness of a tightrope walker, I made my way down the muddy path, every slip and slide ratcheting up the pain.

When I reached the house, I squatted down, trying not to bend from my waist and picked up my keys and cell phone, groaning with the effort.

The phone was wet but still worked. Just as I was about to call Alex, I saw his car coming up the road. I flipped the phone shut and waited for him to park and get out. The sight of him coming toward me drained all the tension from my body.

"Geez, what happened to you? You look like you've been mud wrestling." He ran his fingers lightly across my forehead, then wiped the mud on his jeans.

"Jimmy Braun knows about the murals. He attacked me in the woods. I shouldn't have followed him. But he's been in the house. I don't know how. He's been in the house." I bit off the tears that were building in my throat.

"C'mon. Let's get you outta the rain and into some dry clothes. Then you can tell me about it."

He put his arm around my shoulder and guided me up the porch steps. When he opened the door, I took in a deep breath, inhaling the scent of cigarettes.

"Do you smell that?" I asked, pulling away from under his arm. "Cigarette smoke. He's been here. He's been in my house."

"No sense of smell," he answered, touching the side of his nose. "Occupational hazard of working with chemicals."

Did he think I was making this up? Did that explain the doubt on his face? "I'm not imagining it, if that's what you're thinking."

"What I think is you're scared and you're tired."

"Yeah, but that doesn't mean I'm wrong."

"Are you calling the cops?" Alex asked, putting his sandal-clad feet on the bay windowsill. Like his hands, his toes were long and slender. He'd brought back a bottle of wine from the stop 'n shop, along with a box of saltines and some spreadable cheddar cheese with streaks of pink in it.

I wasn't hungry, but the wine was welcome. With the first glass, I'd downed two analgesics I'd found in Karen's medicine cabinet. The pain in my back was dulled, but not gone.

"I can't call them right now. I need time to think." I put my wine glass on a side table. The rain had finally cooled things off, and a clean breeze filled the house with the approaching night.

"He's not going away," Alex reasoned. "And if he's on drugs, he's dangerous. I don't understand why you went after him."

Now, in the aftermath, I wondered the same thing as I rubbed at the dull pain. "You didn't see the hatred in his eyes when he said Karen's name." I turned and stared at Alex. "He said, 'Look what happened to her,' as if he was implying he had something to do with her death."

He shifted his feet on the window seat. "And you chased him into the woods. You know how insane that was if you thought he killed Karen?"

"You weren't there," I said defensively. "I couldn't just let him let him walk away after he'd said that. And he knows about the murals."

Alex swirled the wine in his glass, coating the inside. "Karen died in a fall. Jimmy's just trying to scare you."

Karen's broken body, mangled and empty, flashed into my mind. "I know what I feel. And he knows about the murals. How does he know about them unless he's been in here?"

"He assaulted you. You should make a report."

I reached across and rested my hand on his hand. "Tomorrow."

He looked at me, a question forming.

"Any chance you'd hang around tonight?" I'd managed a light tone.

"It's your house," he answered, his stare slipping away.

It hadn't been the answer I'd wanted. "I'll find you some bedding. You can sleep on the settee."

Chapter Nineteen

A foot pressed into my back and I tried to scream but nothing came out. Everything was black. I tried to see through the blackness but I couldn't.

Then someone was shaking me. "No!" I cried, flailing my arms.

"Rose, wake up."

Alex was standing over me in the dark, murky bedroom. I blinked, took in a deep breath and choked. The room was smoky.

"What's going on?" I pushed back the sheet, jumped out of bed and slipped on my flip-flops. With Alex sleeping downstairs, I'd finally found the courage to sleep in Karen's bed.

"We've got to get out of here. There's a fire. I've called nine-one-one already. But there isn't time to wait. The fire is moving too fast. It's already near the stairs. I barely made it up here."

He grabbed my arm and led me to the landing where the smoke was so dense it was impossible to see.

"Damn," he said looking down the staircase where flames were shooting up.

A wave of nausea came over me, making me dizzy.

"How are we going to get out of here?" I asked, swallowing the nausea down.

"The ladder in the study? Is it still there?"

"Yes, but it isn't tall enough," I argued.

"It'll have to do. Get down on your hands and knees and crawl to the mural room."

He did the same, but in the direction of Karen's study. The mural room door was shut. I reached up, turned the doorknob and crawled inside. There was no smoke yet in the room. Quickly I shut the door behind me, stood up and went to the windows, opened them and peered out into the night, but couldn't see much. At least no flames were licking this side of the house.

The chemicals, I thought, looking for Alex's tool case. I found it shoved in a corner, dragged it to one of the side windows. I couldn't free the screen, so I grabbed a tool and punched the screen out. Then I heaved the case out the window in an arc as far away from the house as I could. The case hit the ground in a loud crash of breaking glass and scattering tools.

"What was that?" Alex asked, slamming the door and hauling the rickety ladder across the floor to the window where I'd just thrown his case.

"Your chemicals. I had to get them out of here."

Two white towels were draped over his shoulder. He hurried back to the door and shoved the towels under the door, sealing out the smoke starting to snake in through the bottom. Then he strode to the open window.

"You really think that's going to help?" I asked him as he struggled with the ladder, guiding it through the window and lowering it so it rested against the house.

"If the firefighters can get to the fire before it reaches the second floor, yeah, I do." He gestured toward the window. "Okay, let's go."

I looked down at the ladder. There was about a four-foot gap between the window and the first rung of the ladder.

"You've gotta be kidding," I said, as the unbidden memory of Karen's splayed body shot into my mind.

"Unless you've got another idea, this is our only way out. Just don't knock the ladder over. Because then we'll have to jump."

He looked me up and down, his eyes resting on my feet. I'd slept in my running bra and hip-hugging shorts, which left little to the imagination. "And lose the flip-flops."

I kicked off my flip-flops and grabbed on to the window's center post with two hands, positioned first my right foot on the sill, then my left foot. Squatting and clutching with hands and feet, I carefully inched around so I was facing the house and then put my left foot on the other side of the post.

"Good," Alex coaxed. "Now ease your body down off the window sill. Then I want you to transfer your hands to the ledge, one at a time, and make sure you have a good grip before you ease your body off the sill."

My arms were shaking uncontrollably. "I can't." My stomach tightened into a hard ball. Panic shot into my mouth. I couldn't get enough air.

"Look at me," Alex said sternly. He put his large hands on my upper arms. "I'm holding you. Now let your right foot off the sill, and then your left."

I kept my eyes riveted on Alex as I took my right foot off the sill, then my left. "Now ease your right hand off the post and grab the sill." Alex was still holding my arms. Once I let go, he'd have to let go. I froze. Would my arms hold me once they had to bear my full weight?

"Rose, c'mon," Alex urged.

For a split second, I looked down and thought of bones breaking.

"Don't look down. Do it, now!" he yelled at me.

Gingerly, I let my right hand off the center post and quickly grabbed onto the ledge, my body swinging and off kilter. In a grasping panic, I let the other hand go and tried to grab for the sill, but I missed. For a moment I hung by one hand.

Alex lurched for my wrist but gravity pulled me away, the

fingers on my right hand let go as if they had a will of their own.

I tried to grasp at the wood siding with my fingers as I fell, knocking over the ladder and hitting the ground with a loud thump, all the air knocked out of me.

I lay there motionless drifting in and out of consciousness, gazing up toward the window. Where was Alex? He hadn't followed me out the window. I forced myself to stay awake. Then I saw him, squatting on the ledge, something bulging from the front of his shirt. For a second, his long, lanky body dangled from the open window, and then he let go, landing beside me with a loud thud.

"Rose, are you all right? Can you get up?" he called to me.

When I didn't answer, he reached under his shirt and pulled out what I now saw was his camera and swung it behind him. He gathered me up in his arms and jogged away from the house, which was being devoured by smoke. In the distance I heard a siren whirling its way through the dark morning.

He placed me carefully on the ground and then ran back toward the house. I lay there in the wet, cool grass, afraid to move, the damp seeping into my bra and shorts. Slowly I moved my feet, my legs, my arms, to see if anything was broken. All good. Then I pushed myself up on my elbows. A sharp pain pierced the back of my head. I touched the painful spot. It was oozing warmth. In my fall I must have gouged my head on something.

The fire truck tore up the grassy drive, and within minutes was pumping water on my house. Alex must have somehow moved the cars, because they were both parked in the field. I watched the firemen work, dousing the flames on the porch so they could hatchet through the front door. It wasn't hard to imagine the damage the smoke and the fire had done, and now the firemen would be finishing the house off in their effort to save it. All Karen's beautiful restoration destroyed. And the murals: had they gotten there in time to save them? I wondered.

As if waking from a dream, my mind spiraled around the obvious question. Who had started the fire? I could think of only one answer: Jimmy Braun. If he couldn't have his house, then nobody could have it.

I sat on the lip of the ambulance while the EMT cleaned and bandaged the gash in my head. The fire was out, but the smoke lingered, trailing up into the morning dawn. Somehow the house was still there. Most of the damage seemed to be contained to the first floor. The second floor merely looked singed.

One of the firemen had told me the fire had started on the porch near the front door. No gasoline or accelerant was used, just some kindling and matches.

"First floor's in bad shape. But the second floor's mostly smoke damage." He cocked his head and smiled. "Anybody smoking on the porch last night? We found cigarette butts."

I'd pulled the oxygen mask away from my face. "I know who started the fire."

He'd put the mask back on my face. "Tell the police."

"You're lucky nothing's broken." The EMT had a kind face and small, competent hands, which were at odds with his linebacker body. He pressed the large bandage to the back of my head. "But you should have an MRI."

Alex and Officer Dade were a few feet away from me, and I was trying to hear what they were saying.

"I'm fine, really. Thanks."

I hopped off the back of the ambulance a little too fast and swayed with wooziness.

"Whoa, not so fast there, speedy," the EMT said, grabbing my arm before I fell over. "You've got a nasty gash to your head. It doesn't appear to be a concussion, but, like I said, you should have that MRI."

I waited for the wooziness to leave. "I'll think about it." I disengaged my arm and walked over to Alex and Dade.

"It was the smoke that woke me," Alex explained. "I ran upstairs and got Rose. By then the fire had reached the bottom of the stairs."

"I know who started the fire," I blurted out. Both men gawked at me as if I were an unruly child who'd interrupted the grown-ups. "One of the firemen told me there were cigarette butts on the porch. I don't smoke. Neither does Alex. It's Jimmy Braun. My sister had a restraining order out on him. He's been hanging around here threatening me. He started this fire."

Dade looked at Alex for confirmation. When it didn't come, he asked, "Did either of you see him?"

"Like I said, I was asleep," Alex answered, shifting from foot to foot nervously.

Before Dade could ask me, I said, "Look, he attacked me yesterday in the woods over there. He said threatening things to me. You can't tell me you're not going to at least question him." The nausea had returned. I swallowed it down.

"I didn't say that," Dade said, annoyed. "Did you see him near the house before the fire?"

"No. I was asleep. But he's been creeping around here. Getting into the house." My voice had gone up two octaves, and I knew I sounded hysterical.

"You caught him in the house?" Dade questioned.

"No, but I smelled his damned cigarettes. And he knows about the—" I stopped not wanting to draw undue attention to the murals. "About all the restoration work Alex is doing."

"Okay, take it easy. I'll track him down. See what he has to say. Might want to get a restraining order against him." Dade nodded at Alex and went to talk to the fire chief.

A lot of good it did my sister, I thought.

"What's the diagnosis on your head?" Alex asked.

"Why didn't you say something about Braun?" I spat at him.

Alex took my arm and led me over to his car where we couldn't be heard.

"What am I going to say? I'm not the one who went running after him into the woods, was attacked and then refused to call the cops. Do you know how that looks?"

I pulled my arm away and felt another wave of dizziness ripple through me. "What am I going to do?" I cried. "The house is destroyed."

The dark had lifted and yet the smoke held on to the night. Even the grassy fields were hushed with smoke, making everything unfocused. It was like being in an Impressionistic painting.

"We're going to get in my car, drive into town, buy us some clothes, have breakfast and then figure it out."

All the tension drained from me as we drove away from the ruined house. In the side mirror I watched it grow smaller and smaller and then disappear, as if it had never existed.

"What now?" I said, pushing the empty plate away. I didn't think I was hungry, but I'd devoured the eggs, bacon, hash browns and wheat toast, and even the orange slice as if I hadn't eaten in days.

"Once I can get inside and take a look at the murals, I'll know whether I can save them. The towels under the door might have mitigated some of the smoke damage." Alex was toying with his knife, turning it back and forth as if it were one of his restoration tools.

"And if there's too much smoke damage and you can't save them? Then it's all been for nothing." I folded the napkin into a tight square and shoved it under my plate. My head throbbed a slow, steady pain. I'd yet to take the pain meds. Later I could relax, I told myself, but now I needed my wits about me.

"Everything's documented, remember, on my digital and SRL camera. The lab in Boston has copies of everything, and I've e-mailed the digital photos to my personal computer."

"Even if they can be salvaged, I can't afford to pay you to restore them. Like I said, all for nothing." Waves of depression were overtaking me. I wanted to put my head down on the table and sob. It was over.

"Don't worry about paying me."

Alex's phone trilled. He stared at the screen a minute, then answered the phone.

"Helene, I didn't expect to hear from you so soon." There was a warmth in his voice I hadn't heard before.

I watched his face change as the woman talked, his smile turning serious. As he listened, he stared at me.

"Why can't you tell me over the phone? Okay, let me see what I can do. I'll call you back. I've got a few things I need to do here first."

He closed the phone and placed it on the table. Before he spoke, he chewed on his lower lip, as if his words needed softening.

"That was Helene Roundoak, the woman who's an expert on Native American culture." He spun his cell phone around in tight circles. "She thinks she's found something, as she put it, 'extraordinary,' having to do with the strange Native American mural."

"What? What did she find?"

"She wants me to fly back to Boston as soon as possible. She says I have to see it. She didn't go into any details, other than to say if it is what she thinks it is, it could change history."

"Change history? How?"

"Like I said, she wouldn't elaborate. She needs me to see whatever it is."

I leaned back in the booth and gazed out the window that faced Route 146. The day shimmered heat down on the passing cars. Something was off in his explanation. Why did he have to fly back to Boston? What was I missing? "I'm going with you," I said emphatically.

He must have heard the determination in my voice. He shrugged his shoulders, then picked up his cell phone. "I need a flight from St. Louis to Boston." He took a napkin and wrote on it. "Uh-huh. Yeah, okay, book that. Two adults." He looked up and smiled at me. "Alex Hague and Rose Caffrey." He gave the airline his credit-card number.

"I'm good for it," I said after he hung up. "The money."

He waved his hand, dismissing my offer. "Our flight leaves at eight forty-five P.M." He glanced down at his watch. "Plenty of time to swing by the house and check out the murals, unless you're still hungry?"

"No, not anymore."

The twelve-foot ladder Alex had bought at the hardware store in Anna rested against the side of the house where the mural room was located. Though the entire house was scorched, this side showed the least damage. He steadied the ladder a few times and then offered me his hand.

"Ladies first." His lopsided grin made me smile. Since talking to Helene Roundoak, his whole mood had lifted. This was the side of Alex that made me careless, his good humor like a tonic against all caution.

My eyes traveled up the ladder that seemed to reach to the sky. The last thing I wanted to do was climb the ladder, but I wasn't going to let him know that. With both hands firmly planted on each side of the aluminum ladder, I quickly made my way to the second-floor window, my eyes riveted straight ahead. When I reached the window, I leaned my body forward on the ladder and peered into the room.

A veil of smoke lingered, making the room vague and unfocused. "Hold it still," I called down to him. "I'm going in."

"Rose, don't," he shouted in alarm. "The floor might not be safe. You could fall through. I just wanted you to see if the murals were intact."

I ignored his warning and grabbed the center window post, put one foot then the other on the sill, edged around and stepped down into the room. Standing there with the sunlight cutting through the smoke, swirling and dancing in the light, I saw the murals. They'd darkened, but they were still there. I let out a sigh of relief and choked on the smoke.

When I stepped off the ladder into the grass, Alex said, "Well?"

"See for yourself."

While he inspected the murals, I walked around the house, assessing the rest of the damage. Just as the fireman had said, the fire had been contained to the first floor. The front porch was gone and the front of the house was black and charred. Forming in my mind were doubts I didn't want to entertain.

Alex came around the side of the house, walking briskly toward me.

"There're salvageable," he said. "Just have to clean them up."

"That's great," I answered, looking back at the porch. "It's almost as if Jimmy set the fire so as not to hurt the murals," I offered tentatively. "That is, if he set the fire."

Alex's took a step back as if I'd hit him. "Now you don't think he did it? You were so convinced. What changed?"

"Just look at the porch. The fire was started here with matches and kindling, which ignited the wooden porch. No gasoline or accelerant, which would probably have destroyed the whole house, and maybe us along with it. If he wanted to get rid of me, he would have done a better job with the fire."

"Listen, leave the speculation to the cops. Be thankful you're okay. Now, let's go. We have a plane to catch." Alex's mood had turned sour.

As I walked to the car and got in, I continued, "Maybe what he wanted was to scare me off so he could claim the murals." I was no longer talking about Jimmy Braun.

Alex turned on the ignition and headed for the road. "You're not going to let this go, are you?"

"Would you?"

He switched on the radio, filling the silence with a country-western song about praying and love lost.

As the song ended he said, "You're talking about a drugged-out alcoholic. Isn't that what you told me? What would he know about historical murals and their value? What would he care?"

"That's what I can't figure out." I stared at his handsome profile, that fluttering in the pit of my stomach like a warning light. Yet he'd given me the answer I wanted to hear.

It would be so easy to reach out and move his dark hair off his forehead, to massage his neck, to lean over and distract him with my lips. Instead I concentrated on my sister and how much I missed her steadiness and her impossible love, wondering how we'd each arrived at this place of no return.

Chapter Twenty: Boston, Massachusetts

Everything about Helene Ramirez Roundoak was sleek and bright, from her silky dark hair to her burnished skin to her silver hoop earrings. With a pedigree as an expert on Native American culture, I'd been expecting a dowdy middle-aged professor type much like my sister. Helene was Karen's antithesis—model thin, young and oozing enthusiasm.

After our plane landed at Logan around eight-forty A.M., we'd driven straight to Boston University to meet with Helene. Alex had filled her in on the house fire and what else we'd learned about Emily Braun and Talking Bird/William Silk as we walked from her office to a lecture hall.

She listened intently, nodding her head but saying very little.

Alex's recitation brought back everything I'd been trying to shove into a corner of my brain. What was I doing here? The question kept repeating like a strange mantra.

Did I believe what I told Nick last night on the phone when he protested my flying to Boston? "Whoever's behind this is not going to let it go," I'd insisted.

Nick had murmured another protest, but all the fight was gone out of him. He knew I was right. "How much do you trust this Alex guy?"

I'd been asking myself the same question and hadn't come up with an answer. I'd glanced over at Alex where his lanky body was slouched in one of the waiting-area chairs at O'Hare. We'd decided to spend the seven-hour layover at O'Hare instead of a nearby motel. He was dozing, his head on his hand.

"Enough," I'd said, hoping enough was right.

The lecture hall was a vast theater of tiered seats. At the front was a raised dais and a podium, behind which was a screen.

"This is going to blow you away," Helene said, slipping a disc into the computer and turning off the overhead lights with a remote.

Two large images appeared on the screen. The one on the right was the strange mural of the half-naked, heavily tattooed natives with the clawlike fingernails, and the one European-looking woman kneeling before the stone altar begging for the child's life. Behind her a woman carried the naked infant toward the altar while a man with a knife glanced away. In the foreground another native man sat, his arms folded, with that look of grim righteousness on his face that had shocked me when I first saw it. As if the mural needed to lie hidden under the paint and the wallpaper, like the worst kind of remembering.

The one on the left was an engraving I'd seen before but couldn't quite place. This drawing depicted a similar scene, except there were native women dancing around one woman who held an infant aloft. Another woman knelt by a tree stump, not a stone altar, her head in her hands. In the background was a man holding a club. On either side of him were other native men. In the foreground was a seated European man and what appeared to be a native chief adorned in tattoos, feathered headdress and beaded necklaces. All the natives had European features. Though the theme of both murals was similar, everything else about the mural on the left was different—the circle of dancing women, the tree stump, the club, the seated European man. Yet the basic composition was the same.

Alex broke the silence first. "That's a Jacques Le Moyne engraving."

"Right," Helene said, drawing out the word as if encouraging a student.

"Wasn't he one of the first European artists to depict Native Americans?"

"Uh-huh."

"You've got to be kidding."

Helene tapped the remote on her shoulder. "I didn't make the connection at first. But something about your mural was gnawing at me. Not just that you found it in a nineteenth-century Illinois farmhouse. Which is beyond baffling. Once I concluded that these were Southeastern Indians, based on the flora and fauna and the depiction of the natives, it hit me. You know there's been some doubt that the Le Moyne engravings were done by him. Some art historians think Theodor de Bry was the artist. Various inconsistencies have been noticed. If you look closely, you'll see that the seashell in the engraving credited to Le Moyne is a nautilus shell commonly found in the Pacific. What's a nautilus shell doing in a drawing of Southeastern Indians? Also the Native Americans resemble Europeans more than Timucuans, the tribe living in the region at the time Le Moyne was, around fifteen sixty-five."

"But check out your mural. The seashells are whelks, which is what you'd find in Florida. The Native Americans are consistent with descriptions we have from the Spanish missionaries of the Timucuans."

Alex put his Styrofoam cup down on the podium and stared at the two images, his head moving back and forth. "There's no way. All accounts say the original drawings were destroyed when the Spanish burnt down the fort."

I had no idea what they were talking about. "What fort? When was this?"

Helene took in a deep breath and explained. "Fort Caroline. The French Huguenots' failed attempt to settle Florida in the sixteenth century. The Spanish got wind of it and slaughtered everyone at the fort and then burned it to the ground, ending France's hopes of a permanent settlement in this region of the new world, years ahead of the British. Le Moyne managed to escape the slaughter, along with the fort's commander, Rene Laudonniere, and his mistress and a handful of others. Le Moyne returned to England. Where he lived out the rest of his life doing botanical drawings for pattern books used by embroiderers and other craftsmen. He'd been part of the colonization as an artist and a mapmaker.

"It seems fantastical," Helene said, "but I think we're looking at a copy of his original drawing. Since you sent me the murals, I've been pouring over everything I can find about Le Moyne, the French colony, and the Spanish missionaries. And there are two other anomalies in your mural that are puzzling. One is the altar stone."

"You mean those weird marks? Aren't they decorative?" I asked.

"Could be, but my gut's telling me they're more than decorative. I'm not an epigrapher. But I do know the Timucuans didn't have a written language. I did some preliminary research into stone inscriptions and symbolic alphabets, but nothing quite fit our markings. And, like I said, the Timucuans had no written language. So the altar-stone marks are curious. Which brings me to the other anomaly. The word written on the mural, *Confesionario?*"

"It's Spanish for confessional," Alex said.

"Right, but it also has another meaning. And this is where it gets even more fantastical. It was a manual for confessors. A catechism of sorts that missionaries wrote to educate the converts on various aspects of the Roman Catholic faith, written in the language of the converts."

"Why do you think that word would be in this drawing?"

Helene asked, again sounding like a teacher.

"Because it was copied verbatim from the original," I obliged. "Which means Emily Braun had Le Moyne's sketch. But if Le Moyne did the drawing, why was there a Spanish word written on it?"

Before Helene could answer, Alex countered, "Even if it had survived the burning of the fort. How could it have survived for four hundred years? Where was it in all that time? And how did it end up in the hands of a nineteenth-century woman living in Illinois on a farm?"

"Ever watch Antiques Road Show?" Helene answered, her youthfulness a part of the answer. "Alex, my dear skeptic, part of that answer may be the word, *Confesionario.*"

"C'mon, Helene, you're not saying one of those Spanish missionaries saved Le Moyne's sketches?"

"I'm not saying anything. I'm trying to explain what I see in this mural. You have another explanation?"

"So what if you're right? It's meaningless now. If Emily Braun had that drawing, there's no way to know what happened to it. We don't even know what happened to her or, for that matter, her body," Alex reasoned.

"The drawing could still be out there," I said as if talking to myself. Had Karen known about the hidden drawing? Was that what was in the lost diary pages—the key that unlocked the mystery of the murals—a history that spanned centuries?

Alex stepped back from us as if he wanted no part of this discovery.

"If it still exists and you find it, you will have made one of the most remarkable discoveries in American history." Helene addressed her remarks to Alex. "It would be extraordinary to have the original Le Moyne drawing or drawings giving us a glimpse into a time and a people who have vanished. By mid-eighteenth century, the Timucuans had been obliterated by disease and genocide. The drawing would be a window into a past long gone." All lightness was gone from her voice.

"We have to find out everything we can about Emily Braun; she's the key to this mystery." I said, responding to Helene's enthusiasm.

"You mean Emily Lord Braun," she corrected me, turning on the overhead lights. "There was something familiar in that mural of the formal buildings and the town in the valley. I've been doing research on female academies founded in the late eighteenth and early nineteenth century because I came across some evidence that a few Cherokee sent their daughters to the Wolcott Female Academy in Connecticut prior to their forced relocation."

Electricity went through me at the mention of the Cherokee.

"There's a book called *To Ornament Their Minds*. And in it is a drawing of the academy and the surrounding countryside. It's not exactly like your mural. But close enough for me to take a look at their registration records. And guess what?"

"Emily Lord was a student there," I piped up.

"Yeah. From eighteen thirty to eighteen thirty-one. And she's mentioned as one of the assistant teachers of what they called back then the ornamental arts, painting. That's as far as I was able to get in such short time."

"Which puts her in New England when Rufus Porter was working as an itinerant painter. Which means they could have met. And she could have been one of his students, which would explain her painting style," I added.

Alex rasped, "It's all conjecture. And it doesn't explain the Le Moyne copy or what happened to her or the Cherokee boy. I appreciate what you've done, Helene. But you have to admit you've made some pretty big scholarly leaps here."

Why was he being so contrary? It was as if he wanted to put roadblocks in our way. "What is your problem?" I snapped at him, my exhaustion and stress overcoming me.

"My problem? I'm not the one who's been assaulted, not once, but twice. We were lucky to get out of your house alive."

Helene looked incredulous. "You've been assaulted? Because of the murals?"

"Maybe. I can't be sure." I didn't want to talk about the assaults. I didn't want anything to deter me from seeing this through to the end. Karen had died either directly or indirectly because of what lay hidden in the farmhouse, ticking away like some ancient bomb.

"Could be someone else found out about the possibility of a Le Moyne original," Helene said. "It would be worth millions, maybe more."

Alex had gone stone silent.

"What about William Silk or Talking Bird?" I asked.

"Ran out of time. I did a quick online check using both names, but came up with nothing. But if you want to pursue this, contact the leaders of the Cherokee nation in the east and out west. You can use my name as an entrée. I wrote down who you should talk to and their phone numbers. I leave tomorrow for a conference in the Caribbean. But if anything comes up, call me. I don't care what time it is."

She took the disc from the computer and slipped it back into its sleeve. "I know what this could mean for you, Alex. I always thought someone screwed you over."

As we walked across the BU campus, the lush green trees shadowed our path. Neither one of us spoke. Like me, Alex probably was sorting through what Helene had revealed. My mind felt like an electric current was sparking it.

"You know this has to end here," Alex said as we neared the parking lot.

I stopped under a large maple tree and put my hands on my

hips, a raw rage churning inside me. "Are you going to tell me what's going on?"

"You don't get it, do you?" He grabbed my arm so tightly I winched. "You're a pawn. Can't you see it? We're both pawns. When Helene laid it out in there, I realized that we've been set up from day one."

A guy was walking by talking into his cell phone. When he saw Alex holding my arm, he stopped. I pulled my arm away and waited until he passed before I answered.

"You're wrong," I objected defensively, not wanting to cede anything to him in his anger.

"Think about it. Whoever assaulted you has the diary pages. They have one piece of the puzzle and we have the other—the murals and their meaning. They're watching our every move. They may or may not know about the Le Moyne drawing. But they know something of great value is involved. It's too dangerous. We turn everything over to the cops. Let them sort it out. I'm done."

He stormed away. I didn't catch up to him until we reached his car.

"Are you part of this?" I said, standing by the passenger door but not getting in. "Is that why you don't want me to continue? Did someone hire you? Or are you working alone?"

He wouldn't even look at me, clicking the remote to unlock the doors.

I was beyond fury. "Once a thief, always a thief, is that it?"

He shook his head at me as if I were an unruly teen and got into the car, starting the engine. Then he rolled down the window. "Get in," he demanded.

I stood there, my arms over my chest and looking across the parking lot. The morning sun painfully glinting on the cars. I could call a cab. And then what? My return ticket wasn't until

Friday. I could call Nick and beg him for help.
I yanked the car door open and got in.

Chapter Twenty-One

Alex's row house was on a side street in the heart of Charlestown. The flowerboxes out front still held the dried stalks of last year's flowers. A few newspapers lay on the stoop, faded by sun. From the outside the building looked old and tired, smashed between two equally old and tired looking row houses. He'd managed to squeeze his silver SUV into a parking spot meant for a compact, gently nudging and bumping the two other cars.

As I waited for Alex to open the vestibule door, the low moan of a tugboat sounded in the distance. I inhaled the not-unpleasant mixture of diesel and brine. Though I couldn't see it, I knew the Mystic River was nearby.

We'd driven in silence from Boston University through the tangle of angry traffic, the tight whirl of rotaries, the summer heat of too many people and too little space. The only thing keeping me awake was anger. I suspected the same about Alex.

He pushed open the weather-beaten door, and we stepped inside the cool hallway. There was another locked door leading up to his condo on the second floor. As I followed Alex up the highly polished wood steps, our footsteps only intensified the silence that had fallen between us.

The stairs led to a dining-room area, which had been converted to a workspace. A large table took up much of the room, strewn with books and papers. A computer sat in the middle of the mess like an island.

Light filtered into the dark room from the living room, which overlooked the street. Flanking the dining room on the other side was a kitchen.

I let my backpack slide to the floor and went into the kitchen. Everything was cutting edge: stainless appliances, black granite countertops. Off the kitchen was a redwood deck with table, chairs, and umbrella. I didn't need to ask because it was visible in the small things, like the gingham potholders hung on the fridge and the matching kitchen towels, that this had once been home to Alex's wife and daughter. I felt uncomfortable, as if I'd walked in on a moment of marital intimacy.

Alex mumbled what sounded like "something to drink" and disappeared upstairs to what I assumed were the bedrooms.

I heard the whoosh of air-conditioning turn on and smelled dust. Inside the refrigerator were soda, beer, a half bottle of white wine and not much else. I grabbed a soda, slid open the sliding glass door and went outside onto the deck.

A large tree shaded the deck, and dead leaves and seedpods were everywhere. I pulled out a chair, brushed it off and sat down, putting my feet up on another chair.

Sipping on the soda, with the filtered sun speckling my arms and face, I realized how close I was to the heart of the mystery.

Helene had supplied the secret of the murals. The very potent possibility that a lost art treasure had survived and might still exist. But we, Alex and I, had given her the keys to that secret—like an onion peeled away to its core, each layer more pungent than the last. And it all started with my sister, Karen, and the diary she found.

What had she felt, holding Emily's diary, reading her words, the elegant dance of her letters from a time when the act of writing was beautiful? It must have moved her to the core. Now, sitting on a cedar deck in Charlestown, the blare of traffic, the smog of summer pollution making it all too real, I had only a few remaining layers left to peel away.

How had I come this far? After the loss of my parents, I'd never committed to anything again, except the fluidity of my art.

Something had changed inside me. I'd peeled the remaining layers away for Karen, for us. In this, we would be sisters again. The mystery of Emily's empty coffin, and the Cherokee boy, Talking Bird, would be known. I would complete Karen's work. Finally, I would atone and put her to rest.

Idly, I ran my fingers over the warm, splintery redwood table. The rough surface was like the plaster road where Emily had pressed the ribbon so long ago. A ribbon that had meant something to her that I could only guess at. I glanced at the sliding glass door. Where was Alex? What was he doing?

What it now came down to, and there was no escaping it—did I trust him? Karen had paid him a great deal of money to restore the murals. But then after the fire, he'd offered to restore them again for nothing. "Don't worry about paying me," he'd said. And the fire. Had Jimmy Braun started it? Or had Alex made it look that way? I rubbed at the knot at the back of my neck.

But what motive would Alex have to start the fire? To get me to leave and go back to Chicago? From the photos he'd taken of the murals, he had everything he needed to solve the mystery. I was excess baggage.

It all circled back to trusting myself to know if a man was lying to me.

There was something outrageously pathetic in that.

I reached in my pocket and took out the paper on which Helene had written the numbers of the Cherokee chiefs. She'd also written a kind of script of what to say. I smiled at her careful instructions, dug out my cell phone and called Austin Richards in Oklahoma.

I was transferred several times and finally Austin came on the line. "Helene Ramirez Roundoak said I should call you," I began. "My name's Rose Caffrey. I'm an artist from Chicago who's doing research on the Trail of Tears. I inherited my sister's house, which is connected to the trail."

"How the heck is Helene?" he interrupted.

"Good," I said. "What she thought you could help me with is any information you might have about a Cherokee boy, named Talking Bird or William Silk, who came on the trail, but was taken in by a white family, name of Braun, in Anna, Illinois. Anything about him or his family."

"Let me ask around, and I'll get back to you."

I left him my cell-phone number and thanked him. Then I called Scotty Parker, in Gatlinburg, Tennessee. He answered on the second ring.

After I explained why I was calling, he said, "You're a friend of Helene's? She never mentioned you." The suspicion in his voice was palpable.

"Well, she wouldn't. I just met her. And I'm more a colleague than a friend. But she gave me your number and told me to call."

"How do I know you're who you say you are? Anybody could get info on Helene from the internet and about me for that matter."

I put my feet down on the deck and sat up straighter. "Has someone else contacted you about William Silk or Talking Bird?" It was the only explanation I could think of for his obvious mistrust.

"What's your name again?"

I told him my name. "If you check out, I'll call you back. If not, like I told the other guy, I got nothing to say."

He hung up before I could ask about the other guy.

I finished my soda and went inside, found some crackers in one of the cupboards and went back out on the deck. I must have fallen asleep, because the trill of the cell phone woke me.

"Helene says you're okay. Look, Mrs. Arthur is up there in age, almost ninety-three. But she's the woman you want to talk to. She's always claimed that one of her ancestors by the name of Bird That Talks was on the trail and made the journey back home. She's from the bird clan and she's a history buff. It's all anecdotal, mind you. Nothing's written down, but her mind's as clear as water."

"Can I have her phone number?" My heart was thumping in my chest. Bird That Talks, Talking Bird. I'd found William Silk.

He laughed as if I'd said something particularly funny. "That's the thing. I can give it to you, but she doesn't hear so well. How about you mail her your questions? Or the next time I'm out by her place, I'll stop by and ask her. So what do you want to know exactly?"

"How soon would that be?" I was trying to hide my growing impatience.

"Maybe next week."

"What if I came out there now and talked to her?"

"You could do that." I could hear the amusement in his voice. "Make sure you bring your hiking boots though."

"Why's that?" I asked, playing along.

"She lives up in the mountains. It's about a three-mile hike off the Appalachian Trail. You know, the Great Smoky Mountains."

"Will she talk to me if I just show up at her door?"

"That I can't say. Depends on if she likes the way you look. She's pretty ornery. I always kid her that's why she's lived so long."

I took down directions to Mrs. Arthur's house and then drew a question mark.

"You said something about a guy who called you asking about William Silk. Do you remember his name?"

"Ben Jones. I'll bet my last dollar that wasn't his name. 'Cause he hesitated before he answered, as if he was making it up."

"When did he call?"

"A few days ago. Helene says you're researching some lost document or something connected to this William Silk. Who's this other guy?"

"I wish I knew." The only people, besides Alex and Helene, who knew about Silk were Emery Wallace and maybe Reverend Likely.

"Come by my place before you head up to Mrs. Arthur's. If I'm around, I'll hike up with you. I could use the exercise. Any idea when you expect to get here?"

"Tomorrow." Close; I was so close.

"You want to leave right now?" Alex said, as he watched me print out directions from Boston to Gatlinburg, Tennessee.

"Look, I'm not asking you to go with me. Drop me at the nearest car-rental place." I took the printed map, folded it in two and stuffed it in my backpack. It was foolhardy not to wait and leave tomorrow. I needed a good night's sleep, but I felt an urgency I couldn't quell.

"Why are you so sure this old woman knows something?" Alex fingered a stack of papers on the table. The room suddenly felt too close, as if all the air were gone.

"Why are you so sure she doesn't? And don't you find it the least bit coincidental that some guy who called himself Ben Jones called and asked the same questions? Maybe you're right. Maybe someone has been trailing us from the beginning. We have to get to this woman before someone else does."

He grabbed me by my shoulders and turned me toward him, staring into my eyes as if he could read something there. It took all my strength not to push him away.

"Rose, I'm not the enemy," he said, his body leaning into me. Then his mouth was on mine, warm, and full of doubt.

I stood stone still, waiting for him to finish, shoving down my jangling feelings. "I'm going to see this thing through," I said, as if that were an answer to his kiss. "It's no longer about the money."

"I know," he whispered, kissing me again, all the doubt gone.

His one hand slid from my shoulder toward my breast. It was too easy. I grabbed his hand and stepped back from what felt like gravity.

Did I see hurt in his expression or surprise?

"I'd better go now if I want to beat rush-hour traffic."

I picked up my backpack, slung it over my shoulder, and headed for the door.

"Too late for that," he answered. "It's after four. It'll be a nightmare getting out of the city now. We need to sleep and recharge. We'll leave early tomorrow morning."

He was right; we'd be stalled in traffic for hours, and my body felt stupid with exhaustion. "Okay, but we're outta here before dawn."

"Aye, aye, captain." He saluted me as if I was in charge.

I smiled weakly at his joke, its irony almost funny.

Chapter Twenty-Two: Gatlinburg, Tennessee

The interstate was a blur of traffic and cities glimpsed from a distance. Once the radio cut out on us, Alex popped in some jazz CDs, which were like another silence, fraught with some emotion neither one of us wanted to explore.

Not until the towns fell away, replaced by trees and rivers and small flashes of lakes bunching the highway, did I break the silence.

"How well did you know my sister?"

I could feel his eyes on me. "Are you asking me if we were lovers?" He sounded amused by my question, which I sensed was a cover.

Now that he said it, maybe that was what I was asking. "Were you?" I stared back at him, and he looked away.

"Would you believe me if I said no?"

"I might."

John Coltrane's nervous sax started in on "A Love Supreme," and I felt myself shift inside, which way I wasn't sure. My gut told me they'd never been lovers. He wasn't her type, too volatile, too erratic. Karen thrived on control. Alex would never be controlled. But she'd trusted him enough to hire him to restore the murals. His past was her control over him. Why was I hashing and rehashing this? Was it because Karen was usually right about men, and I was usually wrong?

"Did you know Karen chose you specifically because you'd been accused of theft?" I wanted to hurt him, to break through this barrier between us so I could see him, know him, dispel my doubts or confirm them. The tension was electric, and I was glad we were moving fast down a highway with things green hurtling past the windows as if needing to be broken to be put back together right.

He laughed, which infuriated me.

"I suspected that. After all, Chicago has some fine restoration artists. Why would she hire a guy from Boston?"

"But you were flattered. You thought maybe the past was behind you." I kept pushing at him.

"Look, I don't know what you're getting at. I liked Karen, but that was it."

Coltrane's sax echoed itself into quiet as his deep voice repeated the song's title over and over as if it was a mantra.

I was through with talking. Trust him, not trust him. It was too late for such speculations. I'd asked if they'd been lovers, because I wanted him for myself. He'd said no. I was choosing to believe him, at least about that; about the rest I still wasn't sure. And until I was sure, he was a contagion I had no defense against except avoidance.

We reached Scotty Parker's house around seven o'clock at night. His brick, two-story colonial on a quiet suburban street on the outskirts of Gatlinburg surprised me. Where he lived seemed so banal. I chided myself. What was I expecting, a teepee? Helene's ironic comment came back to me: "Most Americans' knowledge of Native American culture comes from movies like *Dances with Wolves.*"

I rang the doorbell several times, listening as it made a hollow sound.

"Doesn't look like he's home," I said to Alex.

He walked to the side garage door. "Car's here," he remarked as he joined me on the front-porch stoop.

I called his cell phone and left a message when he didn't pick up. "Rose Caffrey. I'm at your house. It's seven-ten; we're heading up to Mrs. Arthur's."

"Maybe he went out for a walk," Alex surmised.

"Yeah, maybe."

In case he didn't pick up his cell-phone messages, I wrote a note telling him we were here and stuck it inside his screen door.

We got back in the car and followed Scotty's directions to the road leading to Mrs. Arthur's cabin. As we climbed higher and higher, the road narrowed until it was only one lane. Like a magnet, my eyes kept glancing at the sheer drop below. If another car were coming down the mountain, it would be a very tight squeeze. When the road finally ended, I let out a sigh of relief.

Alex parked the car in one of the two slots overlooking the Great Smoky Mountains. I grabbed my backpack, slammed the car door and stood for a moment, letting the vista wash over me. It was as if I'd passed through to another world. The mountains were ethereal with the blue shadowed mist rising from them. The fading sky, a mirage of blues and oranges and purples, names failing to describe what I saw.

Alex came up beside me. The click and release of his camera seemed like a trespass.

"Kinda makes you believe in other worlds." He sounded breathless.

"If only," I said turning away. I was fighting his every attempt at connection.

"Parker said the trail's near the parking lot on the right. It should be marked." I walked right and found the trail marker partly covered with dense shrubs.

"Here it is." Not waiting for Alex, I started up the trail, with the heavy backpack. I wanted Mrs. Arthur to see the mural photos, Karen's research notes, all the pieces of this historical puzzle she was a part of. Then maybe she would tell me what she knew about Bird That Talks.

The three-mile hike seemed like ten as the rough trail ascended, full of cutbacks and hummocks, jagged rocks and tree roots. My breathing was becoming labored, and I was feeling dizzy from the altitude. I could hear Alex's raspy breathing behind me.

Then the log cabin came into view. It stood at the end of a long wooden walkway, like a house in a fairy tale. A curl of smoke wove its way into the twilight. The tin roof shimmered with the falling light. A few stars punched the darkening sky.

"What if she won't talk to you?" Alex piped up, breaking the spell.

"She has to." I started down the long walkway toward the front door, convinced of nothing, driven by movement.

The sounds of katydids and birds filled the air with welcome—or was it warning?

There was no doorbell, so I knocked on the solid weathered wood door. Nothing. I knocked again, only harder. Then I heard a stirring within the house.

"Keep your shirt on," a woman shouted. "I can only get there so fast."

After another few minutes, she eased the door open a crack. "Lost, are you?" she said, a wry smile on her pleated face. The sharp nose practically sniffing me.

"Mrs. Arthur, Scotty Parker sent me. I'm Rose Caffrey and this is Alex Hague. We'd like to talk to you about your ancestor, Bird That Talks."

I could feel Alex's breath on the back of my neck. We'd agreed that I'd take the lead. He was there along for the ride.

She gave me a keen look, her dark eyes impenetrable. "Why you asking?"

I shifted the backpack from one shoulder to another. "I have reason to believe that Bird That Talks was taken in by the Braun family. Do you know about them and how they nursed him back to health?"

She held perfectly still, showing no reaction. "What's it to you?"

"I now own the Braun farmhouse, and Alex has restored the murals in the house, and we believe two of them tell the story of Bird That Talks."

"I doubt that very much, young woman." Then she turned away and hobbled back into the room, leaving the door open.

Alex shrugged his shoulders.

"It's cold tonight. Shut the door and come warm yourself by the fire," she called to us.

The room smelled of old fires and cooked meat. A large sofa, two rocking chairs and a coffee table were the only furniture. A woven rug graced the dark hardwood floor, an intricate Native American black-and-white basket pattern.

"Sit, sit," she said, gesturing toward the sofa. She eased herself down into one of the rocking chairs flanking the fireplace; a green afghan hung over the back of the chair. She took the afghan and put it over her shoulders.

Her white hair was tied back in a bun at the base of her neck. She was wearing khaki pants and a long-sleeved, pale-blue sweatshirt. Her feet were clad in blue leather slippers. Though she was hunched with age, she was still a tall woman, and there was a solidness about her square face and large frame.

She rocked back and forth, not saying a word. Finally I spoke. "What can you tell me about Bird That Talks? Scotty Parker said he was your ancestor."

A sly smile broke the solemnity of her face. "You have proof of these murals?"

I glanced at Alex, who raised his eyebrows as if to say, "It's your party."

I pulled the other rocker next to her and, from the backpack, took out the photographs of the murals and explained everything I knew about them, about how Karen found the diary, and about the missing pages. Not wanting to upset her, I left out the arson and the attacks on me.

When I came to the photo of the last mural, the one of the Native Americans that Helene suspected was a copy of a Le Moyne drawing, I felt her body tense.

"Bird That Talks was my great-grandfather." She paused to let that set in. "He was the only member of his immediate family to survive the trail on which they cried. Mother, father, two sisters, grandmother, grandfather, all gone, as if a wind blew them into dust. He saw terrible things. A woman laboring with child who couldn't ford the Ohio River, bayoneted by a soldier. The old left to die like dogs, where they lay." Her dark eyes glowered in the firelight. "When they finally crossed the big Ohio River, his mother, Aggie Silk, was sick with fever. The townspeople spat on them as they walked the lonely trail. And the snow fell, and the sleet rained down, and still they trudged on. They were the last of the people to leave their homeland. Trapped between the two big rivers in the worst winter to befall them. Their feet blue-black with cold, their stomachs empty pits, their memories ripped and torn. Then, his mother Aggie Silk could go no further, burning with fever. And then he too burned with that same fever. The man with the blackest hair let them camp on his land. Every day he came, bringing blankets and food. 'Please,' begged Aggie Silk, 'take my son. Don't let him die.' And so, Bird That Talks was saved. And the strange woman with the chicory eyes brought him back to the old land. In the night they left, taking the same trail. She dressed him as her son. She brought him home. It was not easy. But she brought him home to these mountains."

She gazed into my eyes with gratitude. "You have given her a name, this Emily Braun."

"What happened to her?" I asked. "Do you know?"

She grinned and nodded. "Oh, yes."

Alex stirred and was about to say something, but then leaned back.

The old woman would tell her story in her own time and in her own way. "She too went home."

"You mean back to Illinois?" I asked, trying to make sense of the intertwined stories of Emily and William.

She folded her gnarled hands as if in prayer. "Home is not always a place, young woman. Surely you know that. Sometimes it is where the heart lives. That is where she went. East, toward the rising sun, where her heart could live."

"East? Where east?"

"I have no idea. Nor did William Silk."

Her hand covered mine as if to console me. It felt light and cool.

"This is why you came." She tapped the photo of the Southeast Indians' mural with her finger. "One day, my grandfather said our ship would come in. Is that what this means?"

I wasn't sure what she was asking. "I don't understand."

She pushed herself out of the chair with the afghan draped over her like a shawl, and left the room. When she returned she was carrying a dark cedar box, battered with age.

She eased herself into the rocker and opened the box's lid. Her hands shook as she took out what was inside.

"It's time" was all she said as she removed the yellowed piece of parchment and handed it to me.

One edge was singed, the paper wrinkled and torn, water-stained, the colors faded. But there was the Native woman carrying the naked infant, the man with the knife, the stone altar, the weeping European woman and the fierce chief.

I sat stunned, not believing what I was seeing. My eyes roved the old drawing, seeing and not seeing it, as if everything had suddenly disappeared except this magnificent drawing. I shook my head in disbelief.

In the far right corner near the bottom were the initials JLM—Jacques Le Moyne. I was holding an original Jacques Le Moyne, over four hundred years old. Delicately, as if I were coaxing the drawing to sing, I ran my finger over the creased surface lightly.

"What is it?" Alex asked.

I looked up. "I think it's an original Le Moyne watercolor sketch. It matches the mural exactly; even the word *Confesionario* is here. And so are his initials."

Alex leapt from the sofa and stood over me, his eyes devouring the sketch. "Oh, my God," he gasped. "Do you know what this means?"

Something in his tone must have alerted Mrs. Arthur, because she slid the sketch from my hands and placed it in the box. "It means nothing to you," she said gruffly, glaring up at Alex.

"Mrs. Arthur, do you have any idea what this might be worth?" I asked, trying to keep the excitement out of my voice. "We think this drawing is over four hundred years old. And that it was drawn by the first European artist to depict Native Americans. It's a window into a lost past. We'd have to have it authenticated, but we're talking millions of dollars. You would be a rich woman."

A log snapped sending sparks flying up the flue.

"Young woman. Rose. Forgive me if I don't trust you. I'm not giving you this."

There was a knock on the door. Mrs. Arthur didn't move. Then came another knock, this time louder.

Not waiting for Mrs. Arthur to answer it, Alex walked to the door and swung it open.

"I see you got here okay. How's everything going?" I

recognized the distinct cadences of Scotty Parker's voice.

He entered the room, followed by Alex. Scotty Parker was a big, robust man with a shaved head. He was sweating, and there were dark stains under his armpits. His bulging belly hung over his jeans like a beach ball.

"Mrs. Arthur, I hope it was okay to have these people come talk to you about your ancestor."

"Did you know what she has hidden away here?" Alex asked, his frustration evident in his tone. "A lost art treasure that's over four hundred years old."

Scotty looked like he'd been doused with cold water. "Is this some kind of a joke?"

"And she refuses to let us have it authenticated," Alex continued.

I wanted to slap Alex just to shut him up. He was going about this all wrong. Instead of cajoling Mrs. Arthur and winning her trust, he was alienating her. Now she was clutching the box to her chest.

"What Alex means to say is that this drawing that's been passed down through her family could very well make her a rich woman. We think it was done by the first European artist in North America. His name was Jacques Le Moyne."

"I thought you people wanted to know about her family. What are you trying to pull here?" Scotty's jaw was rigid with anger.

"We had no idea this drawing still existed," Alex said, exasperated.

"The hell you didn't," Scotty snapped back.

"Okay, everyone, just calm down," I said. "I'm going to make a proposal that I think will be agreeable to everyone. Scotty, how about you take guardianship of the drawing? You go with us to have it authenticated. If it's what I think it is, then you and Mrs. Arthur can decide what to do with it, whether you want to sell it or keep it in her family."

Alex was pacing back and forth, his arms crossed over his chest, letting out impatient grunts.

Mrs. Arthur said, "Would you be willing to do that, Scotty?"

Scotty didn't hesitate. "What do I have to do, and how long will it take?"

Alex said, "Best place to have this authenticated is the Museum of Fine Arts' laboratory in Boston. I know people there who can expedite the whole process. We can drive back tonight. Hand over the drawing. You'll get a receipt from the museum, and then you can fly back home."

Scotty knelt beside Mrs. Arthur. "What do you want to do, Grandmother?"

She patted Scotty on the arm and then stood up. "Come, we need to talk about this," she told Scotty, clutching the box in her two hands. "You two wait here."

They walked out of the room toward the back of the house.

Alex looked like he was buzzed on caffeine, nervously pacing around the room, picking up knickknacks from the fireplace ledge, then putting them down, arranging and rearranging them.

"There's nothing we can do now," I coaxed. "It's her decision."

"She'll let us take it. She has to." He jabbed his finger at me.

"Alex, she doesn't have to do anything." I didn't like his threatening tone or the way he was acting.

When they came back into the room, Mrs. Arthur was still holding the cedar box, which I took as a good sign. Scotty escorted her to the rocker and then he sat down in the other rocker.

"Okay, I advised Mrs. Arthur that she should do this," he explained.

"I don't want the money," she interrupted him, her lips knit tight.

"Yes, Grandmother, as we agreed. I'll make sure of it. If this drawing proves to be authentic, the money will go to the tribe for our children."

"You won't let it out of your sight. Promise me, Scotty." She rocked back and forth in the rocker.

"I promise," Scotty said, making an X on his chest. Then he stood up.

"Too late to drive down the mountain tonight. You can all stay here," Mrs. Arthur said. "There's plenty of room."

Alex rejected the invitation. "If we leave now, we'll be in Boston by late morning. The sooner we move on this, the better."

I knew what he was thinking, he was afraid the old woman would change her mind.

"Okay," Scotty said. "Let me stop by my place, throw a few things in a bag, and then I'm ready. Been needing a vacation lately anyway. This is the kind of adventure gets my juices going. Maybe I'll stick around Boston for a few days and take in the sights. Walk that freedom trail." He let out a jittery laugh.

Chapter Twenty-Three

After Scotty packed a bag, we fueled up on caffeinated drinks and fast food at a strip mall in Gatlinburg, and then got back on the interstate. I volunteered to drive the first shift, needing the feeling of control driving gave me. My nerves felt electric, my mind spinning and spinning around what we carried, casually resting on the backseat beside Scotty as if it were a cheap souvenir and not a priceless cultural artifact.

Just after connecting to Route 41, Scotty fell asleep, the staccato sound of his snoring at odds with the steady hum of the SUV's tires on the dark highway, a black ribbon pierced only by passing cars and towns.

It wasn't until Scotty's snoring had deepened that Alex spoke. "I'm sorry if I came across too strong back there," he whispered. "It's just that I saw it all slipping away. This discovery could restore my reputation. Then maybe I could get my kid back, or at least see her more often."

I couldn't fathom how this drawing could restore his reputation. "It's not ours. You know that. We have no claim to it."

"But we do. If it hadn't been for us, one of the greatest lost art treasures would be moldering in a cedar box. I'm not talking about money. I'm talking about posterity. Forever, our names will be linked with Jacques Le Moyne and the first French colony in America."

I glanced at him, trying to read his intention. His face was as unreadable as the night. "What if it turns out it's not authentic?"

Shouldn't he be the one questioning its authenticity, not me? Why was he so convinced the drawing was authentic?

"The whole thing's too unbelievable for it not to be."

I looked away, back at the highway, not wanting to argue with him. A light rain began to fall. I switched on the windshield wipers. A car passed on the opposite side of the road, its headlights like a brief whisper across the rainy night. It was almost midnight and few cars were on the road. The rhythm of the wipers, the dark highway, and the steady rain were starting to have a hypnotic effect on me. The muscles in my back and shoulders relaxed, my fingers eased on the steering wheel; now I just had to stay awake.

Suddenly, the car's interior was blasted with light. Blinking, I looked in my rearview mirror and saw a pickup truck tailgating us. Where had it come from? The last exit had been over a half hour ago. It was as if the truck materialized out of thin air.

I slowed down, hoping the truck would pass. But it didn't. It was now inches from the rear bumper, playing some bizarre game of how close can I get without hitting you.

"What's with this guy?" I said. "Why doesn't he pass me?"

Alex turned around in his seat. "Just ignore him. Probably some drunken hick on his way home from a bar."

"Yeah, maybe." I accelerated slightly and so did the truck.

"Something's not right," I said.

Alex shifted in his seat. "You're tired and you're imagining things."

Just as I turned toward Alex to protest my imagining things, a hard thump jerked the SUV forward, jarring us.

"Am I?" I pushed down on the gas pedal. "Hold on."

Now I was driving over eighty, tearing down the interstate into the darkness, gripping the steering wheel as the SUV shuddered with speed.

"Slow down," Alex demanded, holding onto the dashboard

with both hands.

"What? And let this nut job ram us off the highway into a ditch? No way."

"You're going to get us killed," Alex pleaded.

"Not if I can help it." Up ahead I saw an exit ramp. The sodium lights like an oasis, and I debated whether to get off. What if the truck followed us down some isolated road? At least on the interstate, there was the chance of reaching a more populated area. I glanced in the mirror, and didn't see the truck. Where was it?

"I'm getting off," I said, sounding more determined than I felt.

Still hovering around eighty, I took the ramp too fast, barely keeping the SUV on the slick pavement. Without stopping, I turned right onto the one-lane road, my eyes flicking back and forth between the mirror and the road. I still didn't see the truck.

Not until we flew past the sole gas station/mini-mart did I slow down. The road had turned dark, lit only by our headlights.

"Do you see him?" I asked Alex.

Scotty had stopped snoring but was still sleeping.

"No," Alex answered. "Like I said, some drunken yahoo."

Did he really believe that? Why would a drunk ram our bumper? It made no sense.

"Whoever was in that truck knows about the Le Moyne." I was shaking with adrenaline, and Alex's nonchalant attitude was making me want to fight him.

"We're staying on the back roads from now on. Get the map out of the glove box," I ordered. If he fought me on this, I didn't know what I would do. Slug him? Scream?

He folded his arms across his chest. "Turn around and head back to the interstate."

Abruptly, I pulled onto the shoulder, leaned over Alex and

popped open the glove box, rummaging around for the map and wondering if he was right or was something else going on here.

Just as I grabbed the map, he yanked it out of my hands. I reached for it, but he said, "I'll do it. Just drive." He switched on the interior light and unfolded the map. "If we stay on this road," Alex began, when suddenly I saw headlights coming fast behind us.

"Crap," was all I said as I turned back onto the road and floored it.

We were flying down the county road, which twisted and turned, the truck's headlights getting closer and closer.

Alex was gripping the dashboard again and Scotty was awake.

"What's going on?" Scotty asked.

"Someone's chasing us" was all I had time to say before the road made a sharp veer to the left and the SUV's wheels hit the gravel shoulder, causing me to steer the SUV sharply to the right. My fingers were digging into the steering wheel, and my shoulders were bunched as I tried to right the SUV. Just then the pickup slammed into the rear bumper, jerking us forward in our seats.

"Shit," Alex said.

I heard the click of Scotty's seat belt and pushed the gas pedal to the floor and felt the surge of speed hurl us forward, the SUV shaking as if it would implode.

Just ahead on the right, I saw a gravel road. "Come on, come on," I urged the SUV.

The road came up too fast, and I wrenched the steering to the right too sharply. For a moment, the SUV teetered on two wheels, and then it righted itself. Breathing a sigh of relief, I sped down the road, glancing in the rearview mirror. The truck was nowhere in sight.

"I think we lost him," I said, my eyes still glued to the mirror.

"Rose," Alex shouted, but it was too late. The road veered sharply left, then right. I yanked the steering wheel left, then right, but couldn't hold the road. The car hit the dirt shoulder on two wheels, I leaned my body away as if I could right the car myself. But it flipped over with a shattering sound, rocking back and forth until it came to rest, the tires spinning into silence.

I was hanging upside down by my seat belt. I took in a deep breath, the smell of gasoline filling my lungs. For some reason, the airbags hadn't deployed.

Everything was too dark and too quiet. Alex was hanging beside me. His eyes were closed and blood oozed down his face.

"Alex," I whispered. But he just hung there, unmoving.

I tried to see into the back seat, but couldn't get my head far enough around. "Scotty?" No response.

I pressed my seat-belt button trying to release it, but the pressure of my hanging body was jamming it. I pressed and punched at it several more times but couldn't dislodge it. Okay, now what?

Looking down, I saw something shiny—my silver pen, which must have fallen out of my purse. Wiggling my body right, I reached down for the pen, and a spasm of pain shot up my left leg, making my stomach churn. I touched my knee and felt a warm wetness soaking through my jeans. My knee was bleeding. Gently, I felt around my knee; it didn't seem broken. When I pulled my hand away, it was sticky with blood.

I wiped my hand on the car seat, and then reached down for the pen, this time steeling myself for the pain. Breathing through it, my fingers grasped the pen. Using the writing end, I punched at the seat-belt button until it snapped open, and I fell forward onto the inside roof of the SUV.

Shifting my body sideways toward Alex, I felt his neck for a pulse. He was still alive. Looking into the backseat, I saw Scotty's crumpled, motionless body. I had to get help fast. I wasn't sure where my purse was with my cell phone, but I'd remembered that I'd last seen Alex put his cell phone in his front pants pocket when he'd checked for messages after leaving Gatlinburg. In the cramped, hanging position, his body was folded over his pocket and I had to work my fingers into his pocket to retrieve his cell phone.

"What is the nature of your emergency?" the nine-one-one operator asked.

"There's been a car accident. Two people are hurt."

"What's your location, ma'am?"

I closed my eyes and tried to remember the exit.

"Ma'am, what's the location of the accident?"

"Right off Route One-Oh-Nine, the first road on the right after the gas station. We're on a gravel road. Our SUV flipped. Please hurry. They're unconscious."

"We'll be there shortly. Don't move anyone."

"Okay, just hurry."

I looked over at Alex, whose eyes were now open and staring at me. At first I thought he was dead, his stare was so intense. "Alex?" I whispered.

Suddenly he took in a deep ragged breath and said, "Don't."

"It's all right," I reassured him, "the ambulance is on its way."

"No." He began gasping for breath. He tried to lift his arm, but the pain of the effort caused him to moan. "Don't."

"Alex, take it easy."

"Promise me."

"Promise you what?" There was desperation in his voice.

"The drawing, don't give it to anyone, anyone." He was agitated and breathing hard.

"Calm down."

"Keep it. Promise. No one. Don't trust." Then his eyes closed.

"Alex," I said in a panic. "Alex."

When he didn't respond, I felt for his pulse again. Faint but steady, it beat against my fingers.

Suddenly a sweep of headlights lit up the SUV's interior and I turned and looked out the shattered window into the dark open field. Just as suddenly the lights went out. In their place, I heard the slow crunch of tires on the gravel, creeping toward me. My heart started thumping against my chest.

It's the truck that chased us, I thought. It's found us. And now it's coming to finish us off.

Frantically, I pulled back on the driver-side door handle and pushed on the door, but it creaked with resistance.

I've got to get out of here, I told myself as I inched back against Alex's seat. As I bent my knees, I felt the pain again in my left knee. Ignoring it, I brought my legs back, heels forward, and then thrust my feet at the door with all my strength. The door groaned open a few inches, not enough to allow me to escape, and the broken window's glass was too jagged to squeeze through safely.

Again I tried, but the door only gave another inch or so. As I heard the crunch of gravel and the truck coming closer and closer, my heart was racing. My purse, where was my purse? Even if I found it and dug out the pepper spray, how could I defend myself, trapped inside like a sitting duck?

Suddenly I didn't hear anything except the rattling hum of an engine. Then a door slammed. I held still, barely breathing as the sound of footsteps moved through the field toward the SUV. Whoever had chased us was coming for the drawing. I peered through the darkness, trying to see him. But the grass was too thick and tall. All I could do was listen helplessly.

Then like an answered prayer, the wail of a siren broke through the night.

I strained to hear over the siren. But I heard nothing else but the siren's whirling noise. Had he left? Was he still there, still walking toward the SUV? Did he think he could get the drawing before the ambulance arrived?

Headlights shot into the SUV like a laser beam, making me shield my eyes. Then the lights swept past, down the road, in the opposite direction, away from the loud wail of the ambulance.

I let out a deep sigh and said, "We're going to be okay. We're going to be okay." No one answered.

As I sat on the gurney in the hospital, I watched the shadows of the doctor and the nurse behind the blue-and-pink-striped curtain, trying to decipher their muffled voices as they worked to stabilize Scotty. He'd sustained a head injury, and there was bleeding in his brain.

Alex had already gone to X-ray for confirmation of the doctor's initial assessment—two fractured ribs. His head wound was superficial. The hospital was keeping him overnight, but he was expected to make a complete recovery.

In the ambulance on the way to the hospital, Scotty had coded once, and now he had a tube down his throat, a machine breathing for him, and blood pooling in his brain. I was sick with guilt. Scotty's life was in jeopardy because of me. I'd been the one who'd suggested he come with us.

"Do you think he's going to make it?" I asked the ER intern who was stitching the gash on my knee.

"They're transporting him to Mercy. It's a stage-three trauma center. They're used to dealing with head traumas like this. He's going to have the best of care."

He'd answered my question in doctor-speak, meaning Scotty might not make it. I'd been asking that same question since the EMTs arrived. And no one had given me the answer I wanted.

"You called his sister in Gatlinburg?" I asked.

"She's already on her way to the trauma center."

I winced as the doctor snipped the end of the stitches and placed a gauze bandage over my knee.

"Keep it dry for a week and make an appointment with your internist when you get back home."

He pulled the curtain open. "She can talk now," he said to the two cops waiting at the nurses' station.

Officer Somerville and Officer Walls were an odd pairing—a middle-aged white man and a young black female.

I explained that a man driving a pickup truck had been chasing us on the interstate; that I'd exited, hoping to lose the truck, and that it had continued chasing us. Then I'd turned too sharply on the gravel road, and had lost control of the car.

"And you didn't recognize the driver?" Somerville asked, arching his eyebrow in disbelief that I thought might be a chronic condition.

"No. All I could see was a baseball cap pulled low over his head."

"And you have no idea why anyone would be chasing you down the interstate, Ms. Caffrey? You didn't cut someone off or do something to incite this driver?"

I shook my head no. "Maybe the person was drunk," I offered. There was only one reason someone would be chasing us, and that was the Le Moyne drawing. But how this person knew we had the Le Moyne, I still hadn't figured out.

"And where were you and your friends going, ma'am?" Now Walls had decided to jump in.

"Virginia Beach." It was the first place that popped into my head. "Alex, Scotty and I are old friends." I was improvising as I went along. "You know, from college. We're on a road trip." The doctor had given me a mild painkiller, which seemed to have loosened my tongue and my imagination.

"Uh-huh," Somerville nodded. "Well, we have your information. If we need to talk to you again, we'll be in touch. And next time someone's chasing you, call the cops." He touched his hand to his head in a kind of salute.

"Wait. There's something else. I think the person waited around after. I saw headlights, and then when the ambulance was coming, the headlights went in the opposite direction."

The two cops looked at each other. Somerville's eyebrow went up again.

"Could have just been someone who stumbled on the scene and when they heard the ambulance decided to leave."

I was about to protest, to tell the two cops everything: from Karen's death, to being assaulted at the Newberry, to my suspicion that the driver had wanted to kill us. The whole nightmare. But that would mean telling them about the Le Moyne.

Alex's words echoed in my head: "Don't trust," meaning don't trust anyone.

"You're probably right. By the way, what happened to the stuff in the car?" I tried to sound casual, my fingers running up and down the edge of the bed.

Walls answered. "The car was emptied out and then towed to the police-station lot. You can pick up your things at the station in the morning."

"Can you take me there now? The hospital's discharging me, and I'll need to find a place to spend the night. I'd like to have my stuff."

"Sure," said Walls.

After the police drove me to the station, where I collected everything from the SUV, I'd signed a release form, taking ownership of the items. To my relief, the cedar box was there, undamaged. Scotty must have shoved it under the front seat when he'd put on his seat belt. Officer Walls suggested a bed-

and-breakfast in town where I could stay the night.

The bed-and-breakfast was a two-story Victorian house, called The Victorian Era, with lace curtains, brass beds, and rooms named after famous Victorians. I'd been given the Darwin Room. It seemed apt after everything I'd been through: Survival of the fittest. There was a portrait of Charles Darwin as an old man hanging over the bed, looking paternal and wise.

As I sat on the lacy duvet gazing at the portrait, I felt a vibration against my hip, reminding me that I still had Alex's cell phone.

I slipped it from my pocket and looked at the screen: Unknown caller. Who would be calling Alex at four thirty-five in the morning? I opened the phone and pressed send.

"You'd better not be fucking with me." I waited for the harsh voice to continue.

"Alex, you know the deal." Then the line went dead.

I stared at the phone's screen as if I could summon up the man's face, my stomach tight with nausea. Then I closed the phone and placed it on the bed as if it were a bomb. Rocking back and forth, hugging myself, I tried to stop shaking, tried to keep the nausea down. But it was no good. I ran to bathroom, flipped up the toilet seat and vomited. A cold sweat had broken out all over my body. I curled into a ball on the bathroom floor, staring at the white tile floor, that sick feeling still with me.

"You know the deal." The rasp of his words, like sandpaper inside me.

What deal had Alex made with this man? And when? From the first day Alex stood on my porch? Or later, when he realized what we'd found? Did it matter when? I'd been played, and he'd done the playing.

I got up slowly and ran the sink's tap, splashing water on my face, which looked gray and lifeless. Then I walked back into the bedroom and picked up the cedar box I'd placed on the doily-covered dresser. At least I'd had the presence of mind to retrieve it. As I opened the box, I inhaled its sharp cedar scent.

Carefully, I took out the drawing and held it up by the edges, marveling at its beauty and existence. How had it survived nearly 500 years? What stories could the drawing tell me about the people who'd possessed it? Now my story was a part of the other stories, as if we were all guardians of this moment when Le Moyne had put brush to paper, recreating the colors and forms of that day of what he saw and felt.

I was about to put it back in the box when something in the mirror caught my eye, something on the back of the drawing. I turned it over. On the back was a crude map of a coastline. Along the coastline ran a narrow shelf of land. Punctuating the drawing, printed in small uneven letters in three areas was the word *Confesionario*. The words formed a lopsided triangle—two points were on land and one was in the sea. In the middle of the triangle was a sinking ship. I had no idea what any of it meant or if it had any relationship to the drawing.

My cell phone was scattered among my stuff, and it was three fifty-seven A.M. Chicago time. I found my phone shoved in my backpack and speed dialed Nick. The phone rang and rang and just as it was about to go to voice mail, Nick picked up.

"This better be life or death, RT."

"There's been a car accident. Someone chased us off the road. Alex and this guy Scotty are in the hospital. I'm in big trouble, Nick. I have to get back to Chicago as soon as possible. You're not going to believe it, but I've found an original Jacques Le Moyne drawing. And there's this strange map on the back."

He let out a deep sigh. "What do you need?"

I picked up Alex's cell phone with my free hand. "To come home now."

Chapter Twenty-Four:
Chicago, Illinois

"You're going to the cops," Nick said. He had that knitted look around his forehead that meant he wasn't taking no for answer.

The Le Moyne sketch rested on a Plexiglas cutting board, where he'd put it after letting down the kitchen's bamboo shades against the intense afternoon light.

My knee was throbbing, and I was nursing a beer in lieu of pain pills. I'd slept the entire flight from Knoxville to Chicago, the cedar box stowed in my carry-on luggage. It wasn't liquid, you couldn't make a bomb out of it, and so it got through security with no questions asked.

"Too late for that," I countered. "I'm meeting Peter Morant at his loft in Printer's Row at seven tonight to get his opinion on the drawing." I'd called Morant from the airport and explained everything. I could hear the contained excitement in his voice. "It could very well be a fake," he'd cautioned me.

"On the back of the drawing, there's also a crude map of a coastline, with a sinking ship and the word *Confesionario* written three times," I'd countered as if I needed to prove to him the drawing was real.

"Then you called the right person. Maps are my specialty," Morant had said.

"And I'm going with you." Nick glanced at me, then resumed looking at the drawing. "I just can't believe this." It was the fifth or sixth time he'd said that. Then he ruffled my spiky hair as if I'd brought home a stellar report card, making me wince from pain. My head gash was still tender to the touch.

"Don't you have to be at the theater?" I didn't want Nick tagging along. A cab was picking me up on Southport at five-thirty P.M., allowing me plenty of time to get to Morant's place in Printer's Row.

A one-woman show was opening on the weekend. The show was based on the life of Jenny Cashier, the woman who'd served in the Civil War as a man. It was titled "Whose Side Am I On?" It was a comic rendition of the woman's life.

"I'll have Margaret run things until I get there."

I laughed. "You really hired her?"

"She makes thing happen. Not to mention that she scares everyone, even me. And her relatives, have you met her cousin the gangbanger?" He leaned back in his chair. "What about that bastard Hague? I wish he'd ended up in intensive care, not that poor guy Scotty."

Before I'd caught my flight to Chicago, I'd learned that Scotty was going to make it. But, until the swelling in his brain went down, no one could be sure if he'd have permanent damage. Alex was being released today.

"Once I know the Le Moyne is authentic and it's safe with Morant, then I'll deal with Alex," I said.

"Meaning?"

"That's when I call the cops."

"I don't get why you don't do that now. You know he was in on it. That phone call proved it."

"You don't have to get it," I snapped, instantly regretting my short temper. "Sorry. My nerves are fried. And really, Nick, I think it's better if I see Morant alone." I should call the cops. I should have Alex arrested. Was I holding out hope that I was wrong about Alex? Doubting my initial reaction that I'd been played? Too pitiful for words.

"Have it your way," Nick conceded, that knitted look evaporating.

"Don't I always?"

There was nothing industrial about Morant's loft, the openness filled with massive furniture and thick oriental rugs. The colors were a soothing blend of greens and browns and mauves, conducive to contemplation. Pen-and-ink lithographs graced the walls. Was that an original Turner? I wondered. Everything felt expensive and overly worked. His loft was in contrast to his casual Mick Jagger persona.

He'd greeted me holding a brandy snifter, a sly grin on his face.

"In celebration," he said, raising the snifter in a salute. "Would you like one?"

From the slight flush on his face, I suspected this wasn't his first of the evening.

"Maybe later," I said, wanting to keep my wits about me.

"Business it is," he said, ushering me down a long hallway into his study, a large room dominated by a big rectangular teak table and a library of books that spanned two levels. The curtains were already closed and the lights dimmed.

"So let's see it." He put his brandy snifter down on a side table and rubbed his hands together. His laid-back demeanor was replaced with nervous agitation that put me on edge.

Was it a mistake coming here? I questioned. After all, I'd been attacked at the Newberry on his watch. But if he wanted Karen's notebooks, he could have taken them before I showed up. In fact, I didn't even know about them until he told me.

I took my time opening the cedar box and taking out the drawing, holding it by its edges, and placing it in the center of the table.

"Hmm," Morant muttered to himself as he roved the drawing with a magnifying glass, meticulously examining it as if it were a body about to be autopsied.

Finally, he put the magnifying glass down and folded his arms, puffing out his generous lips. "Limning, or, as we say today, watercolor. That's what I think we have here. The pigments are made from naturally occurring colored earths. What the artist did was modify dyes from plants and insects. Which is right for the period."

I let out a deep breath, as if surfacing from under water.

"The paper shows discoloration, which, of course, could be easily faked. But, the style appears to be consistent with Le Moyne's work, and it has his signature."

There were a pile of books on the table, and he opened the top one and showed me Le Moyne's signature. As far as I could tell, the two signatures were similar.

"Of course, I'll need several months for more analysis. I'll send it to the lab the Newberry uses. They'll do paint and paper analysis, study in more detail the way the figures and landscape are drawn." He drummed his finger against his full lips.

"But you're thinking there's a chance it's authentic?" I asked.

Morant flickered a smile. "Oh, always a chance. Always that. But if I were a betting man and I'm not, I'd bet against it."

"Why?" I pouted like a kid who'd just been told she's been grounded.

"Two things: improbability and greed. From all historical accounts of the destruction of Fort Caroline, the Spanish under the direction of General Pedro Menendez de Aviles burned everything, including all the Le Moyne drawings. We have a firsthand account from a Father Alvarez, who in his journal claims to have found the work of 'a great mapmaker and necromancer,' which he fed to the fire. The Catholic Spanish thought the Lutheran French were devils needing to be slaughtered. How could a drawing survive?"

"And the greed?"

"A clever art forger trying to pass this off as the real thing," he added.

It felt like all the air had been sucked out of the room. "But no one knew this drawing existed or what it was until I found it hidden in a cedar box in an old woman's house, passed down through generations of her family. And it still would be there if it hadn't been for the murals and Emily Braun."

Morant moved his head side to side. "Provenance will be a part of this analysis as well. If what you say is true, then it might indeed be authentic."

"And the map on the back, what about that?"

"Yes, that intrigues me even more." He carefully turned the drawing over. "Definitively not drawn by Le Moyne. Much too crude, and *Confesionario* is a Spanish word." He was talking very deliberately, drawing out his words.

"I didn't think Le Moyne drew the map," I said impatiently, trying to goad him on.

"Ever since you described the map to me, Rose, I've been pouring over sixteenth-century maps of the American coastline. Your description of the ship is what sent me in that direction."

He bent down and retrieved a twelve-by-twelve leather artist portfolio, which was leaning against the table. From the portfolio he took out a nine-by-twelve map and placed it next to the crudely drawn map.

The map was fantastical, with large sea creatures swimming in the ocean, a full-masted galleon sailing toward a coastline littered with French names. On the right side, encased in an ornate frame crested with a fleur-de-lis, were a series of French words. I couldn't decipher most of the words except Floridae, Americae, Provinciae and Jacobo Le Moyne.

"Both maps are depictions of Florida based on sixteenth-century exploration. But what's most extraordinary about your map is, not only does it somewhat replicate Le Moyne's drawing of the coastline making it a map of exploration, it also is a map of experience."

"You mean it represents something that happened? That's why the ship is upside down. It's a shipwreck, right?" I could feel the rush of excitement.

He straightened up. "How much do you know about the ill-fated sixteenth-century French colony and Captain Jean Ribault?"

"Not much," I answered. "Just that the French Huguenots tried to found a colony in Florida, and the Spanish burned down their fort and slaughtered everyone."

"Uh-huh," he answered as if he hadn't heard me, his eyes still roving the map. "I think this map shows where one of Captain Jean Ribault's ships sank. And I think it was made by someone who was either a witness to the sinking or knew someone who was a witness."

"Jean Ribault?" I asked irritated.

"He was the French Huguenot captain who was carrying supplies to Fort Caroline. His fleet was destroyed in a hurricane, and he and his men were massacred by the Spanish at Matanzas inlet. Matanzas is the Spanish word for massacre. Some accounts of the massacre say that Menendez ordered Ribault's face cut off to be displayed in Spain as a trophy."

"Are you saying this is a treasure map?"

"Depends on what you call treasure," he said. "There wouldn't be any gold nuggets or large gemstones. But there could be dinnerware, personal jewelry, medallions, weapons, swords, and pikes. And if this happened to be Ribault's flagship, the *Trinité*, then you'd have his personal items. The historical value would be beyond compare. If any of these ships is found, it would be the oldest French shipwreck ever discovered in the New World. The monetary value, well, let's just say, maybe not a Mel Fischer find, but close."

"You mean the guy back in the eighties who brought up the *Atocha* and made millions?"

"Four hundred and fifty million dollars and lost his son and daughter-in-law in the process," Morant cautioned. "Look, this is all speculation, so I wouldn't get too excited. And this map could be inaccurate. Not to mention that coastlines change over time."

"But we have to pursue it. We can't just let it go." Why was he trying to discourage me?

"Let me handle it, okay? I'll fax a copy of the map to Matthew Singer in Saint Augustine, Florida. He's a marine archaeologist who's been searching for the lost fleet for years, but I don't think anyone's looked here." He pointed to the upside-down ship. "From all accounts, the ships went down between Cape Canaveral and Matanzas inlet. This map indicates that the ship sank north of Saint Augustine."

Morant picked up the old drawing and slipped it into a plastic sheath. Then he turned toward me. "It'll be a while until I know anything for sure."

"No," I said, my eyes fixed on the drawing in his hand.

Morant stared at me. "Like I explained, I need to have it analyzed. It'll be safe, if that's what you're worried about. I'll give you an official receipt from the library."

"That drawing belongs to Mrs. Arthur. You can't take it."

"I thought you wanted it authenticated? I can't do that unless I have the drawing."

"People have been hurt because of this drawing," I argued.

"And now they won't be."

"Someone wanted this enough to kill for it." My fingers itched to grab the drawing from Morant.

"All the more reason to let me handle this."

"No, I'm not leaving it with you. It was entrusted to me.

Give me Matthew Singer's information, and I'll contact him." The closed room, the brandy fumes, the casual way he was downplaying the drawing; something was wrong. My gut was telling me to take the drawing and run.

"You're making a mistake," Morant said, placing the drawing on the table as he jotted down Singer's phone number and e-mail address on a sheet of paper. "I'm telling you it'll be safe with me. You take it, and who knows what will happen to it and to you."

"I'll take that chance." I grabbed the drawing, the sheet of paper, and the cedar box and started for the door.

Morant called after me, "It's a mistake, what you're doing. That could be a priceless work of art. It needs to be protected. How are you going to do that?"

Chapter Twenty-Five

The sun was nearly down, and a gritty haze hung over the city as I ambled away from Morant's loft looking for a cab. Luckily, I spotted one on the other side of the street.

As I waited for the light to change, I thought of a dress I'd created for a public performance called Prophets—yards and yards of gray voile shot with yellow silk. I'd draped the long dress down the steps of the Mercantile Exchange. I lay there waiting, wishing someone would muddy the fabric with their shoes, make it all worthwhile. But everyone walked around the long dress and me as if I were the one contaminated, as if I were insane.

With the cedar box clutched in my arms like a baby, I wondered if I were sane.

Why hadn't I let Morant have the drawing? Because something in his demeanor was off. Nothing obvious, nothing I could name.

The light changed and I ran across the street to the waiting cab.

"Where to, lady?" the cabdriver asked as I sat back in the seat. Not sure what to do I gave him Nick's address and sat back, running my fingers up and down the worn wood grain of the cedar box, wondering how I was going to protect the drawing.

I was holding an art treasure of immeasurable value, heading to Nick's empty loft and a dark walk down a deserted alley.

Whoever was after it knew where Nick lived and where his theater was, so I'd have to think of somewhere else quickly.

Calling Nick was out. His phone would be off because of the rehearsal. Alex had betrayed me. Though he'd tried to warn me off, saying that we'd been set up from the beginning, it was clear from his cell phone caller he was working with or for someone.

What I needed was someplace unlikely, and someone I could trust. Once the drawing was safely stowed, I'd figure out what to do next.

As the cab wove its way through traffic, I kept glancing over my shoulder, trying to think of a safe place and a safe person.

"Something wrong?" the cabdriver inquired as he turned onto Lake Shore Drive and I craned my neck again to see who was behind the cab.

"What?"

"You keep looking out the back window like someone's after you."

"Actually," I paused, "my ex has been harassing me."

The cabdriver let out a disgusted grunt. "Men like that give all of us a bad rap. You take out a restraining order on the creep?"

"Lotta good it does." I was thinking of Karen and the restraining order she'd taken out on Jimmy Braun.

"What's his car look like?"

"Black pickup truck."

"Figures," the cabdriver said. "I'll let you know if I spot it."

"Thanks."

"No problem, lady. You want I should do a little detour, just in case he's back there?"

"Sure." As he turned off onto Fullerton, it hit me.

Quinn's Irish Pub and Restaurant, and Michael Quinn. Nick and Quinn went way back when they'd jointly owned an improv comedy club in the loop area on Washington Street. Quinn was the father Nick wished he'd had—kindly, street smart, a guy who'd made his money by working for it, not inheriting it like Nicholas Baxter, II.

I leaned forward. "And drop me right in front of Quinn's Pub on Southport. You know where it is?"

The cabdriver laughed, "You're kidding, right?"

The Cubs must have played a late afternoon game, because when I exited the cab in front of Quinn's Pub, the sidewalk was jammed with gaggles of twenty-somethings smoking and sporting Cubs wear, talking too loud and well into intoxication.

"You take care," the cabdriver cautioned as he counted his generous tip.

The door of the pub was propped open, and the bar was so crammed with people, I couldn't even see the stage where a soft tenor voice was singing a lilting tune about loss and green valleys to the accompaniment of a guitar. Whoever he was, he was one of the countless countrymen Michael sponsored in America over the years. "My way of paying back for all my success," he once told me.

As I elbowed my way through the tightly packed crowd, carefully clutching the box to my chest, I spotted Michael Quinn behind the bar, his shock of white hair and red-rimmed glasses a familiar beacon.

He must have seen me, because he waved and nodded in my direction. I was almost to the bar when someone poked me hard in the back.

"Hey, watch it," I said, turning my head around, shocked to see the greasy face of Jimmy Braun; his baseball cap pulled low, his large watery eyes boring into me with menace.

"Gotcha," he said grinning. Then he leaned in close. "That's a gun up against your spine in case you think I'm happy to see ya."

He put his free hand on my shoulder as if we were friends who'd just run into each other. "You're gonna walk outta here slow like. No fuss, no muss."

He shoved the gun into my back to make his point.

When I didn't move, he threatened me, "I'm not screwing with you, bitch." A cold sweat washed over me as I realized that I had no choice but to go with him.

"Now, move it."

My legs were trembling as I pushed my way through the wall-to-wall crowd, wanting desperately to catch Michael's eye, to let him know that I was in trouble. But Jimmy kept his hand on my shoulder, propelling me forward, his grip digging into my flesh. My only chance for rescue was if Michael saw me leave with Jimmy and thought it suspicious.

"Excuse me. Sorry," I kept repeating as I bumped into people hoping someone would hear the terror in my voice.

But no one did.

"Keep moving," he said as we emerged onto the sidewalk.

"Just take the box," I offered as he kept prodding me in the back with the barrel of the gun as we walked down Southport toward the dark alley. Why wasn't anyone noticing? Because they were all celebrating the Cubs' win.

"Too late for that."

When I reached the dark alley, I started to turn, but he stopped me.

"Keep walking until you reach the next corner, then go right."

I could scream and run, but he'd shoot me in the back. My only option was to wait for an opening. Jimmy Braun was careless, and careless people make mistakes.

As we turned onto the next street, I saw his black pickup truck ahead, parked away from any streetlamp.

"What are you going to do?" I asked when we reached the truck.

He pressed the remote. "Get in."

I climbed up into the cab, still holding the box. He kept the gun trained on me as he came around to the driver's side.

Once he was sitting behind the steering wheel, he took the box from me with his other hand and placed it carefully on the floor behind him.

"Put your seat belt on," he demanded.

Just as I clicked the belt in place, I saw his hand with the gun pull back sharply and then a terrible pain exploded on the side of my head. I felt myself slump into darkness.

Chapter Twenty-Six: Boston, Massachusetts, 1843

Emily's eyes fluttered open, the light from the windows making her blink several times as she slipped back into her body as if finding her way through a ravaged landscape. Her flesh felt flailed, her head throbbed; she had no idea where she was.

"You're awake," someone said, the voice too shrill, too close.

She turned her head on the pillow; she felt an aching in her neck. Lucy Nash Hyde sat beside her. What was she doing here? Lucy's blonde hair had faded to a drab brown, her once-rosy skin now pasty white and creased, all girlishness worn from her face. Even her blue moiré dress with its lacy collar looked matronly on her bony frame.

"Lucy?" she managed to say.

"Have I changed so much these past years?" Lucy gently pushed Emily's hair back from her forehead, letting her hand rest there for a moment. "Your fever's gone. Now we have to get your strength back. Annie's made some broth. I'll bring it up to you."

"How did I get here?" Emily asked, raising her arm as if she needed to assure herself that she could.

"I was hoping you could tell me that."

A jumble of images shot through her head, the last one, stepping down from the stagecoach in Boston. "Is it still September?"

Lucy laughed that same tinkling sound Emily remembered. "Barely just."

At the sudden realization of the two weeks she'd lost, tears trickled from the corners of Emily's eyes.

"Once you've eaten something and rested, I'm sure you'll remember." And then Lucy was gone as if she were a shadow that had flickered across the room.

Emily stared up at the plaster ceiling, her eyes following the rivered cracks that led nowhere. She raised her arm again and studied her hand, turning it back and forth as if it didn't belong to her. On the back was a deep wound that had scabbed over, still red and angry. As she examined the wound, the man's menacing face rose up, and his words hissed like snakes.

"What's the Injun boy to you, missy?"

Then she let her arm drop and she fell helplessly into sleep.

She was walking barefoot up a jagged, rocky trail that kept ascending and ascending, making her breath ragged and her head light. The boy led the way, his small frame was rippled in shadow, and she kept thinking he would disappear if she didn't keep up. Suddenly the trail ended in a cave where moss greened the stone and the boy stood, carving into the wall. The sound grated; the hunch of his shoulders looked feline. When he turned to show her what he'd carved, he was holding a knife—no longer the boy, but the man with the tobacco breath and pocked face, the man who meant her no good. She screamed and woke to too much light and Lucy standing in the doorway holding a tray, looking at her with a startled expression.

The broth tasted greasy and turned her stomach, but she let Lucy feed her. With every spoonful, she felt a rush of heat, and her body responded as if she had no control over it.

"Imagine my shock when you showed up at the back door in such a condition. It was well past nine o'clock at night. Your clothes, well, I've burned them. At first I didn't even recognize you." Lucy dabbed at the drop of broth running down Emily's chin, then raised another spoonful for her to sip. "I'm only glad Wendell was away on business. What would he have thought?" She tsked. "There would have been no end to his questions. You know how lawyers are."

Emily choked on the broth. "What have you told him?"

"What could I tell him? He already knew you were expected." Lucy shook her head. "As to your missing luggage and your state of"—she ran her tongue over his lips as if the word were there—"disarray, I said you were ill and somehow your luggage was lost. That was right, wasn't it?"

"Yes, I guess. I don't know." Emily searched her memory, but it was like a closed door. It was as if she'd stepped down from the stagecoach into blackness.

Then she remembered something. "What did you do with the book?"

"You mean those scraps of paper tied together with a ribbon and shoved inside your corset?" She shook her head from side to side. "They're over there." She pointed to the dark mirrored dresser on the far side of the room. "Why you hid them, and in your corset of all places, I don't understand. Who would want them anyway?"

"No one." Except me, Emily thought. The book, the drawings, were like shreds of her former self, a girl she'd lost touch with, a girl who had no idea what lay ahead of her. Some nights, she'd caress the pages lovingly, remembering how she'd begged the artist, Jacob Painter, to take her with him. If only he'd consented, how different her life would have been.

As if she too were lost in their past, Lucy said, "Weren't we foolish girls back then?" She let the spoon rest in the bowl and stared off toward the morning light.

"When your letter came asking to visit, I knew we would be friends again just like before."

How like Lucy to think the past could disappear as if it had never happened. "It was a long time ago," Emily said evenly, with no emotion in her voice.

Lucy idly turned the spoon in the bowl. "I was so sorry to hear about your son Charlie. Last fall, we almost lost Wendell, Jr., to typhus. But thank the Lord he recovered and has returned to boarding school." Lucy pursed her lips in a strained smile. "So how is Edward?"

At the mention of her husband's name, Emily felt her muscles tighten, a sick feeling in her stomach. This was the moment she'd wrestled with after she'd sent the letter to Lucy. What to tell her when she arrived; how to explain what she'd done?

For the first time, she really looked at Lucy, her delicate complexion, her unblemished hands, the fine fabric of her dress, all in harmony with the opulence of the room's thick Persian carpet, mahogany four-poster bed, tiger-maple side table, marble fireplace, heavy silk draperies. Lucy lived a life Emily had never known, even growing up on her family farm in Ohio. What did Lucy know of hauling water from a stream or chopping wood or losing a son?

She shifted in the bed. "I'm afraid that I wrote you under false pretenses. I'm not here for a visit. I'm here for your help."

"Has something happened to Edward?" Lucy looked aghast, her pale blue eyes wide.

There was so much to tell her, and so little belief she would understand. "No, Edward is well. At least he was when I left him."

"Left him? Emily, what have you done?" There was censure in her words.

Emily pushed herself up. "Lucy, you must let me say it in my own time and in my own way. You of all people know me best. When I left the academy so many years ago, it set me on a path, one that was without deviation." She wanted Lucy to know that the past was still with her and it carried a price. "I often thought that maybe Miss Wolcott was right about the teaching, and that's what I should have done. If only." She stopped herself. "No, too late for that."

If she'd the strength, she would have gotten out of bed and walked over to the windows that looked out on the other fine brick homes lining Beacon Hill with their wrought-iron gates and cobblestoned walkways. What she had to say needed distance. But she was trapped in this bed, clad in Lucy's cotton nightgown that smelled of lilac water and starch. She could stop now and spare Lucy. She could recover her health and leave. But where would she go? Where do women like her go?

"I have left my husband. I have traveled from Illinois to the hills of Tennessee with a Cherokee child who lost his parents during that horrible march. I nursed him back to health. And Lucy, he filled the hole in my heart that Charlie left. I thought in time I would do the same for him. But I came to see that I could never be his mother. No matter what I did, no matter what I said. I have lied and stolen to get here. And now you must help me. Because so many years ago you betrayed our friendship." Her tone had hardened, and she was sweating again. She knew she was being unduly harsh, and that the blame for what happened to her rested squarely on her own shoulders. But she barely knew herself anymore. The scar on her hand stood as a testament to what she was capable of doing to survive.

"Did Edward beat you? Is that why you left him?" Lucy's hand went to her breast, as if she were a character in a theatrical.

She wanted to say yes to ease Lucy's mind, but she was tired of her life of lies. "No, he never beat me. We were ill-suited from the start."

"I don't know, Emily. What will I tell Wendell?"

Emily watched the thin blue vein pulse in Lucy's temple.

"I'll leave that up to you."

Lucy shook her head as if she could dislodge everything she'd heard. "You ask too much. After all this time, to show up and ask me to condone you leaving your husband."

"Please, Lucy, just until I can make other arrangements. Maybe Wendell can help. He's a lawyer. He knows people. He can ask around, maybe someone needs a governess or a teacher. I have nowhere else to go." She should have lied. The anxiety on Lucy's face was palpable.

"But I would have to write Edward and let him know you are here. He must be going mad with worry. What if he comes here looking for you?"

"I left him a letter telling him I was taking the child home and would not return. That is all he needs to know. I said nothing about you."

"Why should I believe you after what you've done?"

"Because we once were friends."

There was a soft knock on the door followed by a man's voice. "Lucy?"

"Come in, Wendell. Emily's up and wants to meet you."

Before Emily could protest, Wendell Hyde strode into the room. He was a tall man with a long face and a prominent nose, a profile that would look good carved in stone. His ruddy complexion extended all the way to his domed forehead and into his thinning hair.

"So how are you feeling, Mrs. Braun?" He was flushed, clearly embarrassed by her state of undress.

"Much better, thanks to Lucy." Emily gazed pleadingly at Lucy, who looked away.

"Good. Well, you are most welcome in our home." He kept his eyes fixed on his shoes. "Well, I'll leave you ladies. No doubt you have much to catch up on. How long will we have the pleasure of your company, Mrs. Braun?"

"That's up to Lucy," Emily answered, her eyes still on her friend.

"We were just discussing that when you came in. It seems something tragic has happened." A pale blush crept up Lucy's neck to her face. "Emily's husband died suddenly. She's come here hoping we can find her a position."

Wendell's eyes widened. "My condolences on your loss, Mrs. Braun."

She could see from his quizzical expression that he knew his wife was lying, but he had the decency not to confront her in front of company. "Let me think on it," was all he said and then left the room.

"You are a poor liar," Emily accused.

"No matter. He'll help you. I'll make sure of it. He has a good heart. You have no idea how many cases he takes on for no money or in barter. And now he has joined forces with the abolitionists. Though I worry for his safety. Only last week he was pelted and booed at a rally. And this Friday he addresses the Anti-Slavery Society at the Lyceum."

"He fights for the freedom of slaves, and you worry about telling him I've left Edward?" Emily questioned.

"To Wendell, marriage is sacred and for life. Abolishing slavery is something altogether different." Lucy stood and picked up the tray. Her eyes narrowed as she said, "You've not changed at all, Emily Lord, not one bit. Still headstrong and feckless as ever."

Then she stomped out of the bedroom. Emily listened to her emphatic footsteps on the carpet like a rain of fists on her head. She might not like it, but Lucy would help her, of that she was sure, if only to be rid of her.

Chapter Twenty-Seven

Wendell Hyde punched his fist in the air and thundered, "In the face of danger our animal instincts compel us to be physically brave. But it takes a much higher and truer courage to be morally brave." His voice echoed up toward the vaulted parlor ceiling and drifted out through the large open windows fronting the cobblestone street into the warm October evening air.

As applause burst from the women, he dabbed at his sweating forehead with a handkerchief, then tugged on his cravat, waiting for the clapping to die down.

Again, Emily glanced toward the windows behind her and then at the two former slaves, Angela Wright and Pauline Perkins, sitting across the aisle from her. Did no one see the danger? She wondered, as panic coursed through her, gaining in momentum as every word and every sound reached the street feeding the frenzy of the gathering mob.

She tried to take in a deep breath to calm her nerves, but Lucy's borrowed dress was so snug, she couldn't. Nervously, she clutched at the dress's silky black fabric, working it between her fingers, shuttling down her fear.

The ruse of changing the Anti-Slavery Society meeting from the Lyceum to the Moreland house on Beacon Street had failed. Right now there had to be fifty men outside. Some were holding torches; others were shouting epithets. And Wendell seemed oblivious to it all.

Prior to his speech, Angela and Pauline had shared their

stories of whippings and lost children, and finally freedom in voices as strong and powerful as Wendell's.

As Emily had listened to their stories, unbidden memories erupted, and though she gnawed on the inside of her mouth so hard she'd drawn blood, she couldn't stop herself from remembering that afternoon on the mountain trail—the rocks digging into her back as the man held her down, the knife at her throat, his hand moving under her skirt, the way he said *whore* as if it were a reason; the crack of bone as she bashed his skull, the blood spewing, erasing his brown eyes, the slump of his body, the leer of surprise. She'd left him there on the trail and grabbed Talking Bird's frail arm, yanking him forward, not looking back to see if the man lived. Neither of them saying a word. Not until they'd walked for a long time did she notice the wound on her hand.

Now she thought she'd jump out of her skin if Wendell didn't stop shouting. If only she could clamp her hands over her ears to block the fevered pitch of his words, which were like needles going in and out of her brain.

For the past hour he'd argued for disunion, and though Emily was persuaded by his fiery oration and sympathetic to the slaves, her attention had been riveted on Charlotte Moreland, who sat on the makeshift dais beside Wendell and who, according to Lucy, might be able to find her a governess position in East Weymouth. Mrs. Moreland's sharp nose fitted her thin lips that looked as if they could bite snakes. She would be a hard woman to fool, thought Emily.

"I've told her all about you," Lucy had said that morning, beaming. "And she's agreed to meet you. If you attend Wendell's lecture, she'll think your heart is in the right place."

Even if it isn't, Emily had wanted to say, but instead said nothing. Lucy was helping her find a position as she'd promised. That she did it grudgingly was of no consequence.

The angry hum of the men increased in intensity, interrupting Emily's musings.

"Lucy," Emily whispered as Wendell ended his speech to enthusiastic applause. "Maybe we should leave now. The mob outside is growing."

"They just want to intimidate us." Lucy dismissed Emily's concern with a wave of her hand. "Don't you want me to introduce you to Charlotte? Come."

Reluctantly Emily followed Lucy across the parlor to where Charlotte Moreland was chatting with Pauline Perkins.

As Emily waited for Mrs. Moreland to finish her conversation, she studied her impeccable dress and coiffed hair more closely. Lucy had told her that when Mrs. Moreland first joined the antislavery movement, others thought her a spy. But her dedication and fervor won them over.

"Charlotte, this is the old friend I told you about," Lucy said. "Emily Braun."

Charlotte reached out and took Emily's hand in hers. "My condolences on the loss of your husband," she said.

"Thank you, Mrs. Moreland." Emily kept her eyes down, afraid the woman would read the truth there.

"Please call me Charlotte. Now, I know of a family in East Weymouth that is looking for a governess for their two young children. They've had the hardest time finding someone suitable. Come to my house tomorrow for tea and we'll chat."

"I would be most grateful," Emily answered, taken aback by the woman's directness.

"Then it is settled. Tomorrow at one o'clock. What did you think of Wendell's lecture and his proposal for disunion?"

"I'm not sure if—" Emily began when a loud explosion sent shards of glass into the room, followed immediately by loud pounding on the front door.

"They're breaking in! They're breaking in," one of the women cried.

All at once the women began rushing from the room and out into the hallway. In hurried frenzy, several women stumbled and fell. Emily saw one woman was bleeding profusely where a shard of glass had pierced her cheek.

"Ladies, ladies!" Charlotte's deep voice bellowed through the panic. "Do not let them see you are afraid. Then they have won."

Charlotte's butler pushed through the crowd of frightened women to Mrs. Moreland. She whispered something to him, then he hurried out of the parlor.

"I've sent for the police," she told the women. "I'll distract the mob. The rest of you exit out the back of the house."

The room quieted as Charlotte walked out, her footsteps clicking on the green marble floor with Wendell close behind her. Emily watched from the parlor doorway as Charlotte opened the front door to the surprised looks of two men who were holding a large wooden log as a battering ram. Behind them, gathered on the stone steps and down into the street, were the rest of the mob, some holding torches, some guns.

"This is a private residence," Charlotte said, her shoulders back, her voice stern. "The police will be here shortly. Now, go home before they arrest the lot of you."

"Who do you think you are, telling us what to do?" The larger of the two men standing on the stoop shouted at her. "We know for a fact that you have runaway slaves in there. Bring them out and we'll leave you be."

Wendell stepped in front of Charlotte. "We'll do no such thing. This is a free state."

The man spat in Wendell's face, then shoved him in the chest so hard he fell backwards into Charlotte, causing them to tumble to the floor.

A cheer went up from the mob as the man walked inside the foyer. He was holding a rope. "Jed, let's get him."

The two men reached down for Wendell and hoisted him to his feet, dragged him outside and down the stone steps to the waiting mob. Lucy started to scream, "No, no!"

Emily scurried into the hall and helped Charlotte to her feet. "Are you all right?" she asked.

"We have to stop them." Charlotte ran down the steps toward the unruly men.

For a moment, Emily stood still, not knowing whether to chase after Charlotte or see to Lucy. Then she heard Charlotte shout over the jeers of the men, "You will not do this. Let him go!"

Emily hiked up her skirts, ran to the door and down the steps just as one of the men was slipping a rope around Wendell's waist.

"Stop, I demand you stop," Charlotte continued.

The men ignored her as they tightened the rope and pulled on it, making Wendell lose his balance and fall face-first in the street. He struggled to his feet while the men laughed at him. Then they began dragging Wendell down the street, stumbling and lurching as he held onto the rope, trying to remain upright.

Charlotte started after them, but Emily held her back. "There's nothing you can do now. To follow will make things worse for him and for you."

Charlotte let out a deep sigh of resignation.

When they reentered the house, Emily found Lucy collapsed on a settee, sobbing uncontrollably amid the scattered glass and overturned chairs. The rest of the women were gone.

"I'm sure the police will find Wendell in time." Emily tried to console her.

"What do you know?" Lucy hissed at her. "You're nothing but bad luck."

A horrible silence fell between them once they arrived home. Lucy refused to change out of her dress or go to bed and insisted on sitting in the parlor to wait for news of Wendell. Exhausted, she finally fell asleep in Wendell's chair, snoring softly, with her mouth open and her head back.

For Emily, sleep eluded her as she watched the night deepen, heard the patter of rain on the windows, the heat finally breaking as a cool breeze shuddered into the room. Lucy's words haunted her. How often she'd thought the same thing: that she was bad luck. That whatever she touched soured, from her marriage to her son to the Indian boy—every impulse seemed fated and tinged with sorrow.

As the room lightened with dawn, she came to a decision. If Wendell didn't survive, she would return to Edward. It would be a just punishment.

A loud rapping at the front door startled Emily from her thoughts.

"Wendell," Lucy said, suddenly awake. They both hurried to the door, opening it to a bruised Wendell.

"Oh, thank the Lord, thank the Lord," Lucy cried out as she threw her arms around him. "Are you hurt? What happened? Did they let you go?"

"Let me come inside, dear, and I'll tell you everything."

Lucy led Wendell into the parlor and sat him down in his chair, taking off his socks. His shoes were gone as well as his jacket, his shirt torn and bloody. He was covered in a thin layer of dirt that caked around his mouth and the creases in his skin. Both eyes were blackened, one swollen shut. His nose looked broken.

"If the police hadn't gotten there in time. I'd'a been strung up in Market Square, of that I have no doubt."

Lucy let out a stifled cry. "You can't do this anymore, Wendell. It is far too dangerous. Charlotte will understand."

She was kneeling beside his chair. He patted her head paternally. "I'll take more care, that's all. Now I am parched and in need of something to drink."

Emily still stood in the doorway, uncertain of her place. "I'll make tea."

When she came back into the room with the tea, Lucy's head rested on Wendell's arm. There was such intimacy between them, Emily had to look away, then felt the familiar sour loneliness.

"I'm glad you're home safe," she said, putting the tray down on the side table and pouring tea for Wendell and Lucy.

"Join us, please," Wendell requested wearily.

"It's been a long night," was all she said, then left and went to her room.

I will not think of it, she schooled herself as she undressed, slipped into Lucy's nightgown and climbed into bed. Yet the scene would not leave her, nor the jolt of what she saw, the raw love of their marriage, how lonely it made her feel. As she lay staring at the light pressing against the windows, she thought of how much she desired to be gone.

Chapter Twenty-Eight

"I'm so relieved to hear that Wendell has escaped with only minor scrapes," Charlotte Moreland said as she leaned forward in her chair and took a cherry tart from the silver platter. "Now, tell me about your drawing abilities. Lucy says you're quite good." She bit into the tart before placing it on her china plate, then licked the tiny bit of jelly at the corner of her mouth. Decorum was not something she concerned herself with, Emily observed, immediately feeling herself relax.

The question seemed to hover over Emily as she tried to think how to answer it. Explaining her drawing was as difficult as explaining the silk Persian carpet at her feet—borders within borders, reds and oranges and blues woven, every knot a secret tied tightly and held.

"Could I show you instead?" She placed her china teacup and plate on a table and took from her reticule one of the drawings she'd kept hidden inside her corset during her dangerous journey from Illinois to Boston. It was a portrait of Jacob Painter as he was that day when he sat painting Carrie's death portrait. After she'd written Edward, accepting his proposal, she'd drawn the portrait so she wouldn't forget Painter's expression, the intensity of his body, the coldness of the room. Even now the sight of it brought it all back to her in a flurry of emotions.

She stood and handed the drawing to the woman.

Charlotte's eyes traveled over it as if she needed to memorize every detail. "You drew this?" she asked doubtfully, looking up at Emily.

"Yes. Some time ago, but it is my work."

"This is most surprising—and mysterious," Charlotte said, now smiling slyly, arching her dark eyebrows. "Most mysterious indeed."

"Mysterious? What do you mean?" A prickling of fear shot through Emily.

"Come with me," Charlotte directed. "You'll understand when I show you."

Emily followed Charlotte out into the marbled foyer, up the spiral staircase to the second floor, where every room she walked past seemed dedicated to light. Finally they reached the end of the hallway where Charlotte walked into the last room on the right. Emily stepped inside, then gasped, putting her hand over her mouth, barely breathing.

Surrounding the exquisite bedroom with its pristine white silky linen, rich furniture, and bay windows were three walls of murals.

"I can see it in your face. You know him, don't you?" Charlotte's voice filtered through her amazement.

She tried to deny it. "What do you mean?"

"Why, the man whose portrait you drew here." She hit the paper with the back of her hand. "Jacob Painter. You recognize his murals."

Hearing his name after all these years made Emily feel light-headed. She grasped one of the bedposts to steady herself.

"When did Jacob paint these?" she asked, all sense of propriety gone.

"Last year. He came round with his uncle, Rufus Porter. Maybe you've heard of him?"

Emily nodded her head yes, not trusting herself to say more.

"Now, you must answer my questions. If I'm to recommend

you to my friend, Grace Smart, in East Weymouth, I must know what you're about." She sat down in one of the white damask wing chairs by the bay window, patting the companion chair for Emily to join her. "Sit and tell me how you came to paint his portrait and what was he to you?"

Emily perched on the edge of the chair, the lace curtains softening the sunlight across her face as she told Charlotte about Jacob Painter and Miss Wolcott, Carrie Barnes and Lucy, leaving out her suspicions about Dr. Clayton; and ending with that awful day she begged him to take her with him. With each word, each sentence, she felt lighter. All those years of never speaking about that time now washed clean. If Charlotte was shocked, there was no trace of it on her strong handsome face.

"I'm not going to recommend you to Grace right now," Charlotte stated with finality. She rose from the chair and started for the door, motioning to Emily to follow. "I'd like you to do something for me, in trade."

Why didn't I lie? Emily reprimanded herself as she hurried after Charlotte. Now what will I do when Lucy tires of me?

They walked down the hall to the staircase leading to the third floor, which opened into a large room with bare whitewashed walls.

"Jacob Painter was to paint these, but he and his uncle left suddenly. Before you ask, I don't know why. One day they were here, and the next they were gone. Take this commission, and you can live here while you do the work, and then if I'm satisfied with you and the murals, I'll write Grace. What do you say?"

"You really mean it?" Emily could hardly believe what the woman was offering—a place to live, a place to paint.

"Oh, Emily, I never say things I don't mean. You'll soon find that out about me. Life is too brief for pretenses. We share that belief, don't we." It wasn't a question.

She turned to leave, then stopped. "You were the only person beside Wendell not afraid of the mob. I don't care what you've done in your past. You have courage."

"You said in trade?" Emily asked still hardly believing the woman's offer.

Charlotte smiled. "Why, the rest of your story. The parts you didn't tell me."

Chapter Twenty-Nine:
Anna, Illinois, Present Day

Everything was still except for the sound of a shovel slicing through the ground, followed by dirt falling with a thump. Slice, thump; slice, thump. I'd awakened when Jimmy Braun had stopped somewhere well off the highway, feigning unconsciousness as he tossed me into the bed of his truck, afraid he'd finished me then and there. After he'd tied a plastic tarp snuggly around me, my head roiled with dizziness and I felt sick.

Then I must have fallen asleep. Because now I lay on the ground, encased in a chemical-smelling shroud, listening to Braun dig what I guessed was my grave.

Where I was, I had no idea. Some isolated place where the crickets paused with every slice and thump. And the trees creaked with the wind. Even if I shouted, no one would hear me. And then the business end of Braun's shovel would come crashing down on my skull.

Did he think I was dead? I wondered. If I ripped through the plastic and started running, could I get away? I'd rather die trying to escape than suffocating in my own grave. I just had to wait until he'd dug down deep enough that he couldn't get out of the grave easily and I'd have a running chance. By the muffled sounds of the slice and thump, it wouldn't be long now.

Suddenly I heard footfalls off to my left. "Took you long enough," Braun barked, his voice echoing up from the hole.

"Why didn't you get rid of the body in Chicago?" The man's voice was clipped with anger. "You could have thrown it in the lake." I froze, afraid to breathe, afraid to give myself away.

"No one's gonna think of looking for her here," Braun answered. "You gonna help or what?"

"You're sure she's dead?"

"If she isn't, she soon will be." Braun chuckled. "You can check if you want. If you have the stomach for it."

No, I cried inside. Please, please don't.

Again, the shovel sliced into the ground, the dirt landing near my head this time. Who was Braun's accomplice?

"Shut up. You screwed this up from day one. You weren't supposed to kill her. I told you, just get the box with the drawing. Why'd you have to kill her?"

A wave of nausea erupted into my throat. I swallowed it down. I recognized the voice from Alex's cell phone. This was the man Alex had been working with, or for. How was I going to get away from him *and* Braun?

"What's the matter, Professor? I thought dirty work was your specialty? Oh, I guess that's what you've got me for, huh? You better come up with the money, or your ass is mine."

Professor, dirty work. Lawrence Grey—he was behind this.

"Are you really that stupid?" Grey spat back derisively.

"Don't call me that. If it weren't for me, you'd never have them diary pages. So who's stupid, huh?"

"That's deep enough," Grey said. "Let's get this over with."

I heard Braun grunt as he climbed out of the hole, the slap of his hands flinging dirt on the tarp. "Could use some help heaving the bitch in."

Silence. I waited. Should I risk running now? I started to tear at the tarp, when Braun yelled, "What are you doin'?" His voice up an octave.

"Back away," Grey demanded.

"You son of a—" The explosion of a gun cut Braun's curse off as his body thudded to the ground. This would be my only chance. I had to take it. Grey had a gun, but I had the element of surprise.

I ripped open the tarp, jumped up, and started running just as Grey was rolling Braun's body into the grave. It only took me a second to realize where I was—a few yards from the woods beside the old farmhouse. I pumped my arms and legs harder. I had to make it to the woods before he got a clean shot at me.

One bullet whistled near my ear. Then another. I hunched and continued running. I was almost there. I could see the path through the trees like an opening to another world. I was going to make it. Then, just as I reached the woods, I felt a sharp sting in my left arm. But I kept running, adrenaline coursing through my body. My arm burned, my head was pounding, but I'd made it. The woods closed over me as I raced down the muddy path.

Grey was close behind me. I had to lose him somehow. At the next curve in the path, I veered off into a dense copse of trees cloaked by the moonless night. Grey ran past me, and then I didn't hear anything.

He must have realized that he'd lost me because I heard him hurrying back my way. I moved farther and farther into the trees, the blood dripping down my arm. As I crept, I searched for a tree branch, a rock, anything I could use as a weapon against Grey. Finally, I spotted a thick branch, picked it up and crouched behind a tree. My heart was thumping, my breathing labored.

The rustling of the leaves as I crouched down must have alerted Grey, because I heard his footsteps coming toward me. I would have one chance to swat him. Hiding behind the tree, I waited, the branch heavy in my hand, the blood moving down my arm.

Then I saw him.

"Rose," he called out. "You're not going to get away. You

should have taken Hague's advice and backed off. Now look where you are? Just where Karen was. Did you know that cow thought I was in love with her? Streets brains, she didn't have any, and it got her killed. But you do."

Shaking with rage and horror, it was taking all my willpower not to leap out at him and give away my advantage of surprise.

"C'mon Rose. You're trapped."

He was standing in front of the tree I was hiding behind. I held very still. Then in the silence, a drop of my blood plopped onto the leaf-strewed ground.

"Gotcha," he said as he came around the tree with the gun extended.

As soon as I saw the gun, I blasted his arm with the branch, heard the crack of bone as he let go of the gun, and he fell to his knees writhing in pain.

I grabbed the gun and pointed it at him. "Get up," I demanded. My arm was trembling and I had to use my other hand to hold it steady.

Slowly he stood, clutching his arm and moaning.

"Now, start walking. And don't think I won't shoot you." I tried to sound tough, but my voice shook.

With the gun trained on his back, we started for the path. As we walked, I studied the set of his broad shoulders, his matted dark hair. What had turned him from an academic to a murderer and a thief?

"Why?" I finally asked. "I have to know."

He kept walking and then said, "Money. What else?"

I needed to keep my mind from the blood dripping from my arm and the searing pain. "You couldn't sell the drawing at auction," I reasoned.

He let out a snide laugh. "Do you know what a collector would pay for the only surviving Le Moyne drawing? Millions. Hague already had a buyer lined up. At least that's what he told me. I never trusted him. But apparently you did."

At the mention of Alex's name, my stomach tightened and I felt sick.

"But you're a respected geologist at a university. You have a long career ahead of you." Even as I said it, I knew how romantically naive it sounded.

He laughed, then groaned in pain. "You know what a respected geologist makes? *Nada.* Do you know how much of your life is eaten up with studying, and research, and students? For what? A tenured job with benefits, a book no one reads. I was sick of living in gentile poverty. I deserved better."

I thought of Karen and how much of her life she'd devoted to her work and how in the end it had gotten her killed.

"It was you who attacked me at the Newberry, wasn't it?"

"Guilty as charged."

"And Alex, where did he fit into all this?" I couldn't help myself. I had to know.

He stopped and turned around. He was smirking. I raised my arm higher and held the gun at his face. "How did he do it?" he asked grinning.

"Do what?" My arm shook. In the darkness of the forest, his deep-set eyes seem to disappear into his face.

"How did he get you to trust him? I never did. Your sister didn't."

"Get moving," I demanded, that sick feeling roiling around inside me again.

He shrugged, turned and continued walking. "Your sister was such a hard-assed bitch."

Was he trying to get me mad so I'd let down my guard? It wasn't going to work.

When I didn't answer, he continued, "I knew she was hiding something, something to do with that house. Then, when Braun showed me the diary pages . . . Well, all I had to do was wait while Alex worked on the walls and you, stripping you both down."

I ignored his taunt. "What was in the missing diary pages?"

We were almost at the edge of the forest. "A description of a very old drawing Emily Braun called *Confesionario* with the initials JLM. Then she went into detail saying something like, 'I'm using it to practice my drawing.' She had no clue what she possessed."

"And Alex kept feeding you our every discovery," I said more to myself than to him.

"Still holding out hope he's redeemable, huh? Well, he isn't."

But Grey had threatened Alex after the car accident, suggesting Alex wasn't going along with their plan. "And the diary pages, what did you do with them?" I said to stop myself from asking about Alex.

"I'm done talking."

We emerged from the woods and walked past Braun's grave toward the burnt-out farmhouse where Grey's truck and Braun's were parked side by side behind the house. I took in a deep breath, inhaling the earthy night smells.

"Where's your cell phone?" All the fight was draining out of me.

He pointed at his truck. "In the glove box."

"Get it."

He retrieved it and handed it to me.

"Nobody was supposed to die," he said, shaking his head as if he were an innocent bystander, all his arrogance suddenly gone.

"Tell it to Jimmy," I countered.

When I reached the nine-one-one operator, I told her there'd been a shooting and then I asked for Officer Dade. "I've got my sister's killer," I said to him, my voice flat as rain as I fought back tears. "I'm at the old farmhouse."

Chapter Thirty:
East Weymouth,
Massachusetts, 1845

The light was nearly gone as Emily stepped back from the mural to view her work. So much of home was there—the biblical scene so like the one she'd drawn in the farmhouse where Charlie died—the enormous trees bordering the edges of the walls, the tropical setting, the inlet spilling out toward the sea that reached nowhere. The billows of smoke, where the altar perched high on the hill, and Abraham obeying God as he prepared to sacrifice his only son, Isaac. And Sarah on her knees, weeping into her hands.

"Are you through, my dear?" A man's voiced called from the next room.

Emily placed the paintbrush on the palette, wiped her hands on a paint-smeared cloth and walked into the next room. Her step felt light and sure as her skirts brushed the wood floor. She thought she'd never felt so whole.

Even at fifty-three, his back was straight and his hair, though streaked with white, was thick. And those piercing blue eyes that always seemed to be sizing something up were still full of intelligence and wit.

That he should come to East Weymouth, she mused. That Grace Smart should introduce them. That he should ask for her help. It all still seemed fantastical.

"What do you think? More blue in the water?" Rufus Porter tapped the end of the brush on his bottom teeth, a habit reminding her of his nephew Jacob Painter. At the memory of Jacob

Painter, she felt a pang of sorrow. She'd never see Painter again in this life. Porter had told her he'd died two months ago in Maine.

She gazed at the scene depicting Moses striking the rock, her head tilted, her hands on her hips. "You seek my opinion?"

"I seek everyone's. That's what itinerant painters do. Now, the waterfall. More blue or not?"

"No more blue, maybe a tinge of white along the edges," Emily answered with more confidence than she felt.

"You're right. Now, let's see what you've done."

They walked into the adjacent bedroom. He'd only glanced briefly at the mural when she'd begun it. He told her, he preferred to let his assistants find their own way. And if they got lost, he'd put them on the path again.

"Fine, most fine," he said, approaching the mural. "You've followed my instructions well."

"Shall I sign it or you?"

For a moment he stared at her quizzically, then answered. "What do you think?"

The question made her pause. Was he really suggesting that she could put her initials to the work?

Emily picked up the paintbrush, dapped the tip in the inky black and printed RP in the lower right corner of the biblical mural.

He chuckled as he saw what she'd done. "You're too modest. Or did you think this is what I wanted?"

"A little of both," she said, a smile playing around her mouth.

"No matter. It is a fine mural. One I'm glad to have my name on."

After he walked out of the room, she gazed at her work.

Some things, she mused, can't be known.

Chapter Thirty-One:
New York, New York,
Present Day
Six Months Later

Sotheby's salesroom was packed. I could almost smell the money as I stood at the back next to the New York arts reporter, George Finley, a paunchy middle-aged man dressed in a navy sport coat and cross trainers, my eyes scanning the crowd.

George whispered in my ear, "Not a haircut under five hundred bucks."

"Who's that man in the pinstripe suit holding the telephone to his ear?"

"You mean the guy who looks like he has a rod up his 'arse,' as the Brits say?"

"Yeah, that one," I chuckled.

"Reginald Browne, Queen Elizabeth's representative."

"It seems Mrs. Arthur's ship is finally going to come in," I responded, glancing at the back of Scotty Parker's shaved head in the front row. He'd made a full recovery, no brain damage, and was at the auction to oversee Mrs. Arthur's interests.

"And yours," George added.

Mrs. Arthur had insisted that I receive a finder's fee, which at first I'd refused. But when she'd said it would be in honor of my sister Karen, I accepted, settling on one percent of the selling price. Depending on what the Le Moyne fetched at auction, I stood to receive anywhere from $100,000 to who knows.

As the gray turntable whirled around and the Le Moyne drawing appeared, restored to its full splendor, a gasp rippled through the audience. Even from here I could see the vivid

The Lost Artist

colors that Jacques Le Moyne applied over 400 years ago, right down to the grooved design on the altar stone.

As if he'd read my mind, George asked, "Received any more fringe theorists' interpretations of the markings?"

"Not since the article came out quoting the consensus of the team of epigraphers, archeologists, and art restorers that the markings were decorative." The discovery of the Le Moyne had garnered international press, along with crackpots who'd been contacting me about the stone altar inscriptions when they'd hit a wall with Sotheby's.

George flipped back a few pages in his notebook. "My favorite is the amateur linguist in New Mexico who claims the inscription is an alien language and means 'live long and prosper.' "

Some of the theories, though, did give me pause. Like the one from the retired professor in Australia who claimed the marks were an ancient Celtic alphabet called Ogam. The alphabet consisted of symbols and was used by the Celts for secret communication and divination. He deciphered the markings to mean Stone of Taranis, purporting that Taranis was a Celtic thunder god. He explained that sacrificial offerings were made to Taranis, so the markings on the altar fit.

His e-mail was so detailed and self-assured, I'd run his theory past Helene Ramirez Roundoak, who'd dismissed it as wishful thinking.

"Yes, there's an ancient Celtic alphabet called Ogam, and there's a Celtic thunder god named Taranis. But the marks don't correspond closely enough to the alphabet to be decipherable." Then her tone turned dark. "I can't believe I was so wrong about Alex."

"He fooled a lot of people," I said dismissively. "Anyway, thanks again for your help."

"Quiet, please." The auctioneer leaned on the small podium, waiting for the crowd to settle down. Then he began, "Lot number seven hundred forty-nine. The only drawing made in America to survive from the work of the sixteenth-century artist and explorer, Jacques Le Moyne, the first European artist to record images of the Native American tribe, the Timucuans. The drawing is a watercolor, done on glazed paper, and depicts a native ritual sacrifice. On the back of the drawing is a map thought to have been made by an eyewitness to the sinking of the lost fleet of Captain Jean Ribault. The opening bid is ten million dollars."

A paddle went up in the second row. It belonged to a gray-haired man with a prominent nose and bushy eyebrows.

"Representative of the Louvre," George explained. "Looks like they want their countryman back home."

"We have a bid of ten million," said the auctioneer. "In the second row, at ten million. Who'll say eleven million?"

As Reginald Browne's paddle went up, I glanced at my watch. Six-thirty. I had an hour before my performance at the Chelsea art gallery Spun. A cab was waiting out front for me.

"Let know me how it turns out." I tilted my head toward George.

"I'll stop by the gallery afterwards."

"I have a bid of eleven million," the auctioneer's voice faded as I left the room and hurried outside to the waiting cab. For the first time in my life, I didn't watch the cab meter. Instead I sat back and thought about what I was about to do.

The red silk dress fit like a second skin. As I fluffed the blonde wig around my face, I listened to the steady hum of voices in the next room. Clare Tyler, Spun's owner, told me that people had started to arrive an hour ago, fueled no doubt by the publicity surrounding the Le Moyne auction, the ancient map, Lawrence Grey's arrest, and the murders of Karen and Jimmy Braun.

As I entered the dimly lit gallery I gasped, overcome with the installation that was my life. The overturned ladder, the strewn books, the mural walls—I felt like I was flung back to that horrible night when I'd found Karen's broken body. The irrevocability of my loss made real. For the umpteenth time I questioned what I was about to do. Though for me the installation was a tribute to Karen, her dedication to unearthing the secrets behind the murals, indirectly leading to the resurrection of one of the world's greatest lost art treasures, would others see it that way?

Then my eyes roamed the walls, letting the murals once again possess me—the farmhouse mural, the mural of Litchfield, Connecticut, the lone house with Talking Bird and his mother in the windows, the Pentimento wall with the overlapping drawings melding time.

I walked to the farmhouse mural, picked up the front hem of the red silk dress and pressed the ribbony trail of the hem to the road that led from the farmhouse to the cemetery ripe with rows of blackbirds. Each blackbird was a feathery V of my shorn hair dyed dark. Then I unfurled the dress slowly and carefully, inching backward to the middle of the room. The dress's train was ten feet long, made of the finest silk and weighing about eight pounds. I felt its weight, and it grounded me as it flowed from the mural like a thick stroke of paint.

"You need help?" Clare asked.

"No," I said, easing myself down onto the floor, flaring the red silk around my body as if it were splattered blood. Then I froze with my eyes staring upward, one hand behind my head, the other flung carelessly by my side.

Clare stood over me. "Looks good," she commented. "Now for the onslaught."

I heard the door open and people file into the room.

"*Sisters,* by Rose Caffrey," she said. "Feel free to interact with the dress. Refer to the catalogue for the story of these remarkable murals, which, as we speak, are being restored at the southern Illinois farmhouse."

Clare had a videographer recording the installation, which she would show as a separate event at the gallery. I lay so still and unmoving that people acted as if I really were dead, walking on the dress, talking freely.

"Doesn't say here, but I heard her sister was murdered. Is that who she's pretending to be? Kinda gruesome, don't you think?"

"Did you read about the map on the back of that drawing? You know, the drawing on that wall over there. Some marine guys are going to be looking for the ships down in Florida. Might be a treasure trove."

"I don't get it. I mean, I get the mural stuff. But"—from my peripheral vision I saw the guy point at me—"what's with her on the floor?"

The crowd was thinning, and it was past the two hours scheduled for the exhibition when I sensed someone standing behind me outside my line of sight. I felt the person's eyes boring into me, causing blood to rush up my neck and into my face.

Finally, he spoke. "I had nothing to do with your sister's death."

A few people were still milling around, and the videographer was still shooting. I didn't move a muscle except to say, "Alex?"

Then a pencil-thin woman with bleached-out hair wearing purple tights and a man's shirt walked onto my dress and said, "Evocative. Really, really evocative." She gave me a thumbs-up and then walked away.

"What are you doing here?" I asked, unnerved by his presence.

He squatted down beside me. "You have to believe me. When

I realized what Braun and Grey had done, I tried to protect you. That's what I was trying to do, protect you."

I turned my head sideways and gazed into those sharp green eyes. "You were trying to steal the Le Moyne." If he was looking for absolution, he wasn't getting it from me.

The videographer moved in closer and turned his camera on Alex. "Yeah, well, as it turned out, the drawing wasn't the real prize." His arrogance was startling.

"What do you mean?"

He kept his voice low and his tone flat. "On the map, that's not a ship sinking. It's a chest, silver, fifth-century CE. You know how I know that? Because I went there and found the chest. I rented a boat along with diving equipment and found it. Inside were carved copper arm rings, solstice stones, ancient gold coins, and Celtic votive wheels, hundreds of them."

I searched his face for the truth. He sounded delusional. "I don't know what game you're playing, but you never saw that map."

He sat back on his heels and smiled. Now the videographer was over Alex's shoulder filming me.

"Oh, but I did. In the old woman's cabin. And when we stopped in Gatlinburg. I took a photo of it with my digital camera, front and back."

"I don't believe you." I struggled up to a seated position, the weight of the dress pulling on me.

He took something from his back pocket. "That's why I brought you this." He placed a small jagged-edged coin in my open hand and closed my fingers around it. His touch felt fevered.

"Rose, do you know what this means? The Celts were in America in the fifth century. I have proof."

The coin felt hot. "Alex, you're an accessory to murder."

At the word *murder*, the videographer swung his camera back toward Alex. "Have it your way," he said, getting to his feet.

And then he was gone.

I opened my hand and stared at the coin in disbelief. Was I really holding a fifth-century Celtic coin found in a chest off the coast of Florida? No, that was impossible. Alex sounded insane. If the coin was authentic, he'd probably stolen it, just as he planned to steal the Le Moyne drawing.

When I looked up, the videographer was still filming. I raised my hand to the camera so he could get a better shot of the coin. My other hand I placed on my chest as if I were taking some strange oath. Finally, I said, "That's enough."

Epilogue:
St. Augustine, Florida
One Month Later

Hey Nick,

I'm sitting in a little bar at the marina, steps from the ocean, nursing a margarita and watching the sun lose itself to water. A hurricane blew through here yesterday, and I thought of Captain Jean Ribault and how weather had been his demise. For a while, it looked like Matt Singer and his crew weren't going to be able to go out today.

But this morning I woke to the most extraordinary sunrise and waters as calm as glass. We were on the ocean before seven A.M. and at the site within the hour.

Are you sitting down? We found Ribault's flagship, the Trinité, *though not where the map showed the sinking ship. Not even close. Miles and miles away. Now, here's the really weird thing. What was left of it was buried beneath a Spanish galleon. Considering what happened to Fort Caroline and the French colony, I thought that was irony to the max. Not to mention the Pentimento mural; treasures beneath treasures.*

Matt used this robotic device to locate the Spanish ship. It wasn't until he and one of the grad students from Florida State dove to take a look did they discover remnants of the Trinité. *They brought up a black plate, which turned out to be silver with the initials JR engraved on the back—Jean Ribault.*

Tomorrow, Matt promised I could go down and have a look. Who knows what I'll find. See ya in a week. Then I have to get *serious about spending some of my $500,000.*

Cheers,
RT

P.S. Showed Alex's picture around the charter boat rentals in the area. No one recognized him. Still don't know what to make of his story or the coin.

I powered down my laptop and finished the rest of my drink, feeling its mellow potency finally quiet my mind, which had been on overdrive since Alex had placed the coin in my hand and then disappeared. The police had yet to find him.

An archeologist authenticated the coin two weeks ago—gold, fifth-century CE, an eight-spoked wheel, with the Celtic symbol of Taranis, god of thunder, on one side. The other side was engraved with a single spiral, a Celtic symbol for the sun.

Had Alex been telling the truth? I wondered. He'd been right about the French ship not being where the map indicated. How could he know that unless he'd gone looking for it and found instead the ancient Celtic chest complete with artifacts?

Just as perplexing was why he'd risked arrest to tell me this if it wasn't true, giving me the coin as proof. True or not, there was nothing I could do about his undocumented discovery. He knew that. Then why risk it?

Because he needed someone to know what he'd found. No matter what amount of money some unscrupulous dealer gave him for the artifacts, the real treasure eluded him. No one would ever know that he, Alex Hague, disgraced art restorer, had discovered verifiable proof that could change history forever.

That sometime in the fifth century, Celts had sailed the Atlantic Ocean from the British Isles and found America. And if Le Moyne's drawing of the altar markings did say, Stone of Taranis, then Celts had settled here long before Columbus or the Vikings. And they'd changed Native American language and culture.

I wanted to believe him. I spun the coin on the glass table as if luck or fate held the answer. I wanted to believe in a world that mysterious and unknown. I wanted to believe that Alex had risked himself to bring me this extraordinary gift of a world undecided, because I was the one person who would understand his loss.

The coin clattered into silence. The single spiral, the sun symbol, landed faceup. The wheel of Taranis, god of thunder and sacrifice, lay hidden from view.

I picked up the coin and held it in my hand, turning it back and forth, marveling at its ancient artistry—the raised golden spokes, the spiral coiling perfectly.

What did it cost me to believe, I thought, as the sun fused sky and water fuchsia? Nothing and everything.

ABOUT THE AUTHOR

Gail Lukasik was born in Cleveland, Ohio, and was a dancer with the Cleveland Civic Ballet Company. Lisel Mueller described her book of poems, *Landscape Toward a Proper Silence*, as a "splendid collection." In 2002, she was awarded an Illinois Arts Council award for her work. She received her MA and PhD from the University of Illinois at Chicago, where she taught writing and literature. She writes the Leigh Girard mystery series. *Kirkus Reviews* described her second Leigh Girard mystery, *Death's Door*, as "fast-paced and literate, with a strong protagonist and a puzzle that keeps you guessing." *The Lost Artist* is her first stand-alone mystery.